HEART OF HONOR

Knights Of Honor
Book Five

Alexa Aston

Copyright © 2017 by Alexa Aston
Print Edition

Published by Dragonblade Publishing, an imprint of Kathryn Le Veque Novels, Inc

All rights reserved. No part of this book may be used or reproduced in any manner whatsoever without written permission, except in the case of brief quotations embodied in critical articles or reviews.

Books from Dragonblade Publishing

Knights of Honor Series by Alexa Aston
Word of Honor
Marked By Honor
Code of Honor
Journey to Honor
Heart of Honor

Legends of Love Series by Avril Borthiry
The Wishing Well
Isolated Hearts
Sentinel

Heart of the Corsairs Series by Elizabeth Ellen Carter
Captive of the Corsairs

Also From Elizabeth Ellen Carter
Dark Heart

Knight Everlasting Series by Cassidy Cayman
Endearing

Midnight Meetings Series by Gina Conkle
Meet a Rogue at Midnight, book 4

Second Chance Series by Jessica Jefferson
Second Chance Marquess

Imperial Season Series by Mary Lancaster
Vienna Waltz
Vienna Woods
Vienna Dawn

Blackhaven Brides Series by Mary Lancaster
The Wicked Baron

Queen of Thieves Series by Andy Peloquin
Child of the Night Guild
Thief of the Night Guild

Dark Gardens Series by Meara Platt
Garden of Shadows
Garden of Light
Garden of Dragons
Garden of Destiny

Rulers of the Sky Series by Paula Quinn
Scorched
Ember

Viking's Fury Series by Violetta Rand
Love's Fury
Desire's Fury
Passion's Fury

Also from Violetta Rand
Viking Hearts

The Sons of Scotland Series by Victoria Vane
Virtue

Dry Bayou Brides Series by Lynn Winchester
The Shepherd's Daughter
The Seamstress
The Widow

Table of Contents

Prologue... 1
Chapter 1.. 16
Chapter 2.. 24
Chapter 3.. 34
Chapter 4.. 43
Chapter 5.. 52
Chapter 6.. 61
Chapter 7.. 67
Chapter 8.. 74
Chapter 9.. 86
Chapter 10.. 97
Chapter 11...107
Chapter 12...114
Chapter 13...123
Chapter 14...133
Chapter 15...143
Chapter 16...152
Chapter 17...160
Chapter 18...168
Chapter 19...178
Chapter 20...185
Chapter 21...193
Chapter 22...201
Epilogue 211
About the Author..215

PROLOGUE

Windsor Castle—August 1369

"I SIMPLY DO not understand why you are not betrothed, Alys. You are already ten and two. Why, I have been betrothed to Christopher since I was seven years of age."

Alys de Montfort took a deep breath and continued grinding the herbs in front of her. This new girl who'd only been present at the royal court for three weeks might drive her to madness.

Especially if Alys had to listen to her speak about this Christopher person. Again.

"A girl who is not betrothed by the time she arrives at court must find herself a future husband soon after her arrival or be subject to gossip," Richessa continued. "'Tis her parents' responsibility as members of the nobility to ensure the most advantageous match." She sighed. "And I could not be more pleased to wed Christopher Emory when the time comes. He is so handsome and well spoken. Father says it's a match that will benefit both the Giffard and Emory families."

Aggravated, Alys pushed harder with her pestle, crushing the rosemary leaves lying in the wooden mortar until they were finely ground.

Yet she knew her mother would urge her to be gracious in such a trying situation, so she said, "You are fortunate, Richessa, to find yourself betrothed to such an outstanding choice."

The younger girl set her pestle down and gazed at Alys earnestly. "You should demand that your father take care of the matter for you. He is being remiss in his duties."

She stifled the laughter that threatened to bubble up at the thought of Geoffrey de Montfort being negligent. Honor and respect were woven tightly into his character, as was the deep love he had for his wife and children. Her father was the best man she knew—and Alys had met hundreds of them during her time spent at the various royal palaces throughout England.

"I can take care of myself," she assured her new acquaintance. "Besides, my parents are close with the king and queen. They have entrusted Queen Philippa to find my betrothed for me."

Richessa's eyes widened in surprise. "I am sorry. I did not know."

"Talk less—and listen more. You will learn much if you do."

Hurt filled the girl's face as tears welled in her eyes.

A pang of guilt struck Alys. She tried to repair the damage she had caused by softening her tone. "I apologize, Richessa. I did not mean to tread upon your feelings. I merely offer advice to you since I have been at court longer."

"How many years have you been in service to the queen?"

"Five years now," Alys replied. "The king and queen came to my family's home on summer progress a few times. The queen asked my parents if I could foster with her, so my father brought me to London at her request." She thought a moment. "'Twas probably best to separate me from my twin brother. Ancel fosters with the Earl of Winterbourne, an hour's ride from my home of Kinwick. Being apart will allow us to forge our own identities."

Richessa's brows knit together. "What does that even mean?"

She saw true puzzlement on the young girl's face. Oh, Richessa Giffard would be a good wife to this all-knowing Christopher Emory. She would do everything her husband asked and let him do her thinking for her—which was the exact opposite of who Alys had come to be. Her mother, Merryn, had raised Alys to be a strong woman. When she did wed, her husband would soon find out his new wife had opinions and a purpose in life—if he did not already know beforehand.

Alys grew wistful. She missed her mother so much. While she realized fostering with the queen was a unique opportunity that few shared, she wished that she could be back home at Kinwick. Each time she returned for Christmas or a summer visit, Merryn de Montfort taught her more about herbs and remedies. As Alys' knowledge grew under her mother's tutelage, so had her reputation at the royal court. Even the king and queen requested she prepare powders for them when they suffered from a headache or loose bowels. Courtiers came to her seeking remedies for everything from sprained joints and queasy bellies to toothaches and bruises. She had even delivered a few babes when a midwife couldn't be located quickly enough.

Mayhap she was not meant to marry, she realized. Instead, God might be calling her to dedicate her life to healing others. Not as a good sister, though. Alys would never wish to be locked away in a convent, but she might serve Him in another capacity. She enjoyed helping the people at court who had various ailments. Permanently serving as a healer in the royal household might be an option to consider, but she would require far more training.

Hilith rushed in, her cheeks flushed a bright pink. "I am happy I located you, Alys. You are needed. Bring your case."

Alys reached for the case that contained the various herbs and medicines she used. It proved her constant companion and was never far from her reach.

"Finish what you are doing, Richessa," she instructed, "and place the herbs in the containers I have shown you. Clean the bowls thoroughly with hot water and then let them air dry. I thank you for your help this afternoon. You did well. Now, please excuse me."

She left with Hilith, who linked an arm through hers and led Alys down the corridor.

"Am I truly needed," she asked, "or are you rescuing me from hearing more tales about Christopher the Great?"

Her friend giggled. "By the Virgin, I swear that girl can speak of nothing but her handsome betrothed. I have almost gone mad listening to her nonsense about a man she barely knows." Hilith gave her arm a squeeze. "But the queen did ask for you, Alys. That is why I sought you out."

"Is she in pain again?"

Hilith shrugged. "If so, she is good at hiding it from everyone."

As they wound their way to the Rose Tower, Alys worried about Queen Philippa's condition, which had baffled the royal physician. Alys had even written to her mother for advice on how to treat the royal, whose feet and ankles continued to swell each passing day. The condition now affected her legs and had spread up to her hands. The queen found it hard to bend her fingers these days and could not do any needlework. Not one to complain, she had grown quieter than usual in recent weeks. Usually talkative and gay, Philippa now spoke little and suffered in silence.

They reached the queen's rooms. Her ladies-in-waiting sat in a circle. Some sewed as Agnes, the chief lady-in-waiting, read aloud to those gathered.

The noblewoman closed her book as they entered. "She is waiting for you, Lady Alys."

Alys saw the concern written on Agnes' face. She nodded and went to the bedchamber door. Rapping lightly, she heard a voice call for her to enter.

It surprised her that Philippa was alone, reclining on the bed. Her shoes and stockings had been removed and her skirts pushed up. Pillows rested under her legs and feet. But what surprised Alys more was the swelling about the woman's eyes and cheeks. Usually, this puffiness only occurred in the mornings after the queen had reclined all night in sleep. Alys came to attend the royal each morning, giving her Petty Morel boiled in water and reduced down, which the queen drank before she arose. She had also begun to create an extract of the leaves and stems, combined with Horehound and wine, for the queen to drink in the evenings before she retired to bed. The concoction proved a strong painkiller and aided the queen as she went to sleep since it made her drowsy.

Alys closed the door and curtseyed. "Greetings, your grace. How may I help you?"

"Come closer, Child. Sit."

She did so, drawing a chair next to the bed as she set her case down beside her. She waited for the queen to speak but could not help noticing how swollen her lower extremities were. It was the worst Alys had seen since the queen's decline had begun.

"How old are you now, Lady Alys?"

"I just turned ten and two last week, your grace, but you know that. You remember everything you are told—and then some."

Philippa smiled, looking pleased at Alys' answer. "I do. And I think it's time I should arrange a betrothal for you. Before I die."

The queen's bold words caused panic to flare within her. Alys dug her nails into her palms and calmly replied, "I hope you will see many more years, my queen. I would hope that you would dance at my wedding feast."

The queen frowned. "Alys de Montfort, you have never been untruthful with me. Do not start now."

Alys felt her cheeks burn and lowered her eyes.

"Does anyone at court strike your fancy?"

She met the queen's eyes. "Nay, your grace. In fact, I may be destined to remain alone."

Philippa snorted. "I will not allow such a thing. You are compassionate and nurturing. You need to care for a great estate as your mother, Merryn, does. Take care of its people. Your husband. Your children."

Alys sighed. "I fear I shall never find love, your grace, and I do want to fall in love with my future husband."

The queen chuckled and then drew in a sharp breath. "Oh, that hurts."

"I am sorry to have made you laugh," she apologized.

Philippa studied her a moment.

"A love match is not unheard of, my dear, but love can grow between a man and wife. Look at the king and me for no greater example. The bishop came to Hainault because a marriage between England and Belgium would be favorable to both of our countries. He was to choose one of Count William's daughters. The bishop selected me, he said, because I was tall and pretty. He thought Edward would be pleased with this choice."

The queen took a stuttering breath before finishing her story. "I came to England and married the king," she continued. "We grew to respect one another, and that admiration eventually turned to love. That love has matured over our decades together, through many children and many victories over our enemies."

"Oh, everyone knows how the king loves you," Alys said.

"And I fear he will miss me when I am gone."

"The king adores you," Alys insisted. "He would be despondent without you as my father would be if he lost Mother."

Philippa looked at her and smiled. "And your parents have loved each other since childhood. I know their story well."

Alys shrugged. "'Tis how things are in my family. My cousin, Raynor, told me that when he first caught sight of his Beatrice, he knew they were destined to wed. He said by the time they did marry, they knew they'd fallen in love with one another."

"And your cousins, Elysande and Avelyn? They, too, made love matches, I recall." The queen shook her head. "I have had this exact conversation with Lady Avelyn, my dear, when she attended me at court several years ago."

"Avelyn and Lord Kenric are most happy, your grace. As are Elysande and Lord Michael." She paused. "I know that you allowed your eldest son, the Black Prince, to marry for love. So it's not unknown even in your family, I suppose."

The queen shook her head. "I thought that boy would never marry," she confided. "But he—like you—wanted to wait for love. He was one and thirty before he wed his cousin, Joan. An old man," she teased.

"But a happy one because he married his soul mate," Alys pointed out.

"Still, though your family has a history of falling in love with their spouses, I promised Lord Geoffrey and Lady Merryn that I would arrange a betrothal for you."

"You will, my queen. I promise that I will look more carefully at the men at court." She sighed. "There's bound to be someone I could love, I suppose."

Philippa laughed again, wincing at the pain it brought. "You do entertain me, Lady Alys. Only you would pass over men with wealth, good looks, and old family names in the elusive hunt for love." She paused. "But I must rest, Child."

"Would you like more of the—"

"Nay. In fact, I think I would like to speak to the king. Will you fetch him here for me?"

"Of course, your grace."

Alys rose as the queen shut her eyes. She picked up her case and slipped from the room, closing the door behind her. As she glanced up, she saw a stranger pacing on the far side of the room. Her insides fluttered in an unusual way as she felt herself grow warm.

He looked to be a handful of years older than she, with dark brown hair and a tall, lean frame. He possessed an energy about him that would draw others to him.

He glanced over at her and called out, "Are you Lady Alys?"

"Aye."

He crossed the room and told her, "The king has need of you, my lady. Come with me."

She followed him from the queen's rooms to the other side of the Rose Tower, where the king occupied a series of rooms for his private use.

As the young man escorted her, Alys found herself tongue-tied. She wondered what ailed her, as she never proven shy with others.

"Are you new at court?" she finally managed to get out.

He looked down and grinned at her, causing her heart to skip a beat. "Aye. My name is Kit. My father was recently named chamberlain to the king. He has been the Chancellor for the Exchequer after working in the treasury for many years. He sent for me to assist him and I arrived at Windsor Castle a sennight ago."

"I see."

They cut around a group of courtiers standing in the hallway. Alys nodded at Lord Sewell Talbot. He had helped guide her cousin, Avelyn, when she served in the queen's household, and the nobleman had also taken an interest in Alys when she arrived in London. She had learned that Lord Sewell knew everyone—and their business.

"Watch that one," Talbot mouthed to her as they passed, nodding his head in Kit's direction.

They rounded a corner and she stopped. Kit took a few steps more and then turned, impatience on his face at her delaying them.

"Why would Lord Sewell warn me about you since you are newly arrived?" she boldly asked.

His sheepish grin intrigued her. He returned to her side. "I thought I could make a new start at court, but if Lord Sewell is a friend of yours, he will tell you all that he knows."

"Are you implying that he is indiscreet?"

"Nay, my lady. He would only be telling you the truth." Kit took her hand and pulled her into a dim alcove mere steps from where they stood.

Now hidden from view, Alys wished she had her wooden sword with her. Her cousin, Raynor, had crafted it for her when she was but six years of age and taught her how to use it, warning her of forward men at court. Raynor also taught her a few tricks to use in case her sword was not handy.

She would put one to good use now.

"My cousin told me I would find men such as you at court," she said, her voice low and honeyed, the better to throw this stranger off. In a swift move, she slammed her foot into his knee, watching pain and surprise flicker in his vibrant green eyes. Before he stumbled, she gave him a hard, swift kick in what Raynor termed *"the family jewels"*.

Immediately, Kit grunted and doubled over.

Alys turned to step calmly from the alcove, gripping her case. No sense running out like a madwoman. 'Twould be embarrassing to her if the circumstances were known. She did not want to become an object of gossip.

But that was her mistake.

Firm fingers latched on to her ankle and pulled, causing her to fall to her knees. She whipped around as Kit toppled over, still clutching her.

She drew up her free leg to deliver the kick of her life.

"Stop," he wheezed. "I . . . I . . . do not wish to harm . . . you," he got out.

Alys wiggled, trying to see if he would release her ankle, but he held fast. He eased himself to a seated position and leaned against the wall. His breath came in short, hard spurts. Seeing he refused to relinquish her, she decided screaming was her best alternative.

"No," he hissed when she opened her mouth. "Do not . . . draw . . . attention."

She met his eyes and realized he was not a threat to her in his present condition. The tension which had built left her body. Then her pulse began beating, the sound rumbling in her ears.

It was his touch. Despite the fact she thought he had wickedness on his mind, something inside her stirred.

"I will let . . . go. But please. Stay, my lady," he begged.

Oddly, she did not want him to release her, though he now did. Alys drew her freed foot close to her. She wanted to glare at him but the peculiar rush of feelings tumbling inside of her would not allow her to do so.

They sat looking at each other a moment until Kit regained his composure.

"I did not plan to take advantage of you, my lady. I merely wished to draw you aside to share something with you."

She frowned in confusion. "What?"

He shook his head. "I had hoped my past would not catch up with me at court, but I am now sure that it already has. Especially if you know Lord Sewell. He sticks his nose in everyone's affairs."

"I like him," she defended. "He was ever so kind to my cousin, Avelyn, when she was at court several years ago. He told her of trouble that brewed and how a supposed friend of hers actually betrayed her in the worst way. Avelyn was grateful to him. In fact, she even wrote to Lord Sewell and asked him to look out for me during my time in the queen's household."

Alys held his gaze with as much seriousness as she could muster. "So watch what you say, my lord. 'Tis the first lesson you should learn if you are to remain at the royal court."

"Then I shall speak the truth. 'Twas why I wanted to pull you aside in the first place. I wished to tell you something of myself." He paused. "My father did send for me—but not to assist him. Only because I had been dismissed from another nobleman's household. Again."

Alys heard something in his voice that tugged at her heart. Without thinking, she scooted over to him and took his hand.

"What happened, my lord?"

Kit shrugged. "What always happens. Since childhood, I have constantly been in trouble. I could never stay still. I went through several tutors, none who wished to remain and teach me. They all said I was a bright boy but full of too much mischief."

He gazed into her eyes. "I have fostered in four households, Lady Alys. And four times I have been asked to leave. I am too bold. I do not follow the rules. I am disrespectful. It's always something." He shook his head. "This last time I'd been placed in the household at a friend of Lord Sewell's. He must have heard about the . . . incident."

She squeezed his hand in encouragement. "Go on."

"I served in Lord Brutus' service. I think my father paid him with several bags of gold simply to take me on. Lord Brutus was especially hard on me. He beat me at the slightest provocation. Everything that went wrong in the household was forever blamed on me." Kit chuckled. "That's why I called him Lord Brutal behind his back—and then to his face."

Alys sucked in her breath. "You didn't."

His green eyes gleamed. "But I did. That proved to be the final straw. He sent me back to my mother at Brentwood. She did not know what to do with me, so she wrote to my father. He requested my presence here at court. I assume he believes I will learn under his tutelage and tame my wild ways. I briefly met the king, though. He praised my boldness," Kit said, pride evident in his voice.

"You must do your best to fit in, Kit," she said softly. Her hand throbbed in his, but she cast aside the thoughts that brought. "The king may have complimented you, but he is strict when it comes to the rules of court. You will not be given special consideration. You must conform in all practices of the court. It won't only affect you, but your actions will affect your father and his position at court."

Kit blew out a long breath. "Then we are doomed. Curbing my restless nature is the last thing I can do. I have always been rash and acted first without thought. Mayhap, I will beg Father to send me home instead of jeopardizing his role at court. I would not wish to harm his relationship with the king."

He slowly drew himself to his feet, pulling her up to her own.

"You surprise me."

Alys wondered at his words and asked, "Why?"

He searched her face as if looking for the answer. "The king demanded you come to rid him of his headache. I expected Lady Alys to be a healer who was older, not a mere girl. And now you have dispensed words of wisdom to me. You are quite an unusual person, Lady Alys."

Her insides glowed with the praise he offered to her. She tamped down the butterflies that fluttered in her stomach.

"I have known the king since childhood and have fostered with the queen these past five years. My mother has a way in the healing arts. She has passed on her knowledge to me. I often prepare potions for the king when his head aches or if his bowels run foul."

"Well, the king is lucky to have you. But come, we must head swiftly to his side. I fear he will be upset at the delay."

"If he is, I can placate him," Alys said. "I will tell him I was with the queen and only recently left her side. He loves his wife very much and knows she's felt poorly as of late. He won't be angry with you, my lord."

Kit released her hand and reached down to retrieve her case. He handed it to her as they stepped out into the corridor and hurried to the opposite end of the Rose Tower.

They arrived at their destination and entered the king's chambers. Kit brought her straight to the royal monarch, bowing and stepping aside as Alys made her curtsey.

"My head hurt before, but I did as you have suggested and ate some fruit and drank a tankard of ale. I feel much better, Lady Alys. I am sorry you made the trip here. But how is my queen today?"

She knew sometimes the king got so busy he forgot to eat or drink. She found if he got something into him, preferably juicy fruits or ale, he seemed to recover quickly.

"The queen asked that you come visit her as soon as possible, your highness. She was in some pain when I left her side just now." Knowing he respected honesty, she added, "The swelling is much greater today. Her feet and ankles are twice their normal size, as are her legs. I think a visit from you would go a long way in bringing her relief."

Edward stood. "Let us go to her then." He motioned to his royal physician. "Hobard. Come with us."

The king strode from the room as assembled courtiers stepped aside, only to fall in behind him. Alys found herself almost swallowed up by the horde.

Then someone grasped her hand and pulled her forward.

She looked and saw it was Kit who had hold of her. He maneuvered them through the crowd till they caught up with the king just before he entered the queen's rooms.

The assembled ladies-in-waiting all rose as he made his way across the room. Edward paused at the door and seemed to steel himself before he knocked and went in. Hobard followed the monarch inside. Kit boldly drew Alys into the chamber and closed the door behind them.

The queen looked pale but smiled as her husband pulled a chair close and took her hands in his.

"We have had a good life together, have we not?" she asked.

"We have, indeed."

"I fear I have not accomplished enough."

The king laughed. "You gave me ten and four children, my love. That alone should be accomplishment enough."

He grew serious. "But you have done far more than that. You founded the colony of Flemish weavers at Norwich and have supported them for years. You brought artists and scholars from Hainault to the court. Your namesake college sits at Oxford and will for decades to come. You have acted as my regent on many occasions when I have left the country."

The king looked affectionately into the queen's eyes. "And you have been my loyal, most loving companion for forty years. Your wisdom and kindness are shining beacons that call out to me in my darkest times."

Edward leaned forward and tenderly kissed her hands.

Philippa closed her eyes and smiled. The room remained silent for several minutes. Then she opened her eyes. Alys saw the pain in them and shuddered.

"I would ask three things of you, Husband. Pay all the merchants I have engaged for their wares. Fulfill any gifts I have made to the church and my servants."

The queen swallowed. "And when God calls you hence, lie by my side at Westminster Abbey."

Tears shone in the king's eyes as he replied, "Lady, all this shall be done." He leaned to kiss her cheek.

Tears sprang to Alys' eyes. She realized Kit still held her hand in his. She glanced up at him, her mouth trembling. He brushed a hand against her hair in comfort.

Quietly, the king said, "I believe she is gone, Hobard."

Alys watched the royal physician move forward to examine the queen. After a minute, he nodded. No other words were necessary.

"'Twill be as she asked," the king said. He slowly trod from the room, followed by Hobard.

She heard him say something to the gathered women in the next room. Immediately, sobs broke out. Alys' tears began to roll down her cheeks.

Silently, Kit wrapped her in his arms. Alys burrowed her face into his chest. They stood that way a long moment without words. She drew strength from him as she remembered the remarkable woman who had passed.

Finally, she drew back. "England has lost a great lady," she told him. "The queen was kind and compassionate and knew how to handle the king like no other."

"I am sorry for your loss," he said. "You seem to have known her well."

Alys nodded. "We should leave."

Reluctantly, she pulled her hand from his and felt at a loss when it was free. She wrapped it around the handle of her case, both hands squeezing it to help ground herself.

They exited the bedchamber. Weeping women embraced one another, seeking comfort from such a tremendous loss.

Alys looked up at Kit. Before she could speak, he said, "You wish to be alone. Let me escort you to your bedchamber."

She nodded and followed him from the queen's rooms, no words between them. They walked slowly down the long corridors until they arrived at the room she shared with Hilith.

"Thank you," she said.

"I am sorry we met under such circumstances, my lady. I did not know the queen as you did, but I realize your heart is heavy."

Alys nodded, words impossible to speak.

Kit pulled her to him again, his arms enveloping her in a comforting warmth. She wished she could stay this way forever.

"What are you *doing*, Christopher?" a familiar voice screeched.

Kit dropped his arms and turned to face his accuser.

"I am giving solace to Lady Alys, my lady. We come from the queen's bedside. She has passed on to a better world."

Richessa Giffard stepped forward and tucked her arm possessively through the crook of Kit's arm. She glared at Alys as if she wished Alys were dead.

At that moment, Alys realized that Kit . . . was Christopher Emory.

CHAPTER 1

London—April 1375

KIT EMORY MADE his way through the palace as only an insider could have. He avoided the usually crowded corridors and receiving rooms, filled with sycophants and foreigners. Instead, he slipped through a little used door that his father had shown him when he first came to court six years ago. The hall he entered served as a holding area for those awaiting their audience with the king.

His eyes skimmed over close to a dozen men grouped in small circles scattered about the room. He sighed and leaned against the wall, wondering how long he would wait before he could speak with his father.

He listened in on the conversation among the trio standing to his right. From what he overheard, Kit gathered that the Duke of Lancaster and a committee of men involved in the signing of the Treaty of Bruges currently had an audience with the king. As one of Edward's closest advisers, Kit's father would be in the thick of things.

A passing servant offered him a glass of wine. He swallowed the sweet brew with a tinge of sorrow. He did not want to be on English soil. He preferred to be back fighting the French—even though he had not seen his country meet with success during this most recent campaign. Kit had been part of the ill-fated group of ships that had sailed with the king and his men three years ago. Every attempt to land English troops in France had been met with contrary winds that finally drove them back home. His father, knowing that the king was in no shape to lead a war party, had called the misadventure a blessing in disguise.

That made Kit even more eager to be a part of the troops when the Duke of Lancaster, John of Gaunt, had led a march through France two years ago. Though fighting had been fierce and laden with heavy casualties, the king's second son had achieved nothing through this endeavor. Unlike his older brother, the Black Prince, the duke did not have a keen military mind. His strategies proved fruitless, and the English troops never maximized any advantage they'd held. The entire venture ended in failure. Subsequent battles Kit had fought in saw dwindling forces falling to the French—including the one where he lost men due to his own stupidity—along with his friend Ralf.

England had failed to keep Aquitaine and only held four coastal cities in France now. Kit wondered if his country would ever return to its former greatness during his own lifetime. From the sound of it, the same thoughts were being echoed by the two men to his left.

Turning slightly in their direction, Kit decided to join in their conversation.

"At least we retained Calais. It's a vital port," said one with piercing blue eyes and the rugged build and air of a warrior.

"But what good are four towns, Michael? By the Christ, we need the Black Prince whole again, to lead us against these French bastards," his companion proclaimed. The man's hazel eyes flickered with anger. A broad chest and muscled arms let Kit know this one was a man to be reckoned with. If in a fight, he would want both of these knights by his side.

"You speak of the treaty?" he asked.

Both men glanced to where Kit stood and shook their heads, their eyes wary. He knew spies could be anywhere, so he kept his own voice low.

"I believe the year's truce the treaty calls for will only give France more time to build up their weaponry," Kit said. "And more time for the Duke of Lancaster to dig himself into a hole."

The one called Michael studied him. "You are free with your tongue, my friend."

He regretted his rash statement. He often spoke—or acted—upon impulse without considering the consequences. His mother termed it his greatest flaw. And with his father as an adviser to the king, he had been privy to information others did not have. Kit shrugged and said, "It's merely my opinion. I fear England is in for hard times ahead with both the king and the Black Prince in poor health."

The larger man nodded and offered his hand. "Kenric Fairfax. Earl of Shadowfaire." He indicated his companion. "This is Michael Devereux. Earl of Sandbourne."

"I am Kit Emory, son of Godwin Emory, Baron of Brentley. I have been with the duke's men in France and have only returned home with the news of this truce."

"We, too, have fought for England these last few years. I am ready to return to my children and my sweetest Elysande," said Devereux.

"You think she will tear herself away from her precious horses in order to greet you?" Fairfax teased.

Devereux punched the nobleman in the arm good-naturedly. "She better. I am starved for her kisses and her touch."

"And I long to embrace Avelyn and never let her go," Fairfax answered. "Other than to hug my own children, of course."

Kit heard something in the voices of both men that caused him an inkling of jealousy.

"You both sound smitten with your wives," he noted cautiously.

Both men laughed. Devereux said, "We married sisters, nieces to Lord Geoffrey de Montfort."

Fairfax added, "They are both beautiful women with quick wits and loyal hearts." He beamed. "I do not care if the world knows. I love my Avelyn with every fiber of my being, and I know Michael feels the same way about Elysande."

"We are both men who married for love and find ourselves constantly challenged by the women we wed." Devereux added. He grinned. "And we would not have it any other way." He paused. "Are you married, Emory?"

"Aye." He thought of his loveless union with Richessa, a woman whose inane chatter drove him to madness—when he could tolerate her presence. She had given birth twice to stillborn children. The midwife had told him after the last one that Richessa could no longer bear any more. Since his wife's health had grown poor, Kit wondered how she had fared in his time away from England. As an only son, he would need to provide an heir for Brentwood.

If he could, he idly wondered if the charming Alys de Montfort might still be available. From time to time, he found himself musing over what happened to the budding beauty he had met when he first came to court. He had caught the de Montfort name when Devereux mentioned it and decided to inquire, hoping to appease his curiosity.

"You mentioned Lord Geoffrey de Montfort. Might he be father to Lady Alys de Montfort?"

"He is, indeed," Devereux said. "Lord Geoffrey is inside now, meeting with the king, along with his cousin, Raynor. Both men participated in the signing of the latest treaty."

"Lord Geoffrey is the best knight in all of England," Fairfax proclaimed. "A warrior like no other and possessing a good heart and keen mind. Alys is his oldest daughter. She favors her mother, Merryn, in looks and has her mother's healing ways. So you know her?"

Kit nodded. "I met Lady Alys briefly at court. Years ago, on the day the queen died."

Devereux nodded solemnly. "God bless the good queen. Poor Alys took her death quite hard."

"I did not see her at court after that event. Did she leave to foster elsewhere?"

"Nay, she returned home to Kinwick Castle," Fairfax said. "She had been with the queen several years and was ready to come home. Lady Merryn knows much about herbs and healing. She has passed on her knowledge to Lady Alys through the years, and Alys' reputation grows each year."

"Do you visit Kinwick often?"

"Aye," Devereux replied. "Both Elysande and Avelyn are close to their uncle and Lady Merryn. Lord Geoffrey's sister, Lady Mary, lives at Sandbourne with us. Visits are made from our households on a regular basis. All the young cousins enjoy being with one another."

Casually, he asked, "I wondered if—"

At that moment, the doors were thrown open. Men began pouring through them.

"It was nice meeting you, Emory," Devereux said. "We must leave now and head for home with Lord Geoffrey and Lord Raynor. If you are ever nearby, stop in at Sandbourne."

"Or at Shadowfaire," added Fairfax, "now that we have a break in this nasty war." He gave Kit a brusque nod. The two men joined up with two older noblemen, both still handsome for their ages and bearing the posture of seasoned knights. He wondered which of the two might be father to Lady Alys.

And if she had wed.

Kit had been about to ask that very question when the meeting with the king ended, interrupting their conversation. He watched as the group exited the hall and lingered as others ventured from the long meeting. Finally, he caught sight of his father and headed toward him.

"Christopher!" his father called in greeting, embracing him. "I did not know when to expect you."

"I came on the ship that brought the duke back to London," he explained.

He studied his father, noting that his beard had gone totally gray, as had most of his hair. New lines were etched into his face since Kit had last seen him.

"Come. We shall go to my chamber and speak in private."

Kit followed his father as they wound their way through the gathered throngs and down crowded corridors before they reached the quiet of the large, airy chamber. His father offered him wine, which he refused.

Pouring himself a healthy amount, Godwin drained it and rested the cup on a table as he sat. He indicated for Kit to take the chair next to him.

"The king is old and tired," his father began. "His health has only grown worse since you were last at court."

"And what of Alice Perrers?" he asked.

A sour look crossed his father's face. "She is still his mistress. Edward is heavily under that greedy woman's influence."

"What of the Black Prince? Has he recuperated?"

His father sighed. "He rallied some after returning from France, but now he only grows weaker as each day passes." He hesitated. "I fear he will be the first Prince of Wales who won't live long enough to become king."

Kit shuddered. "But Prince Edward is a natural leader."

"Not anymore. Our Prince of Wales is sick and old before his time. And his son, Richard, is much too young to assume the throne and rule. I fear the chaos that will follow the Black Prince's death, especially if the present king passes near the same time."

"Richard is but a boy, but he would be the rightful heir, Father. If what you say comes to pass and England finds herself without King Edward and the Black Prince, Richard must be crowned as our monarch." Kit thought a moment, his knowledge of palace politics deep. "Yet I fear his uncle, the Duke of Lancaster, would try to control the boy."

His father snorted. "Lancaster already controls enough as it is. Before he left to fight on the continent, none of his actions on behalf of his father proved to be honorable or successful. Now Lancaster has all but lost every possession of England's in France and brought home to us a worthless truce, not worth the parchment it's written upon."

"I fear this pause in the action will only benefit the French."

"I couldn't agree more, my son. While England's leadership crumbles around us, our war chests have emptied. Taxes will have to be raised in order to replenish them. And everyone throughout the land has grown tired of war. Meanwhile, the French only grow stronger and more fervent since they have won back so much territory in recent years."

"What have you advised the king to do since the treasury is so dangerously low?"

His father shrugged. "It matters not what I say. I believe I am on my way out. The duke is surrounding the king with men loyal to him while he rids King Edward of his longtime advisers. I do not know how long a time I will remain at court."

"Go home with me now, Father. Leave this nest of vipers," Kit insisted. He worried about his father's health more than the king's. Besides the obvious aging his father's face showed, Kit noticed a shortness of breath that concerned him.

"Nay. I will stay as long as I can and hope I am useful. But you should leave at once. Your mother and wife have both been ill as of late."

"Mother is ill? What ails her? And Richessa?"

Kit tried to keep the alarm from his voice, but it upset him to hear such news. He had always been closer to his mother than his father. She had been much more than a parent to him—more like a trusted confidant, supporter, and wise mentor. A steady force in his life and the one person who loved him unconditionally, no matter how many mistakes he made and how often he had been sent back to Brentwood in shame.

His father waved a hand about. "I know not. Dawkin's message to me only said both of them had been struck with something."

It did not surprise him that his father had remained at court despite their steward notifying him of his wife's illness. The couple tolerated one another, with no affection in their marriage. Long separations had only driven a wedge more tightly between them. His father reveled in his life at court; his mother preferred her life in the country. Kit was their only issue. After several lost babes, his mother had never produced another.

Though he never realized it before, Kit now thought that his own marriage echoed that of his parents'. A twinge of sadness pricked at him. He thought back to the two earls he had met only an hour ago. How each man spoke lovingly and longingly of returning home to his beloved wife.

Would he ever experience such a feeling?

He squared his shoulders. "With your permission, I will leave at once for Brentwood. I will write to you of Mother's—and Richessa's—health. I only wish you would accompany me."

His father shook his head emphatically. "Nay, my boy. I'll lap up whatever time I have left in the weak sunshine emitting from our king. I feel, for England's sake, that I must remain in my position as long as possible, before Lancaster casts me aside and replaces me with one of the incompetent fools that he calls friend."

Kit bid his father farewell, wondering if it would be the last time they would meet.

"Go with God, my son."

CHAPTER 2

Kinwick Castle

ALYS DE MONTFORT watched her mother flit from one activity to another, an anxious air about her.

"Father will be home soon," she said, hoping to calm her mother's frenetic energy. "And he'll be staying."

The older woman paused and took a deep breath. "I know. Yet I cannot help but worry until he arrives safely."

"He should be home sometime today according to the missive he sent."

"Father's coming home?"

She turned and saw her sister, Nan, standing in the doorway, a wide grin spreading across her face. The younger girl ran and hugged her mother tightly.

"Do you think Raynor might come with him?" Nan asked. "I want him to see me with my sword."

"Nay, Child," Merryn said. "Raynor will be anxious to return home to Beatrice and your cousins."

"Then we need to go see them soon," Nan proclaimed. "Raynor must watch me fight. Alys has been teaching me. I think I am getting quite good."

Alys thought back to how Raynor had made wooden swords for her and Ancel when they were close to Nan's age and how much fun the two of them had brandishing them about as Raynor cheered them on. She had kept up her own weapon practice over the years. Though not as skilled as a knight of the realm, Alys knew she could protect herself with a sword if she ever found herself in danger.

She decided to continue the sword lessons with Nan so that her sister would also grow up confident in her ability to defend herself.

"Would you like us to go out into the bailey and—"

"Oh, aye!" Nan ran from the room to retrieve her sword before Alys could even finish her sentence.

"Thank you for keeping her occupied, Alys," her mother murmured. She sat in a chair and picked up the embroidery lying on the table next to her and aimlessly turned it over in her lap.

Alys went and dropped a kiss atop her mother's head and then left to find her own wooden sword in order to duel with Nan.

Soon, she was caught up in instructing her sister, who had changed into what she termed her boy clothes. Alys had waited years for her mother to birth a girl child, but Nan preferred swordplay and riding to the womanly arts. Much to her mother's disappointment, Nan showed no interest at all in herbs. In a way, Alys missed passing along to her little sister what she had learned about the healing power of herbs. She had assumed Nan would continue in the de Montfort women's footsteps. At the same time, it gave Alys precious hours alone with her mother as they ground and pressed different herbs and visited the many tenants at Kinwick, addressing their multitude of ailments.

Alys swung her sword at her opponent, glad to see how fast Nan reacted to counter Alys' moves. For a child of six, her sister had an innate sense of balance and a true feel for the weapon in her hand.

"Step to your left!" Gilbert called out as he stopped to study them. "You swing your sword with confidence, Lady Nan, but you need to be quicker on your feet."

"I am quick, Sir Gilbert," Nan retorted to their captain of the guard. "I just prefer the right."

The knight came closer and watched them go at it a few minutes before he interrupted again.

"Lady Alys knows your preference," he warned. "She will take advantage of you if you let her. You never want your opponent to know you favor one side over the other. Practice being equally skilled coming from both directions."

Nan stopped and blew out a hard breath. "You are right, as always," she admitted. She glanced at her sister. "Can we stop, Alys? I am tired."

"My lord captain!"

They all looked up to the soldier stationed on the wall walk.

"Lord Geoffrey approaches," he continued.

Gilbert waved in acknowledgement. He looked at Nan. "Best go in and find Lady Merryn and let her know your father will arrive soon."

"And wash your face and change your clothes after you do so," Alys called after her as Nan scampered away.

Her sister stopped and thrust out her tongue for an answer before running across the bailey toward the keep, her sword swinging by her side.

"She is a feisty one, our Lady Nan," Gilbert said, shaking his head.

Alys laughed. "We all thought Hal was a terror at her age. Can you imagine what Nan will be like in a few years?"

"Master Hal is turning out just fine, my lady. All of you de Montfort children make your parents proud."

"Thank you, Sir Gilbert. Coming from you, that's high praise. If you will excuse me, I intend to ready myself for Father's arrival whether Nan does or not."

She hurried to her chamber to bathe her face and wash her hands before she changed into a fresh cotehardie of pale yellow. Her father always complimented her when she wore the color. Her braid had held up during their practice, so she left it in place and returned downstairs.

As she came outside into the warm sunshine, Alys saw her mother already waiting at the foot of the stairs, Nan beside her. Alys quickly made her way down to them and linked her arm through her mother's. Merryn's face was flushed with excitement and anticipation at her husband's return.

Nan defiantly looked up at Alys, her little, wooden sword still in hand. She hadn't changed into female attire. "Father loves me as I am," she declared. The child wrinkled her nose and turned back, awaiting the horses whose hooves could now be heard thundering nearby.

Alys squeezed her mother's arm. She glanced as their longtime servant, Tilda, came and stood on Merryn's other side.

At that moment, she sighted the returning party as they rounded the corner into the inner bailey and galloped toward them. Her heart swelled with pride seeing her father at its head. The king had great admiration for Geoffrey de Montfort, having once asked years ago for Geoffrey to serve on his royal council. Her father refused to do so, wanting to remain at Kinwick and raise his family far from the scheming courtiers in London. As a compromise, the monarch had called upon the nobleman to serve him in times of need, which was why Geoffrey had been gone to Belgium on the king's business the past few months. Her mother had shared that knowledge with her, stressing for her to keep his whereabouts to herself since the diplomatic mission required the utmost secrecy.

Though now graying at the temples, her father was still a handsome man at two score, tall and broad-shouldered. Alys saw he only had eyes for his adored wife as he drew near.

Geoffrey de Montfort leapt from his saddle and strode toward his wife, a satisfied smile playing about his lips. He cupped his wife's face in his large palms, drinking her in before kissing her soundly.

Alys chuckled to herself. She had grown used to her parents' open affection for one another. She delighted in the fact that they loved each other after so many years of marriage, as well as respected one another.

Seeing their warm embrace, Alys felt a twinge of envy at what they had together. She wondered if she would ever know a great love such as theirs.

Without meaning to, her thoughts flashed as they had so often over the years to Kit Emory, Richessa Giffard's betrothed, the only man she'd ever experienced any longing for. She pushed aside his image as her brother, Ancel, came toward her and wrapped her in a bear hug. As squire to Lord Hardwin, her twin had accompanied the nobleman to France. She had said countless prayers to the Virgin Mary to keep Ancel safe as the two countries warred against one another. Having him back on English soil and at Kinwick brought sweet relief.

Glancing over his shoulder, Alys saw that Hal and Edward also headed their way. Happiness at having all three of her brothers present filled her.

"I have missed you, Alys de Montfort," her twin said, twirling her about before he set her down and released her.

"It was good of Lord Hardwin to let all three of you come home for a visit. Mother will be thrilled to have all her ducklings under one roof."

Her father finally pulled away from his lengthy kiss, thanks to Nan tugging on him. "I see you are dressed for battle, my little lady." He looked to Alys. "I'm sure you have done an excellent job of teaching your sister swordplay while I have been gone."

He hugged Nan, who squealed in delight, and then enfolded Alys in his embrace. "You look lovely as the sunshine, Daughter. But tell me. Was your mother her usual whirlwind while I was gone?"

Alys laughed. Anytime her father went away on the king's business, her mother kept everyone on the straight and narrow. The keep was cleaned from top to bottom. The ledgers were scrutinized and any corrections needed promptly made. Extra candles would be fashioned, and the workers would have their tasks inspected more closely than by any man with the Countess of Kinwick in charge.

"Mother did an excellent job while you were away, but she missed you dreadfully. We all did, Father. Kinwick isn't Kinwick without your presence."

He kissed her cheek. "Then I shall plan to stay and give everyone a break from her tyrannical rule," he teased.

Alys greeted Hal and Edward. "You are sprouting like a weed, Hal," she told him. "I know Ancel was not nearly as tall at one and ten as you are."

"What about me?" Edward demanded. "Was Ancel as tall as I am? I am nine, you know."

She laughed at the eagerness of her youngest brother. "Of course, I know your age, Edward. I have known you since you left Mother's womb. I've rocked you and swaddled you and sung to you."

"And taught me about swordplay," the boy added solemnly. "You are a good sister to me, Alys."

She ruffled his hair fondly. "And you are the best of brothers, Edward."

Ancel slung an arm about her shoulder. "And what am I?" he demanded.

She rested her head against him, happy to be reunited with all of her loved ones. "You are the best twin I could have, Brother. You are my better half and will be the finest knight in the land one day."

"Finer than Kenric Fairfax?" he asked, waggling his eyebrows.

They both laughed. Their cousin, Avelyn, had married an extremely tall, very talented knight who loved to claim that he was the best soldier in all of England. It had become the family joke because they had heard him say it so often.

"Kenric *is* an incredible knight," her father said.

"How is he? And Michael?" her mother asked. "I know they were with you in Belgium."

Geoffrey slipped an arm about his wife's waist and drew her near. "Both of them are well and send you their love. Raynor, too."

"I wish they would have come to Kinwick so I could see them for myself," Merryn said.

"They have their own families they were eager to return to, Wife." He gave her an affectionate squeeze. "Soon, we will have all of them come to Kinwick to celebrate the fact that all of our men have returned to English soil. But for now?" His eyes twinkled. "I am famished, my love."

Alys sensed her cheeks pinkening. She knew her father meant he was hungry in more ways than one. Her mother had explained the ways of men and women to Alys several years ago and she knew after they dined, her parents would feast upon one another tonight.

Tilda spoke up. "I have had a spread laid out in the solar, my lord.

All your favorites are there."

Geoffrey de Montfort looked to his three sons. "Then come. Let us wash the dust of the road from us and dress in clean clothes and then gather as a family. It's been far too long since we have all assembled under our roof."

Ancel scooped Nan up and placed the giggling girl on his shoulders as Alys took Hal and Edward's hands and led them inside.

Once they arrived in the solar, her mouth watered at the smell of freshly-baked bread. Tilda had brought starling and chicken, along with cod and eels, a round of cheese, two cakes, and wine. The family sat at the table, soon devouring everything in sight, as the younger boys spoke of their time fostering at Winterbourne and how they enjoyed serving as pages for Lord Hardwin.

"You must thank Lord Hardwin for allowing you to return to Kinwick to see your father," Merryn said. "Did he say how long you may stay?"

"He told us to remain today and tomorrow, then return after that," Edward shared. "He said he would have much for us to do now that he has returned home to Winterbourne."

"But Lord Hardwin did not take us with him to France," complained Hal. "I wish I could have gone with him as Ancel did."

"Ancel is Lord Hardwin's squire," their father reminded him. "It's Ancel's duty to accompany his lord and help prepare him for battle." He looked to his oldest. "And how did you find the French?"

Before her twin could answer, Hal punched Edward in the arm. Edward hit him back. Nan threw a wadded up piece of bread to distract them, hitting Hal in the face.

"Enough!" Merryn proclaimed. "You younger children have obviously finished eating and are restless." She gave them a solemn look. "You may be excused. Go make mischief somewhere else."

The three children jumped from the table and rushed to the door.

After they exited, her father again turned to Ancel. "I am sorry your brothers have no clue as to how dire the situation is, but they are young. What are your thoughts regarding the French?"

"That they're bastards, each and every one of them. I know our forces could best them, but . . ." Ancel's voice trailed off.

"Go on," urged Geoffrey. "I asked for your opinion and I'll have it."

"We have no leadership at the top, Father. The soldiers know it and dread what is to come."

Her father nodded. "I am afraid this treaty is merely a break in the action before another phase in the war between our two countries begins. I myself worry who will lead our troops when the inevitable fighting starts up again."

"What of John of Gaunt?" Alys asked. "Is the king's son not up to performing his duty?"

"The Duke of Lancaster is a capable man," her father said, his brow furrowed. "But England will need more than that."

"Why?" Alys asked, not understanding.

"The health of both the king and the Black Prince is worrisome," Geoffrey continued. He took his wife's hand and looked from her to Alys. "Neither of you have seen either man in several years, not since the queen's death." He shook his head. "Both father and son are in pitiful shape."

Geoffrey paused for a sip of wine. "The king is now manipulated by his mistress, Alice Perrers, while Lancaster has inserted those loyal to him in positions of power at the royal court." He sighed. "I expect both the king and his eldest son to die soon."

"I fear for a kingdom ruled by a ten-year-old boy," her mother said. "It would mean the Duke of Lancaster overseeing the new king's reign for several years."

"Worse," Ancel said. "The world laughs at us, Father. When you were my age, you fought at Crecy and Poitiers and tasted sweet victory. Now, the French have reduced us from ownership of Aquitaine to only a few coastal ports. England has become a shadow of itself in a handful of years."

Alys had always had a head for figures. "What of money, Father? Wars are horribly expensive—especially now that we are on the losing end, with little to show for our time spent abroad fighting."

"England's royal treasury is sorely depleted. 'Twill mean higher taxes from the king, which trickles down to the common worker." He frowned. "I fear a rebellion from the people."

"Surely not here at Kinwick," her mother protested.

"Nay. We have avoided most of the problems that have surfaced ever since plague and famine hit years ago." Her father's face grew grim. "But since plague killed off so many workers, laborers have more power."

Alys asked, "Would it be as when the barons forced King John's hand at Runnymeade? Would all noble families be in a similar position?"

Her father placed a hand on her shoulder. "I hope not, Alys." He gave her an affectionate squeeze. "But enough talk of politics. How is Kinwick?"

He rose to his feet and they all followed suit. "We should go ride the property, Ancel. You have been away the longest. Ladies, we would appreciate your company."

As the four made their way to the stables to have their horses saddled, Alys fell into step next to her twin.

"So the French are that awful?" she asked.

"The men certainly are." He grinned. "But the women are far different."

Alys playfully punched him in the shoulder. "Better not let Mother—or Father—hear you speak like that. Consorting with our enemy." She sniffed.

Ancel shrugged. "I'm sure Father knows. French whores abound along the edges of both army camps. They will service their fellow countrymen or the English for a coin or two."

"And how many women assisted you during your time in France?" she teased, watching a blush cross his cheeks.

"A few," he admitted. "Lord Hardwin encouraged me to take an hour now and again for myself."

She gasped. "Lord Hardwin? Surely, he didn't—"

"Nay, the earl loves Lady Johamma as much as Father does Mother. But he understands that war is hard on soldiers, physically and mentally. It's difficult being away from home and the ones you love." Ancel paused. "Not only did I prepare him and his horse for battle, but Lord Hardwin also allowed me to enter the fray several times. I have no doubts now about my sword skills when tested by the enemy."

Ancel stopped abruptly and faced her. "Tell me of any news you have. What have I missed while abroad?"

She understood that he did not want to speak of war now. Not when he had just arrived home. Instead, Alys slipped her hand through the crook of his arm and as she spoke, she sensed the tension leaving his body. She told him about the five babes who had been born on Kinwick lands and the upcoming May Day celebration plans, as well as her last visit to Sandbourne to see Michael and Elysande and their three children.

"And the horses?"

"You mean Elysande's other children?" Alys countered.

Ancel laughed heartily. "I know our cousin loves the three she gave birth to but I have never seen anyone, man or woman, who adores horses as much as Elysande does."

They reached the stables and found her parents awaited them with their horses already saddled. As the four of them rode through the gates of Kinwick, Alys hoped the doom and gloom her father predicted would never come to pass. And if it did, she wondered what it would mean for her and her loved ones.

CHAPTER 3

RELIEF WASHED THROUGH Kit as he saw Brentwood in the distance.

He regretted his haste in leaving London alone, something he had done many times in the past. Yet England was a different place from the one he had left when he eagerly plunged into the war in France. Travel had become more dangerous in the last decade. Bands of highwaymen roamed the roads, sometimes led by minor noblemen who had fallen on hard times. Kit had avoided two large groups of men, skirting through the woods when he spied them. Last night, he had camped without starting a fire so that he wouldn't bring attention to himself. Mayhap he was maturing after all and would no longer rush head first into situations without giving them some thought.

Now, as he approached his boyhood home, anxiety over his mother's health returned. Berengaria Emory had always been more friend and ally than parent to him. He admired how she managed Brentwood as well as any man since her husband was gone at court a majority of the year. Kit had no brothers and sisters, so he had remained especially close with her through the years. His father had granted him the privilege of staying home for two years instead of leaving to foster with another nobleman's family in order for him to learn how to run a large estate under his mother's tutelage. The experience had strengthened the bond between them even more.

Once his father deemed Kit ready again for service to a nobleman, he was sent to Lord Brutus' household for a last, ill-fated time spent fostering. Godwin Emory chided his only son to rein in any wild impulses and keep his mouth closed, instructing him to do whatever task Lord Brutus assigned him cheerfully and willingly. The Christ Himself knew how hard Kit had tried to please this ill-tempered nobleman, but the man had earned his nickname of Lord Brutal long before Kit Emory set foot on his lands.

The gatekeeper welcomed Kit with a wave as he rode through the opened gates to the stables, where he handed his borrowed horse to a groom. He had lost his own horse in the last days of fighting in France and would miss the faithful companion that had been with him most of his life.

A flash of the battle crossed his memory. *The blood. The cries. Ralf dying in his arms.* Kit quickly pushed away the images to a far corner of his mind.

No one stood to greet him as he entered the keep, but it did not surprise him, knowing that his mother and wife were both ill. As his eyes adjusted to the dim light inside, he saw Dawkin hurrying toward him. The man had been Brentwood's steward for as long as Kit could remember.

"Hello, Dawkin. 'Tis good to see you."

"Greetings, my lord." The steward lowered his eyes a moment too long. When he raised them, hesitation hung in the air.

Panic surged through Kit. For a moment, he believed his beloved mother had already passed away and that he was too late to see her one more time.

Dawkin must have read his thoughts, for he quickly said, "Lady Berengaria is still with us, my lord. Weak, but very much alive." He cleared his throat. "'Tis your lady wife."

"I saw Father in London before I journeyed home. He said Richessa has been ill."

Dawkin shook his head back and forth slowly. "She is gone, my lord, from Saint Anthony's Fire. We lost her two days ago. I had her buried yesterday morning."

Kit hated that relief was the first feeling he experienced at hearing his wife was no longer alive. Living with Richessa had been as if someone had attached an anvil around his neck. He had dragged the weight of her around in misery. She had been the most empty-headed and vain person of his acquaintance, short of temper and unkind to everyone she met. He could not muster any sorrow upon hearing about her death.

"I see." He paused, his head bowed, but only prayers of gratitude at her passing came to mind. He raised his head and met Dawkin's eyes. "I wish to see my mother now."

"Your lady mother is resting in her chambers, my lord. I know it will definitely lift her spirits seeing that you have returned to Brentwood safe and sound."

Excusing himself, he made his way to the solar. The outer room stood empty. He moved to the bedchamber door and rapped lightly before entering.

Berengaria Emory lay in bed, propped up by pillows. A smile lit her pale face as she caught sight of her only child.

"Kit!"

He rushed to her side, taking her hands in his and covering them in kisses. He could feel the heat in them. Placing a palm against her forehead, he noted how hot the skin burned.

"What ails you, Mother?" he asked as he drew a chair near the bed and sat.

She shrugged. "Father William said 'tis dysorexy, mixed with a fever. I simply have no energy as of late."

Hearing that concerned him. His mother had the stamina of ten men and worked harder than anyone he had ever seen. She ruled the entire estate and castle and its inhabitants, never slowing down.

"We need to bring in a healer," he told her. Theirs had passed on three years ago and had never been replaced.

"I am just so tired," she murmured. "But we must be thankful that you have returned from that awful fighting in France."

He took her hands in his again. "I am blessed to be alive and returned to you. I won't lie. Fighting was fierce. Many did not come home to their families as I have."

"I do love you, my son." She sighed. "I cannot say how long I will be here. Because of that, I believe it's time to find you a good woman. You need to raise sons—and hopefully—find love."

Kit's thoughts immediately went to Alys de Montfort. She always danced around the periphery of his mind. And now that Richessa had passed?

What if she could be his?

"Dawkin told me of Richessa's illness and death."

His mother nodded. "I am ashamed to say I won't miss that child, for that's what she remained her entire life. She never matured, even after you brought her to Brentwood as your bride. She played at being a wife and had to be the most disagreeable woman in all of England."

Berengaria pushed herself up. "I would see you happy, Kit. It seems a lifetime ago since I heard you laugh."

"May I have your permission to bring someone here, Mother? It's a woman I met briefly at court years ago. She was skilled in the healing arts. I want her to examine you and see what can be done for your ill health. If anyone can cure what ails you, I believe she could."

She studied him. "There is more to this woman than you are saying, my son."

Kit nodded slowly, as if reaching a decision. "I believe there is. Not only did she serve in Queen Philippa's household, but both the king and queen trusted her and her medicinal remedies. Many people at court came to her for their own ailments, as well." He sighed. "And she happened to be the most vivacious and charming person I met at court."

"You had feelings for her?"

"I did," he admitted aloud for the first time. "I could not act upon them, thanks to my betrothal to Richessa, but now that I am free?" Kit sensed his resolve strengthening. "I would locate her and not only see if she would come to minister to you, but I would pursue her with everything I have."

"I can see she made quite an impression upon you."

"She did," he said resolutely. "I have thought of her many times over the past five years."

Interest brewed in her eyes. "Could you possibly love this woman?"

He heard hope in her voice. "Nay, for I only met her the one time. It's been years since I have seen her. But I believe, if given a chance, one day I could."

"Yet you have never mentioned her to me."

Kit shrugged. "What good could have come for wishing for someone I could never have? I am a man. I had a betrothed who became my wife. I moved on. But she left an indelible mark upon my heart long ago."

Berengaria reached a palm to his cheek. "Then I can only hope she is free, Kit, and that you have a chance at happiness. What is her name?"

"Alys. Alys de Montfort."

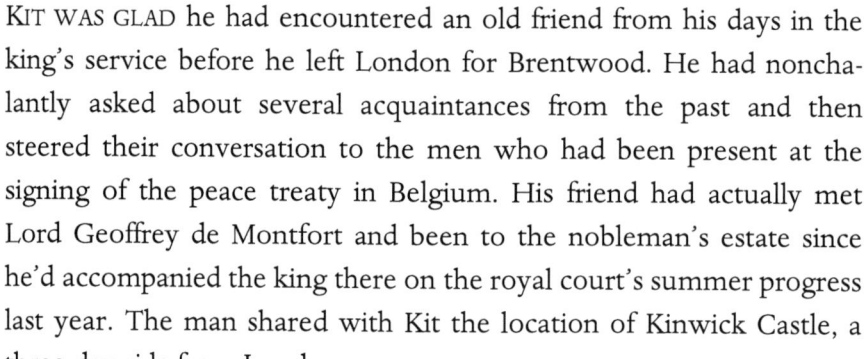

KIT WAS GLAD he had encountered an old friend from his days in the king's service before he left London for Brentwood. He had nonchalantly asked about several acquaintances from the past and then steered their conversation to the men who had been present at the signing of the peace treaty in Belgium. His friend had actually met Lord Geoffrey de Montfort and been to the nobleman's estate since he'd accompanied the king there on the royal court's summer progress last year. The man shared with Kit the location of Kinwick Castle, a three-day ride from London.

Since he had traveled a day and half north of London to reach Brentwood, Kit decided he could carve off at least half a day by skirting around London in order to reach Kinwick. He realized he should have sent a messenger first to see if Lady Alys still resided at her home, but concern for his mother's condition caused him to act hastily. He wished he'd had another few moments with Devereux and Fairfax, for he would already know what had become of her.

Kit prayed to the Blessed Christ that he would find Alys de Montfort upon reaching Kinwick, and that she would agree to return with him to Brentwood and treat his ailing mother. Selfishly, he begged that she would also be free of a husband.

He couldn't put into words why he had been so taken with this young girl and still found himself intrigued by her so long after their brief encounter. Mayhap because she seemed wise beyond her years. The fact that she had earned the implicit trust of both the king and queen at such a young age factored into it. But something about her spirit drew Kit in. Her image had stayed with him all this time.

His eagerness grew since this would be the last day of his journey. By his calculations, he should arrive at Kinwick in the next hour or two. Once again, he had impetuously set off alone in his travels, though he had taken precautions along the way. Kit scanned the road ahead and saw no one in sight. He cantered along at a steady pace in the warm sunshine, the English meadows he passed full of spring flowers in full bloom on this April day.

As he rode, his thoughts wandered to what he might find when he arrived. He would be interested in meeting Lord Geoffrey and hearing his opinion of the peace treaty since de Montfort was a man who had held the king's ear for a score or more. Devereux and Fairfax had mentioned that Alys' mother had taught her the healing arts. He wondered if Alys' rich chestnut hair was inherited from this mother. How he had fantasized about running his fingers through it after their single meeting.

Again, Kit whispered a fervent prayer to the Living Christ that his mother would be saved by Lady Alys' ministrations. Berengaria Emory was the strongest influence in his life, and he had learned everything about how to care for Brentwood and its people at her knee. He needed for her to be in his life many more years, keeping Brentwood thriving—and God Almighty willing—seeing her grandchildren play on the estate. Kit knew it would give his mother a reason to live if he could wed again and provide an heir. It would also give him a new outlook on life to bring home a new bride to Brentwood, one he could respect and even enjoy being in her company. And dare he wish for—

one that might bring love into his life. After all the fighting and ugliness he'd witnessed in France, he longed for a different kind of life with a woman who could bring him happiness and fulfillment.

Watching his parents, Kit had understood from an early age that their union had never been close, much less joyful. They lived entirely separate lives, with his father at court most of the year. Godwin Emory thrived on all the political intrigue court provided and he relished the power given to him by the king. Many years, his father had chosen to go on summer progress with the royal court and had not even returned home during that season.

His mother had the heart of a lion and the head of the wisest counselor. She ruled Brentwood with a firm yet loving hand, never afraid to make an unpopular decision if it was in the best interest of the estate and its people. She had hired multiple tutors for Kit so he would be well versed in languages and history, but he learned the most from her regarding decision making and arranging priorities, as well as how to manage people and what made a great estate work seamlessly.

That was why he wished for her to stay healthy for years to come. He believed he still had much more to learn from her. Besides, he truly enjoyed his mother's company.

Suddenly, he spied a large group ahead on foot. Their bedraggled appearance made him wary, though he didn't spot anyone armed. His daydreaming had caused him to lose focus. Kit decided since none of the men before him were mounted, he would ride quickly by the potentially hostile strangers.

As he drew near the group, they paused as one mass, spreading out across the road. It didn't matter to him if he injured any of them by barreling through their line of resistance. Nothing would cause him to come to a halt. He refused to play things safe and ride slightly off the road away from the troublesome band, for his horse could step in a hole. If it did, the animal might stumble—or worse—break a leg. That would prove disastrous.

One of the men raised a dolon from behind his back. His face looked all the more menacing thanks to the deep scar that cut across his cheek. At least the stranger threatened him with a mere club and not a mace, which held a metal-tipped end. Kit could easily withstand a blow from the club as he rode by. He glanced at the side of the road as he approached, which narrowed due to the trees on each side. He understood that was why the group halted where it had. He realized even if he'd wished to, he wouldn't be able to ride to the side of the group since the trees proved far too dense. That route would cause him to slow his horse too much, and he was unwilling to do so and be overtaken.

Energy coursed through him. He dug his spurs into the horse's side, urging it on and deliberately rode away from the man holding the dolon, aiming to burst through the other side instead. As he reached the haggard group, the line of men he headed toward leapt aside in order to avoid being trampled by his horse. Just before he came even with them, they bent into the dirt as one.

Too late, Kit realized his mistake.

The unkempt band lifted a chain a foot off the ground. There was no time to urge his horse to jump the small hurdle, for he reached it at that very moment. Strung tightly across the path, the horse's hooves hit it, and the animal stumbled. Kit sailed over its head, relinquishing the reins at the last minute so he wouldn't be dragged down with the beast.

The horse struck the ground behind him. He heard a loud snap before he also hit the earth and knew one or more of the animal's legs broke in the fall. The horse screamed in pain. His gut wrenched at the unearthly sound that reminded him of men crying out in pain across the battlefields in France.

But he was already rolling, coming to his feet, drawing his sword.

Slowly, the crew of men—eight in number—fanned out and encircled him. Kit thought he could take out at least half of them if he moved quickly. He turned slowly, noting their positions, then he rushed forward to attack.

He let his sword fly, and two men went down in mere seconds. He slashed at a third, who clasped his throat and fell to his knees, hot blood pouring into the dirt. Another strike, and a fourth man went down.

Then he was slammed from behind with great force. Kit dropped to his knees as shoots of red and gold lightning bolts clouded his vision. Someone ripped his sword away. He tried to stand and retrieve it, but again he was struck in the back of his head. Stars burst before his eyes. Vaguely, he realized the man swinging the dolon had landed the blows. Kit tried to rise, but the ground swam underneath him as another blow connected to the back of his neck. He went down, face first, before the weapon was driven hard into the small of his back. A burst of nausea filled him.

Kit struggled as they rolled him over. Booted feet stomped hard, holding his wrists down. He sensed his cloak being stripped away and tossed aside. He caught a few words of conversation and knew the men would sell it. Next, they ripped his coin purse from him. Then blows rained down upon him. Fists and kicks pummeled him till he heard ribs crack. White-hot pain shot through him.

Then half-conscious, his cotehardie and gypon were torn from him, followed by his pants. More blows struck him as men kicked his back and chest. Kit drew himself into a ball, the pain unbearable, as a loud whack against the side of his head caused his teeth to vibrate. Waves of pain shot through his head, causing his vision to go blindingly white, before a whooshing sound occurred.

Everything went pitch black.

CHAPTER 4

Alys left Mass with Ancel by her side. They returned to the great hall to break their fast.

"I don't see why Father insists on escorting us back to Winterbourne," her twin complained. "It's only an hour's ride to the north. Surely, I can manage my own two brothers for that short a time, even if one of them is Hal."

She took a sip of her ale and set it down on the trestle table. "He isn't questioning whether or not you can handle Hal and Edward. But times are different, Ancel. Even when we travel to Wellbury to visit Uncle Hugh and Aunt Milla, a group of soldiers always escorts us."

"But you don't even have to use a road to reach Wellbury," Ancel said, surprise on his face. "Our properties are adjacent."

"Aye, but it's a long way through the fields and then the forest before you reach the meadow and catch sight of Wellbury. You have been gone from England, Brother. Just as things are troubled abroad, so are they here in the kingdom."

He gave her a doubtful look. "But surely not here at Kinwick. Nor with our neighbors. We are fortunate to have good harvests and hardworking tenants. I cannot see our roads as dangerous. You're exaggerating, Alys."

"Yet you heard Father speak his mind yesterday. Prosperity slips away. Gangs of robbers infest the countryside now, roaming far and wide. They hide in forests in order to ambush travelers, placing fallen trees in the roads to bring a traveling party to a halt. Though Winterbourne seems like a short ride from Kinwick, Father is wise to take precautions."

Ancel shook his head. "I had no idea violence lay at our back doorstep. I thought I had left all of that behind in France." He tore a piece of bread from the loaf before them and chewed it thoughtfully.

"Do you think of the war often?" she asked, remembering his reluctance to discuss it yesterday.

A faraway look came to her brother's eyes. He seemed lost in thought. Then he reached and sliced a bit of cheese from the small round on the table, breaking the spell that had come over him.

"I dream of it," he admitted. "I hear the cries of the wounded. I can smell the blood pooling in the dirt under fallen men. I fought because it's what I have been trained to do all of my life. To defend England and her honor." Sadness crossed his face. "I hope you never have to see the things I saw for they can never be unseen. I have killed, Sister. Numerous times. I watched the life ebb from men whose names I will never know. My nightly prayer to the Virgin Mary is a plea for this fighting to end. For good."

Alys understood his anguish, for anything Ancel felt, she seemed to, as well. Any time he had suffered, be it a physical wound or one deep within his soul, immediately she knew something was wrong. The connection forged between them in their mother's womb had only grown stronger through the years. One morning several months ago, she had shot up from her bed, her heart pounding like the thundering hooves of a galloping horse. Her belly clenched as nausea overtook her for several minutes. Then it eased, though she still experienced discomfort the rest of the day. She had no doubt that Ancel had made his first kill on the battlefield that morning.

She covered his hand with hers and squeezed it sympathetically. "I'm glad you have returned home, Ancel, even if you'll remain at Winterbourne instead of Kinwick. I will be more at peace knowing you are close by."

He sighed. "Mayhap Father is wrong and the truce England and France signed will hold."

Alys had never known their father to be wrong, especially when it came to matters regarding politics. She could only pray that he, her brothers, and cousins by marriage would remain home for the foreseeable future.

"When do you leave for Winterbourne?"

"Father said directly after we broke our fast." Ancel brightened. "Would you like to ride with us? I'm sure Lady Johamma would enjoy seeing you. The boys, too. You know they adore you."

"Hmm. Mother did say she needed to deliver some herbs to replenish the stock she had given Johamma." She smiled. "I think I will. Let me check with her as to what I should bring with us."

"Meet me in the bailey as soon as you can. I'll have your horse saddled for you."

Alys went upstairs and found her mother in Hal and Edward's chamber, packing a few new gypons for them to wear. She explained to her mother that she would ride to Winterbourne and take whatever herbs Johamma needed.

"I will gather what I promised to her," Merryn said, "and meet you downstairs."

Within a quarter hour, the assembled group was ready to ride out from Kinwick.

Edward endured his mother's kisses without comment, but Hal began to protest when she fussed over him.

"Don't cover my face in kisses, Lady Mother," he begged. "It's unseemly for a boy my age. Edward and I will return in less than two months' time for our summer break."

Alys watched as her mother ignored his words and gripped Hal's chin in her hands. She kissed his forehead. "I will miss you every day that you are gone, Hal. Edward, too." Her eyes gleamed at her young son. "And the day will come when you will long for a woman to cover your face in kisses," she teased.

Hal turned crimson and hurried to mount his horse as those gathered had a good laugh at his expense.

The traveling party rode through the inner and outer baileys and sailed through the open gates. They passed workers weeding in the fields, waving as they cantered by.

"I adore spring," she told Ancel. "I'm sorry you will miss the upcoming May Day activities."

His eyes lit up. "We always had good times at the festivities," he agreed. "So how are you keeping yourself occupied besides learning from Mother?"

"Her knowledge is vast. I continue to learn something new from her every day," Alys replied. "But I do visit the workers on the estate and help tend to their needs. Especially Old Davey. He's gone blind now. I also serve as midwife and have delivered over a dozen babes this year."

"You told me you started doing that while at court."

"Aye. I only helped in birthing a few babes in London, but it was good experience. Mother comes with me when she can, but she has been busy with estate matters while Father spent time in Belgium negotiating the truce."

"It reminded me how Father told us that the king asked for him to come to court and serve as one of his advisers," Ancel shared. "'Twas many years ago. Soon after he returned from . . . you know."

They never spoke of that dark time—even amongst themselves. Geoffrey de Montfort had gone missing the day after his wedding, only returning when his twins were almost six years of age. When he came home to Kinwick, he was a stranger to them all. It had taken time to know him. Trust him. And love him.

"But he didn't go."

"Nay," her brother said. "He turned down the king."

"Who does that and keeps his head?" she marveled, already aware of this from what her mother had revealed.

"Apparently, Father did because he wanted to stay home with us. He told the king he was happy at Kinwick and did not want to raise his family at court. In turn, he agreed that King Edward could call upon him when necessary. The king has done so several times over the years. This truce with the French is only the latest example of Father's service."

"I admire that he stood up to the king. You know how mercurial his temper is, Ancel. Father took a great risk by demanding he be allowed to remain at Kinwick."

"I know. It makes me proud of him."

Alys was happy to hear her brother say so. She had come around to her father's presence more quickly than Ancel had. Her brother, though sunny in nature, was more cautious in placing trust in others. He and Geoffrey had mended the fences between them long ago, but it still warmed her to hear how Ancel took pride in their father's actions on their behalves.

They traveled in silence after that, basking in the sun as they rode through the countryside toward Winterbourne on a day that had turned cool. Alys was happy she had decided to accompany her brothers back to Winterbourne, even if it only meant another hour in their presence. Though she enjoyed the time she spent with her sister, Nan, Alys always looked forward to seeing her brothers, especially Ancel. Being twins, the two would always share a special bond.

Riders pulled up in front of them, so she slowed her horse and brought it to a halt. Her father whipped a hand, finger pointed, and Hemmet rode out from the group.

Alys leaned around and saw something in the road ahead.

Bodies . . .

Her throat tightened as her pulse pounded fiercely. She watched the men of Kinwick fan out and encircle the de Montfort children, their steeds facing outward. She wondered if the wandering thieves she had warned Ancel about watched them from the surrounding woods. She turned to observe her father as he assessed the situation, his eyes moving in all directions as he walked Mystery around the outside of the circle.

She focused on Hemmet as he inspected the fallen. The soldier squatted and reach a hand down. He remounted his horse and rode back in their direction and was admitted inside the circle. Her father followed, and the guard closed ranks again.

"Looks like a man was attacked on the road, my lord. I believe he cut four of them down before being overwhelmed. He's alive. Barely."

"Then we must come to his aid," Alys said. "I implore you, Father. Let me go to him."

He surveyed the area once more.

"Don't think it's a trap, my lord," Hemmet added. "I saw no one about."

"Nor I," Geoffrey agreed. "Come," he ordered. "Let us see to this fallen man." He glanced to her. "No rushing ahead, Alys," he warned.

She tamped down her impatience. The guard trotted to where bodies littered the road. As Ancel helped her dismount, Alys saw two had been cut down with a sword. Another had a gashed throat, his head almost severed from his body. A fourth faced the dirt, blood pooled beneath him. A downed horse whimpered softly. Her eyes met her twin's. He strode off in the horse's direction, and she knew Ancel would mercifully put the suffering animal down.

But it was the last man who drew her attention.

He lay curled in the road, his arms raised protectively about his head. The thieves had beaten him severely. His swollen, bloodied face was covered in dust. Fresh bruises appeared over a majority of his muscular body. She could see them because they had stolen not only his sword but the very clothes from his back.

Alys knew for him to cut down four strangers so quickly, the injured man must be a knight. Or a talented soldier, at the very least. The clothing he wore would fetch a high price at market, as would any weaponry he carried.

She bent and touched the man's throat. A weak pulse greeted her fingers. She worked her fingers through his dark brown hair and found a knot on the back of his head. Though unconscious, he moaned as she tenderly felt the goose egg. This blow could have killed him. He was lucky to have survived it.

Her hands lifted his from his head and skated down his arms. Nothing broken so far. She rolled him to his back, trying not to drink in his warrior's magnificent frame. She had tended to many injured men over the years, but this stranger's powerful build was unlike any she had ever seen. Even covered in bruises, he took her breath away.

Alys prodded him and found he'd sustained broken ribs and then discovered a stab wound in his lower right thigh. Throughout her exam, he remained unconscious and the Kinwick men around her were quiet.

She rose and faced her father. "His injuries make it dangerous to put him across a horse. We are but a quarter hour from Winterbourne. Ancel and a few others can go there to retrieve a cart."

"Shall we take him to Winterbourne?"

"Nay, Father, for he will need tending for some time. I'd rather he be under my and Mother's care at Kinwick." She looked to her twin. "Bring back wine and clean linen and place a few blankets in the cart. We need to make him as comfortable as possible and keep any jarring to a minimum."

Geoffrey sent half his guard with Ancel. When Hal demanded to go with them, a single look from his father silenced the lad. Alys knew he wanted to keep Hal and Edward with him to ensure their safety.

Alys unfastened her cloak, glad the day had warranted her wearing it. She draped it over the man. Unsheathing the baselard that she always wore tucked into her boot, she lifted her cotehardie and kirtle and pulled the hem of her smock down. Slicing through the smock's thin material, she created several long strips.

Motioning at two of the soldiers, she instructed them to lift the man so she could wind the cloth about him. The road back to Kinwick was far from smooth. She wanted his ribs jostled as little as possible. She returned the dagger to her smock, removing more material which she used to wrap round his thigh. The stab wound had stopped bleeding, but she wanted it to remain as free from dirt as possible until she could pour wine over it to cleanse the damaged skin.

She sat in the dirt and had the men lower the injured stranger back down, directing them to place his head in her lap. Cradling it, she studied his face as they returned her cloak to cover his bare body. Though covered in the dust of the road, this man seemed slightly familiar to her. Alys wondered if their paths had crossed during the time she fostered with the queen. She had met hundreds of courtiers in London and at the various palaces Edward and Philippa frequented. Mayhap she had seen or even met him during those days long ago.

Not only was his body built for war, but his face was beyond handsome. She guessed him to be a handful of years older than she, possibly five or six. Mayhap he returned from the wars in France and was headed to his home when he was attacked.

Her father knelt next to her. "He'll live?"

"Aye. It will take time for him to heal, but I foresee no problems in his recovery. Mother and I will look him over more carefully once we have him back at Kinwick and clean him up." She paused. "I'm thinking he might be a soldier returning from France."

"I thought the same," he agreed. "It would explain why he was alone on the road. The man was probably eager to return to his family."

"At least Ancel will now understand what I have tried to tell him. England has changed."

"And not for the better," Geoffrey confirmed.

Ancel returned with the soldiers from Kinwick and another ten men from Winterbourne, led by the earl himself.

"Lord Hardwin," greeted Geoffrey.

"My lord." The earl gave a deep bow. Alys noted how the earl had always been respectful—even deferential—toward Geoffrey de Montfort, even though they were of equal rank. She knew Lord Hardwin had sought his neighbor's advice many times over the years.

Her father explained the situation to Lord Hardwin and that they wanted to return the injured man to Kinwick.

"I agree. Lady Merryn and Lady Alys will take excellent care of him." Winterbourne placed a hand on her father's shoulders. "Just as I will do the same for your three sons."

Geoffrey nodded. He called Hal and Edward to him and said his goodbyes. Alys then hugged her twin, hating to let him go, but knowing he must return to his duties as squire to the earl.

"Take care, Brother," she whispered as he brushed his lips to her forehead.

"I will. And I will do my best to keep Hal and Edward out of trouble."

She laughed. "Good luck with that."

Alys went to her horse and untied the sack from the saddle horn. She took it to Lord Hardwin. "From my mother. It's herbs that Lady Johamma needed."

"I trust she will know what to do with them. 'Tis good to see you, Lady Alys. You must come visit us and your brothers once you have healed this injured stranger and seen him on his way."

"Thank you for the invitation, my lord. I will do so. I enjoy your boys and look forward to seeing you all soon."

Her father shook hands with Ancel and saw him to his horse. The earl's men surrounded the three de Montfort boys and set out for Winterbourne.

She turned to her father. "Let me tend to his leg wound with the wine, then I'll ride in the cart and try to keep him steady."

Alys returned to the injured man and unwrapped the strip of cloth from his leg. She poured the wine Ancel had brought back across his thigh and rubbed gently until the blood and dirt had been flushed from the wound. When it did not begin to bleed again, she examined it and saw the cut to be fairly shallow. She decided to let it remain free and receive the healing open air on the journey back to Kinwick.

Motioning to the men surrounding her, she stood and had them place the stranger atop the blankets in the cart. She stood and allowed her father to lift her into the vehicle as Hemmet tied both his and her horses to the back of the cart and climbed up to take the reins.

"I'll set a slow but steady pace, my lady. We will be back at Kinwick Castle in no time."

The guard fanned out as Hemmet popped his wrists and the horse started off.

Alys rested the stranger's head in her lap again and once more studied his handsome face, trying to recall where she might have seen him.

CHAPTER 5

Alys absentmindedly stroked the man's hair as they rode through the gates of Kinwick. She had murmured comforting words meant to reassure him when he stirred a few times. It took them twice as long to return home since the cart moved more slowly than traveling by horseback.

Her mother and Tilda stood waiting as they drew near the keep, an anxious look on both of their faces. Her father had sent a rider ahead to notify Merryn that they were bringing home an injured soul. Alys saw her mother's twitching fingers, a sure sign she was upset.

Hemmet steered the cart toward the foot of the stairs that led up to the keep. As he brought it to a halt, the soldiers in their party dismounted and moved to the vehicle. Two of them jumped up and took the ends of the blanket that the man rested on in their hands. They lifted it, keeping it steady as they handed it off to others waiting on the ground.

"We have a bedchamber ready," her mother said as Alys eased down, her legs stiff from being bent for so long. "Follow Tilda," she called to the men.

Their devoted servant scurried up the stairs, four soldiers carrying their guest atop the blanket.

Her mother linked an arm through Alys' as they followed. "I had water boiled and whatever medicines and herbs we might need to tend to this man brought upstairs. Tell me everything. Messengers rarely relate the entire story."

As they ascended the stairs and moved down the corridor, Alys described the scene they had come upon and the various injuries the man had suffered.

"The only thing I worry about is that he has not regained consciousness," she said.

"The blow to his head must have been severe."

"I agree. The size of the lump is vast. He tried to rouse himself but fell back into unconsciousness as we traveled home. Other than that, we can treat his broken ribs and the bruising on his torso. It's the head wound that worries me most."

"Do you believe he killed the other men you found scattered about?"

"It's the only explanation. He's a most impressive man, Mother. Tall and broad-shouldered, with corded muscles that come from long years of training. I feel certain he swings his sword for a living and was probably returning from France when attacked."

"But why was he on the road alone?" Merryn mused.

Alys shrugged. "You know men. They believe they are invincible. Father thinks this man was anxious to reach his family and had no others that traveled in his direction to keep him company. I believe he must be a nobleman since the thieves stole every stitch of his clothing—down to his boots. They even took the saddle from his horse."

She kept from her tenderhearted mother what had happened to the injured animal. It would only cause Merryn distress to know the horse had to be put down.

They entered the bedchamber across from hers, the one her brothers shared when they were home.

"I thought to place him here. It will be easier to care for him with you close by and the solar but a few doors away."

Servants appeared, carrying buckets of steaming water.

"Set them here," her mother commanded.

The soldiers had placed the man onto the largest bed in the room and awaited orders from their countess. Merryn had them lift the man's limbs as she pulled the blanket from underneath him. A low groan echoed in the room.

Alys ordered everyone out, instructing Tilda to bring broth in case the man awoke. She and her mother examined him carefully, finding no more broken bones other than his ribs.

"We need to wash him first," her mother said. "Then we can better tend to him." Merryn always emphasized cleanliness when caring for the sick and injured, believing they had a better chance for regaining good health this way.

Alys dipped a cloth into the closest bucket and began with the stranger's face, holding his chin steady as she ministered to him. The more she gazed upon him, the more Alys believed she had been introduced to him at some point. She had a good memory for names. Once he awoke and shared his with her, she was certain she would recall the time and place of their meeting.

They washed his limbs and torso in silence. Alys could not avert her eyes during the process. The more she touched the man, the more perfect he seemed, as if chiseled from stone and then made into flesh. She stroked the cloth against his massive chest, wiping away the dirt and blood. Her scalp tingled and her lips followed suit, soon followed by her heart racing. Her stomach bounced about giddily, as if she'd danced too fast, making her head swim.

She avoided touching his manhood, which had come to life under their ministrations. Alys sensed the blush on her cheeks and skipped over his member, moving down his muscled thighs. Even the man's calves spoke of his beauty, curved in such a way that caused her mouth to grow dry.

Her mother had them roll the stranger to his side. "Hold the candle close, Alys." She combed through his hair with her fingers. "The knot is large, but I find no cut anywhere." Her mother gently washed where he had suffered the blow. "Make a poultice for it. Ease him to his back again for now."

While her mother stitched the wound on the man's thigh and then dressed it with Saint John's Wort, Alys created a poultice to reduce the swelling. They lifted him again so that she could place it against his skull and wind thin linen strips around his head to secure it in place.

Once they completed that task, the two women worked together to coat the man's ribs with comfrey and wrapped them tightly in clean linen before they rubbed a salve over his bruised body.

"He will need to eat rose hips for the bruising," Alys said as she drew the bedsheet over him. "I would also macerate cabbage leaves to place on his ribs for tomorrow to further reduce the swelling and encourage healing."

"Crushed parsley will also help," her mother suggested.

"I agree." She thought a moment. "He's a large man. Even taller than Father. If you bring me cloth, I can work on a new gypon for him to wear once he's up and about."

"You plan to stay with him?"

"Aye. I feel responsible for him. I wouldn't want him to awaken alone in a strange place after surviving the attack on the road. I will sit with him. Learn his name and where he was headed. We can send a messenger so that his family won't be worried when he doesn't arrive."

Her mother rose. "Tilda will bring you needle and thread and material. I myself can work on breeches for him." She looked at their patient. "Now that he is clean, he is quite handsome."

"He is," Alys said softly.

"I'll see to the cabbage and parsley, as well. We can apply those in the morning."

The door swung open. Tilda entered, bearing a tray. "I brought a bit of bread and the broth you requested, my lady. Some weak ale, too, just in case."

"Thank you, Tilda."

Merryn said, "I will check on you later and see if you have need of anything. Come, Tilda. We need to find material to make our guest some new clothes."

The two women left the bedchamber. Alys remained seated on the bed. She took the stranger's large hand in hers. It was warm. She touched his forehead and found it slightly warm. She hoped she could keep the fever at bay if, in fact, it was fever. She'd discovered that men tended to run more hot-blooded than women. She and her mother were forever dressing in layers to ward off a chill, while her father and brothers never seemed to grow cold, even in the dead of winter.

Tilda returned a short time later with the sewing supplies. Alys retrieved a chair and sat it next to the bed and placed the candle closer to the edge of the table it stood upon, the better to see as she worked. She occasionally glanced up at her patient. He seemed to be resting comfortably. Her mother brought her the evening meal and checked on her again before bedtime.

"I am happy to sit with him," she offered.

"Nay, Mother. I will remain."

Alys closed her eyes, thinking back on the day's events. She must have fallen asleep for her body jolted, almost pitching her from the chair.

She knew who he was.

Grasping the candle, which burned low, she used it to light another one beside it. Gripping the newly lit candle, Alys brought it close and studied the man in the bed.

"He's Kit Emory," she whispered aloud. "I cannot believe I didn't see it before now."

Alys had dreamed of Kit several times over the years. As she watched the sleeping man, she recognized signs of the boy she had briefly met. Well, not actually a boy. She had been ten and two and Kit at least five years older. He'd been on the cusp of manhood. Obviously, his body had developed since they'd last seen one another. His frame had grown even taller, filling out in a most pleasing fashion. Kit must have left court, despite his father calling him to his side, in order to join the scores of Englishmen who fought in France.

His face had matured, but she grew more certain by the minute that it must be him. She remembered his easy smile and the brilliant green eyes that seemed to see to the depths of her soul.

Would he remember her?

Probably not. Years had gone by since she last saw him at Windsor Castle on the day of the queen's death. And in those passing years, surely he had married that wretched creature, Richessa, who constantly had spoken in glowing terms about her betrothed. Alys remembered Richessa bragging how the match was a most advantageous one and would benefit both of their families. Of course, they would have gone through with a marriage. There would have been no reason not to do so.

A dull ache made her head begin to throb. To have found Kit after all these years—only to lose him all over again.

But . . . where was his family home? She couldn't remember much about the Baron of Brentley, Kit's father, who had been one of many noblemen who advised the king. Wasn't his estate located to the west of London? If so, why on earth was Kit on the road between Winterbourne and Kinwick?

A cough startled her, followed by a heavy groan.

Alys looked down and saw she still held the candle above Kit. She set it on the table.

"You're safe, my lord," she said soothingly, stroking his arm reassuringly.

"I am parched." He tried to sit up and sucked in a quick breath.

"You are injured. Broken ribs. And a dagger wound, though it's not too deep."

"My head. It aches," he complained.

"You have a large knot where someone struck you rather forcefully. Mayhap more than once even."

He laughed weakly. "I fear they struck me other places, as well. My body throbs with pain all over. As if I have been kicked and then trampled."

She chuckled. "You probably were. You are a mass of bruises. Soon, you will be a rainbow of colors while you heal. Black will turn to purple and then fade to a garish green and finally a sickly yellow."

He attempted a smile. "Then I have something to look forward to."

"If you believe you can sit up, I will help you to do so. I have broth and some bread and a weak ale for you to drink."

His stomach rumbled loudly at the mention of food. "You describe a feast, my lady. How can I turn down such tempting fare? Please assist me."

Alys did her best to prop pillows behind him and not jar him much. She guided the cup of ale to his sensual lips. He wrapped a hand around hers as he drank in order to steady it. Her insides fluttered so much that she thought she might take off and soar like a bird around the room.

Tamping down the giddiness, she told him, "Enough. Now try some of the broth."

He looked at her. "I'm ashamed to admit it, but I haven't the strength to bring it to my mouth. Can you help me?"

"Of course, my lord."

It took several minutes, but he finished the broth she spooned for him and ate a few bites of the soft bread.

"I would say that was a successful meal." He frowned. "But where am I? What happened to me? How did I wind up in such terrible shape?" He grinned. "Even if it is a beautiful lady who has come to my aid."

Alys flushed at the flirtation. His green eyes danced with mischief, much as Hal's had as a small boy whenever he'd gotten into something he shouldn't have. She realized that Kit didn't recognize her and understood why. She had been a mere girl at their only meeting. Six years later, she had blossomed into full womanhood.

With all the longings that brought—and which she had never understood—till this moment.

"I accompanied my father as he escorted my three brothers to the Earl of Winterbourne's estate. It's only an hour's ride from here. My two younger brothers foster with the earl and are his pages, while my twin brother serves as his squire."

"You have a twin? How interesting. I have never known anyone who was a twin."

She swallowed, not wanting to share the next part of the story with him but knowing he needed to hear it.

"We approached Winterbourne and found you on the road, surrounding by four dead men. You must be quite the swordsman, striking down so many. We believe you were outnumbered by bandits, though, who beat you and took your possessions."

He frowned. "My sword?"

"Aye." She paused. "Even your very clothes. Highwaymen do this at times and sell the stolen goods, from surcoats to boots, at the local markets. They left you with nothing."

"They stole... *my clothes*?" he asked incredulously. "I cannot remember any of this."

"You suffered a severe blow to the back of your skull. It's possible that is why you do not remember this attack."

He started to reach behind him, but she caught his wrist. "Nay, do not touch it. You couldn't feel it anyway because I have attached a poultice to it and wrapped your head in linen to keep the poultice in place. Leave it be for now. Just know that the lump is huge."

She released his wrist and licked her lips nervously as he stared at her. Alys remained silent, letting him absorb what had occurred to him.

He unexpectedly took her hand. "So your traveling party came along and rescued me."

She grew warm as his large hand swallowed hers. The heat he gave off was tremendous, though his green eyes did not possess the look of fever in them, nor did his face appear flushed.

"Aye. I sent Ancel ahead to Winterbourne for a cart. We transported you back here to Kinwick, my home, so Mother and I could care for you. We have tended to your head and ribs and coated your bruised body with a salve that will work wonders. My mother is known far and wide as a healer. I have learned from her example ever since I was a young girl."

"You have saved my life, my lady. Surely, I would have died if left in the road."

She sensed the blush rising on her cheeks as he gazed at her intently. "We were happy to do so. But you will need to stay with us a short time in order to recover from your injuries. Might we send a messenger to your family and notify them of your whereabouts?"

He gave her a blank look and finally said, "'Twill be impossible, I fear."

"Why?"

"I know not who I am."

CHAPTER 6

*K*IT DID NOT *know who he was.*

Alys took in the news. She realized the blow to his skull must be responsible for this lapse in his memory.

Should she tell him who he was? Better yet, was she certain he even *was* Kit Emory? Doubt festered within her. It had been several years since their one, brief encounter. True, she saw some of the young man she had met in this stranger's face as they now spoke. Yet he was so large. His features seemed different. His voice was much deeper.

What if she was wrong and this man was not Kit Emory? If she revealed his identity to him, he might accept it and not try to recollect who he truly was. That could prove disastrous. And if he truly was Kit, he needed to come to this realization on his own. It would be part of the healing process.

Still, she felt guilty hiding the knowledge from him of who she believed him to be. Part of her wondered if she did so in order to enjoy his company while he mended.

Before he returned to his wife.

Alys saw the expression on his face change to frustration. "You will regain your memory, my lord," she said, her voice trying to reassure him.

"How do you even know I am of noble birth?"

"Because the thieves stole every stitch of the finery you wore?" she ventured, hoping her light, teasing tone would ease his burden.

"I might be one of those thieves," he said. "I might have had a disagreement with the leader and was attacked by the group of them. Mother of God—I might even *be* the leader of this gang, and they rebelled against my authority."

She laughed aloud. "You certainly have a creative mind, my lord. No, by your speech alone, I would know you are of noble birth. From your immense size, I believe you are a knight who has returned from the fighting in France. Now that the truce has been signed, you most likely were on your way home to your family and estates when you were attacked."

"France." He closed his eyes and grew silent—but continued to hold her hand. Alys never wanted him to relinquish it. His touch brought her a sense of peace. And longing. What she wouldn't give to brush her lips against his. Be enfolded in his embrace.

The piercing green eyes opened. "I can remember bits and pieces. The sounds on the battlefield. I think you are right, my lady. I fought in France. That feels like something I would do." He yawned suddenly.

"You're tired. Now that you have eaten, try to get some more rest."

"Will you stay with me?" he asked.

"If you wish."

He gave her a sleepy smile. "And your name, my lady?"

"Alys. Alys de Montfort."

"Thank you, Lady Alys . . ."

She watched him drift off into sleep. His hand still held hers. She left it, not wanting to disturb him. Oh, who was she trying to fool? She wanted never to let go of him. She wished she could climb into the bed beside him and curl up against his large, muscular frame.

Alys could not believe that, in a matter of minutes, she had gone from a self-assured woman with no thought but to help others to one who puddled in her chair, melting at the touch of this man.

One she knew could never be hers.

A little voice told her, *"But he can—even if only for a short while."*

She would take what crumbs she could get. Alys leaned forward and lay her head on the bed next to his hip, her eyes focused on their joined hands. Closing her eyes, she dreamed of what might have been.

HE AWOKE AGAIN, slowly opening his eyes. A single candle burned low, casting a little light about the room. He was in a bed. And God's Wounds, he ached everywhere. By the Heavens above, his body hurt beyond anything he had experienced before. At least, he thought that was the case.

War. She had talked of war. With France. He believed her. He could feel a sword in his hand. Knew he had cut down men with it. The sounds came to him. Horses charging into battle. The screams. Cries of agony. They all held a familiarity.

He was conscious of his hand wrapped around hers—and warmth by his side.

He looked over and saw she sat in a chair, but the upper half of her body rested on the bed. She must have stayed with him all night and grown weary.

Alys. That was her name. Gradually, he recalled what she had told him. What had happened to him as he journeyed... home? He couldn't say. No image came to mind of where he lived or what his family looked like. Did he still have parents? Was he wed? Might he have children of his own?

Everything seemed a blur.

He looked down at the chestnut hair that had come loose from her braid. Long strands spilled about her. Even in the dim light, the rich color drew him in. His free hand reached over to smooth her hair. He left it resting against her head. Touching her brought him comfort. Serenity. He viewed the smooth, ivory skin and rosebud lips, finding great beauty in Lady Alys. Her compassion and kindness he was already familiar with, but now his manhood stirred as he focused on her physical beauty. He would love to see her smile again. No, he desired more than a smile. He wanted to plunge deep inside her. Bring pleasure to her. Have that beautiful mouth call out his name.

Whatever it might be.

He removed his hand from her hair, his fingers reluctantly parting from the silken strands. He didn't want her to awaken and think he took advantage of her in her sleep. He was not that kind of man. At least, he didn't think so—but who knew?

He drew his eyes away from Lady Alys and studied himself. The linen bedsheet had fallen to his waist. He saw he was a large man. Heavily muscled through his battered chest and arms. He sensed the strength within him despite the punishment his body had undergone. Had it been a large group that had attacked him? She said he had slain four men. He closed his eyes and tried to remember, but he drew a blank.

Footsteps. In the quiet of the castle, he heard them. They paused nearby. Then the door to the bedchamber opened. A woman's figure silhouetted in the doorway. He raised his hand and motioned for her to enter.

As she approached, he knew her.

"You could be no other than Lady Alys' mother," he said softly. "So this is what she will look like as she matures." The woman standing next to the bed was tall and willowy, with high breasts and a small waist. A few years shy of two score, but still a remarkably beautiful woman with her luminous skin and chestnut hair.

The noblewoman looked down at her sleeping daughter and smiled. "I am Lady Merryn de Montfort. Since you know Alys by name, I suppose you have already spoken with her."

"Aye, my lady. She told me how the escort party to Winterbourne came across me and what they suspect happened to me during my travels."

"You don't remember the incident?"

"Nay."

"That might be for the best. If Alys didn't tell you, you are at Kinwick Castle, home of the de Montforts. My husband, Geoffrey, believes you are a soldier. He recently returned home from Belgium, where he helped negotiate the fragile truce between England and

France. Are you also returning from the continent, my lord?"

He sighed. "I am uncertain." When she frowned in confusion, he told her, "I fear I do not remember my name, Lady Merryn. I know not where I rode from nor where I traveled to."

She nodded. "That doesn't surprise me. You suffered a severe blow to your head. I've seen this a few times over the years. When we were children, my brother was thrown from a horse. For two days, Hugh was vague on what had occurred and looked at everyone about him as a stranger. He recovered his memories quickly, though. And I tended to a servant once who had climbed into a cart. He stepped backward and fell out, striking his head against the ground. He remained confused for several days, not knowing his name or what had happened leading up to the incident."

"But he regained that knowledge?"

"Aye. It took over a sennight, but everything came to him at once." She chuckled. "He never volunteered to jump up in a cart and remove goods from the village after that. He was content to have others hand items down to him so that he could carry the goods inside the keep."

Lady Merryn nodded reassuringly. "You will be fine, my lord. Alys and I shall take excellent care of you. Your memories will return, and you will be on your way home or to wherever you need to go."

"Your daughter said you—and she—are healers."

"A woman named Sephare trained me early in the healing arts. I have done the same with Alys. I believe her knowledge now surpasses mine."

"Then I trust I am in good hands with the two of you."

Alys stirred, a small sigh escaping from her. She raised her head, blinking sleepily.

"Mother?"

"Good morning to you. I've been speaking with our guest."

Alys looked at him sheepishly. "I am sorry I fell asleep."

"I did the same. And if I had need of something, I could have awoken you." His stomach grumbled loudly. "It sounds as if the bread and broth you fed me were not enough to keep my belly filled."

"Let me go to the kitchens and retrieve something for you, my lord. It would do me good to stretch my limbs." She frowned and twisted in the chair.

As she stood, she pulled her hand from his. Instantly, a sense of loneliness descended upon him. Her hand belonged in his. He longed to bring her to him and kiss her, long and slow.

"I'll return soon with plenty for you to eat," Alys promised him.

Lady Merryn tucked a hand through the crook of her daughter's arm. They began discussing what to do for him next as they left the room.

He watched the swing of Alys' hips as she walked away and caught the sweet curve of her breast as she turned to the side.

Had he ever wanted a woman more? Flashes of couplings with others danced through his head—but none brought the desire that flickered in him for the beautiful woman who had just left the bedchamber.

He believed himself cautious by nature. It was a sense he had of himself. Yet he would throw caution out the window in order to lay himself at the feet of Alys de Montfort. He wondered why a woman he'd only met had such an effect on him.

The one thing he did know—he couldn't let on regarding the attraction he felt to her. He might not be free to forge an alliance with her. Worse, she might have a husband of her own. It wouldn't go well if the man came in and found his wife kissing her patient.

He would bide his time. Figure out who he was. Hope that he might be free—and that Alys was, as well.

If so?

The first thing he would do is kiss her senseless.

CHAPTER 7

"CHECKMATE," ALYS PROCLAIMED, her sapphire blue eyes sparkling with her victory.

"Surely, I can't be as poor a player as I have demonstrated," he said in frustration. "I know how to play the game. I remember the rules. But for the life of me, I cannot seem to defeat you, my lady."

She lifted the chessboard from the bed with ease, balancing the pieces carefully despite their heavy weight. He watched her walk to a nearby table and set the game board down. Though tall and slender, she seemed strong for a woman. Though he could not say what his experience with women had been in the past, he believed they were physically frail creatures.

But not Alys de Montfort.

As she returned to her chair, he commented, "That board and its piece are quite heavy. I am surprised you carried it with such ease."

She grinned. "I may be a woman, but I'm quick and strong. I often carry food and medicines to the workers on our estate, so I'm used to hauling heavy baskets about. I collect herbs and plants from our gardens or gather them from the nearby meadows and forests and grind the herbs with my mortar and pestle, which also takes strength. And I train every week with my sword."

Her words caught him by surprise. "You train with a weapon? As a soldier does?"

Alys nodded. "When we were five or six, my father's cousin, Raynor, crafted a wooden sword for Ancel, my twin brother. He thought himself quite the little knight and went about swinging it every which way in a very superior manner. I begged Raynor for one of my own. At first, he didn't want to provide me with one, but Mother insisted. She thought it important that I learn to defend myself." She paused. "Even if it was from my demon of a brother."

He laughed. "I would have liked to see you then with your sword. Or now," he added. The thought of Alys de Montfort slicing through the air with a sword sparked his interest in her even more—and he had not thought that possible.

"My blade is now of steel. Gilbert, our captain of the guard, puts me through my paces at least twice a week. The weapon is smaller and lighter than one a man yields, but if I needed to defend myself or Kinwick, I wouldn't be embarrassed by my performance. I have begun giving my younger sister, Nan, lessons, as well. Raynor crafted her a sword not too long ago, and she has taken up the practice with a skill I did not believe possible in one so young."

"Is she your only sister?" he asked. He was curious about her. Since she seemed in a talkative mood, he determined to learn what he could about her.

"Aye. She is six years of age. Our Nan is already a beauty, and she is smarter than any of us, I believe."

"You mentioned your brother, Ancel. Where is he? And do you have other brothers?"

"My lord, we discussed my brothers when you first awoke after we brought you here," Alys reminded him.

He looked a little perplexed. "I fear that my memory is a little fuzzy regarding our first conversation. It must be the effects of the attack I suffered."

A smile touched her lips. He wondered if he was brother to another and how they felt about him. An emptiness rested inside of him, leading him to believe he didn't have the type of relationship Alys had with her siblings.

"All three of my brothers live at Winterbourne, to the north of us. The estate is near where we found you. Hal is one and ten and Edward but nine. They foster with the Earl of Winterbourne and serve as pages in his household. Ancel is squire to Lord Hardwin. When Ancel left Kinwick to foster, it was the first time we were separated since the womb."

A wistful look crossed her face. He had to physically restrain himself from reaching out to touch her in comfort.

Then she continued. "Hal is a whirlwind, into everything, but already a leader. Edward has the sweetest of temperaments and follows Hal's lead."

"Whether it leads them into mischief or not?" he guessed.

She laughed. "It sounds as if you have brothers of your own and may have led them astray a time or two."

He shrugged. "I hope we will soon learn of that possibility. But if your brothers all went to Winterbourne, did you not follow them?"

"Nay." An odd look crossed her face. She stared at him intently. "I fostered at the royal court. With Queen Philippa." She paused as if she gauged his reaction.

He frowned. Something tugged at him. A faint memory regarding the queen. Had he ever been in her presence?

Then somehow he knew. "She is dead, I think. Something tells me she is."

Alys nibbled at her bottom lip. "Aye, she is. She passed away some six years ago. I left London at that time and returned to Kinwick."

His curiosity grew. "What was she like? I feel in my bones that I might have seen her before. Or even the king." A picture came to his mind of one with regal bearing. "A strong man. Virile. Shrewd." He thought a moment. "With a quick temper."

"You have certainly described King Edward. He is a most intelligent man and powerful ruler but mercurial in his moods. The queen was his opposite. She was slow to anger and patient to a fault. No one could talk the king out of a foul mood as Queen Philippa could. They were a good match and very much in love."

"In love, you say?" The thought of the king acting like a lovestruck fool didn't fit the image in his mind of the monarch.

"Very much so. Though the marriage was arranged, their relationship grew from one of strangers to mutual respect and then finally love."

He caught the tender look in her eyes as she spoke of this royal couple—and of love.

"So you believe in love?" he asked, wondering if he did.

She nodded with enthusiasm. "I do. My parents loved each other from their childhood. Raynor, the cousin I mentioned, met his wife, Beatrice, and fell madly in love with her—even though he believed her to be betrothed to another."

Alys sat up, a sweet smile lighting her features. "And one of our knights, Michael Devereux, fell in love with my cousin, Elysande, as they delivered a foal." She laughed, the sound a merry tinkling to his ears. "Michael did not even know her name and yet knew he wanted to wed her. And my other cousin, Avelyn, met her husband when he escorted her home from London. They, too, became a true love match and wed."

"You would have me believe that falling in love runs in your family."

"Wouldn't you say so after hearing about all of those couples?" Her heightened color brought out the blue in her eyes and made that rosebud of a mouth infinitely more tempting to him. "Of course, I realize that it's the rare couple who marry and fall in love. Marriage is a duty and a way to unite family fortunes and gain political affiliations. Often, it's arranged to strengthen bonds at court and throughout the nobility."

She sat back in her chair and sighed. "But I have witnessed love firsthand. I believe in it. I hope for it."

"You are not married?" he asked, praying she was not.

"Nay," she said softly. "Nor have I a betrothed."

"That's unusual," he replied. "May I ask your age?" He wondered how old he himself might be.

"I am seven and ten for another four months."

"Why have your parents not chosen a husband for you?"

Alys worried her full, bottom lip again, causing a wave of desire to ripple through him.

"The queen was going to choose a husband for me before she passed. When I came home after her death, marriage was the last thing on my mind." She looked about the room as if searching for an answer. "And I have been content at Kinwick these past years. Father and Mother haven't pressed me to wed. Mayhap I am not meant to." Her last words came out just above a whisper.

"But you must," he insisted. "You are a well-bred, beautiful, interesting woman. You would make an excellent wife, my lady. Just look how well you have cared for me."

She gazed at him a long moment, as if she plunged into the depths of his very soul. "I will know when I have found the right man to wed. It will be a love match for me—or none at all."

Alys rose. "I have kept you from your rest long enough, my lord. Mayhap if you sleep, you will be strong enough in body and mind to defeat me when we next play chess."

The playful light in her eyes and ghost of a smile teased him. A hot wave of fresh desire poured through him again as he imagined her naked, entwined in his arms.

"Then I shall rest all the harder, knowing I won't be entirely well until I can claim victory through checkmate."

"I bid you goodnight, my lord." She slipped from the room and closed the door behind her.

How could he rest when his mind swirled so?

He slammed a hand down on the bed and gasped at the ripple of pain that sprouted from his broken ribs. He wondered how long they would take to mend. He fingered the stitches along his thigh. These, at least, seemed familiar to him. He knew he'd gotten them before, for already the itch at the place of the wound was something known to him. A week had passed since he had been brought to Kinwick. Though the bruises had begun to fade, he could see a few scars upon his flesh where he had suffered prior injuries.

That led him to believe he was a soldier. Alys spoke of the men he'd downed when attacked. Again, vague shadows of him raising his sword crossed his mind. He closed his eyes and could envision himself riding on a horse as he approached—no, charged—a line of men. Flashes of sunlight glinting on his swinging sword flittered by. Then all went dark, as if his mind shielded him from remembering the way he had been injured.

He pushed a hand through his hair and opened his eyes, searching the room. He'd been placed in a large bedchamber, much larger than he had known. That was what he believed in his foggy mind. He lay in a bed, and two smaller ones faced opposite it. He couldn't remember anyone else sleeping in the room since he'd been brought here. Either its occupants had been encouraged to sleep elsewhere, or they were not present. He guessed this room might belong to the siblings Alys had mentioned. The twin brother. Ancel. The younger two. Hal and Edward.

At least he'd finally discovered that she was unwed—and unattached. He sank back into the pillows and allowed himself to think of her. She wore her thick, chestnut hair in a long braid every day. His fingers itched to undo the complicated plait so he could rub the silken strands between the pads of his fingers. Her eyes, a vivid blue, seemed kind—yet sometimes they danced with mischief. Her heart-shaped face called for him to cup it in his hands. He longed to stroke those porcelain cheeks with his thumbs.

More than anything, her mouth called to him. Those pink lips cried out to be kissed. He wished to brush his mouth against hers while he explored the sweet curve of her breasts and hips. Yet how could he act in so coarse a manner? Lady Alys had rescued him. Saved his life. He would never repay her by pawing at her.

For all he knew, he might be betrothed—or wed.

He sensed he must be older than she was. That meant it was possible that he possessed a woman in his life. He couldn't allow his physical yearnings to override good sense when he might not be free.

But what he would give for one night in Alys de Montfort's bed.

He shook his head to clear those wicked thoughts. At least the action no longer pained him, as the lump on the back of his skull had dwindled rapidly, even if it remained sensitive to his touch. He needed to assess his situation.

What did he know?

He knew war. His gut told him as much. With the truce he'd learned about, he must have returned home to England. He would ask Lady Alys where Kinwick lay. For some reason, he could picture London. The streets. The crowds. Wait . . . *he knew the royal court.* He hadn't simply glimpsed the king and queen. He could imagine ladies in their finery and courtiers dressed in rich, vibrant colors. He knew exactly what King Edward looked like because he'd seen the monarch in person. Up close. And the queen. Sadness welled in him, knowing she was no more.

Think.

He brought up the king's image clearly. This time, a newer one came to him. That of an older man, but still imposing. Now another likeness came to him, one that bespoke of age, even frailty. The king was no longer a strong man. Age and sickness marked his appearance.

But if he knew of the sovereign at different times, did that mean he had been to court often? Could he have possibly grown up there or even fostered with a nobleman who spent time at the royal palace?

All this thinking made his head throb. He touched the small, swollen knot at the back of his skull. Still tender. He brought his hands to his face and touched it gingerly. It was a bit puffy and no doubt bruised. A lump over his left brow bowed out. He could imagine what he looked like. He had probably given Lady Alys and her mother quite a fright.

Yet as they tended to him, neither seemed jarred by his appearance. Both women had a competent, light touch. Their assured manner and frank words led him to believe they hid nothing about his injuries from him.

He pulled the linen sheet up and shut his eyes as weariness descended upon him. Sleep would help restore his battered body and aching head.

That . . . and another visit from Lady Alys. That would be the best medicine possible.

CHAPTER 8

ALYS KNOCKED ON Kit's chamber door and wasn't surprised when he opened the door to admit her. He began restlessly pacing the room as she set down the tray she had brought him so he could break his fast.

"I see that you are ready to be up and about, my lord."

He pushed a hand through his thick, brown hair. "I've spent more than a week in bed. I am ready to stretch my legs and see something of your estate, my lady." He looked sheepish. "If you feel I won't frighten anyone with my appearance."

His battered face still held a few bruises from the attack but wasn't affected as much as his body. The garish colors she had predicted covered his torso and limbs in a variety of hues as he healed.

"Your face appears almost normal. I can fetch a small hand mirror for you if you would care to see yourself."

He brightened. "I would. That might help spark my memory."

"I will bring it at once while you break your fast."

Alys left the bedchamber, her heart pounding in her chest. She should have thought to let him view his image. She knew she was being selfish, keeping his identity from him—for she had determined he must be Kit Emory. Though she'd had but a single conversation with him years ago, he had left an indelible print on her memory. The more she spoke with him, the more she could see the young man he had once been.

The one she longed for with all her heart.

She wavered between telling him who he was and believing he

should come to the realization on his own. If she told him now that she had known who he was all along, she couldn't predict what his reaction might be. Nay, she could, for she knew what hers would have been. She would be furious with the person who kept her very name from her. She would lash out at him or her. Curse them.

And never forgive them.

That was why she had kept her secret, for with each conversation she had with Kit, each moment she spent in his company, she became more drawn to his intelligence and quick sense of humor. Alys liked that he treated her as an equal. Many men would not have done so. She enjoyed his company immensely and did not want him to leave Kinwick.

It was wrong. She knew it was wrong. Alys knew she should speak up. But every time she tried to, she became lost in his emerald eyes. Bewitched by his handsome face. Drawn to him as she had been to no other man.

She knocked on the solar door but received no answer. She supposed her parents remained in the great hall, breaking their fast after mass. Alys entered and went inside the bedchamber. She lifted her mother's mirror to her own face and studied herself, something she rarely did. Her cheeks had color in them. Her eyes looked bluer than they normally did. She wondered what Kit thought of her looks.

That thought made her tear her eyes away from her image. Nay, she should not think in this manner. Kit was married to Richessa. It did not matter if he thought her pretty or interesting looking. He had a wife and probably children by now. Selfishly, she was keeping him from his family and home.

The sudden thought of him returning to them—leaving her alone at Kinwick—caused her knees to buckle. She dropped to the ground. Hot tears sprang to her eyes.

"Alys?"

Her mother's voice undid her. The tears began to flow rapidly, spilling onto the stone floor.

Wordlessly, her mother's arms came about her, bringing her close.

She gave in to them as her mother stroked her back, murmuring sounds of sympathy and encouragement. Alys cried till she had nothing left. She took a cleansing breath and wiped her cheeks with the back of her hand.

"It's this stranger," Merryn said. "You have feelings for him."

"Aye," she admitted, her voice a hoarse whisper. "And I should not."

Her mother drew Alys to her feet. "You cannot contain your feelings, my sweet. It's like saying you could control the wind or the rain." She kissed Alys' forehead. "I hope he will remember who he is soon. Then we can explore whether the two of you could have a future together or not."

Alys clung to her mother. She should tell her mother that she knew who Kit was. That he was not free. That she lied by omission and kept the truth from him.

But she couldn't. Shame filled her at what she had done. She had never disappointed her parents in any way. She was embarrassed to admit she had kept such a wicked secret.

Her mother drew back. "I see you have a mirror."

"Aye. He thought if he saw himself, it might help his memory return."

"It could. That and all the ginger we have given him to eat. Sephare always told me that would aid a person's memory. I hope she was right." Merryn cupped Alys' cheek. "Bathe your face in some cool water before you go back to him. And remember, whatever happens, you know your father and I love you and will support you."

"Even if I choose not to marry?" The thought sprang to her head. If she couldn't have Kit as her husband, she didn't want any other man.

Her mother frowned. "Why would you say that, Alys? You nurture everyone about you. You will make a fine wife and mother someday."

She swallowed. "I may wish to return to court. To be a healer. For the royal family and those who reside there."

Disappointment flickered across her mother's face. "I know the king would be happy to have you back. Your skills now outshine my own." She paused. "But do you truly want to go back into court and all the politics?"

"I am only considering it."

Her mother nodded wisely. "You believe this man might have a family. And you have fallen in love and believe you could be happy with none but him."

Alys bit her lip and held back her tears. "You know me well, Mother."

Merryn put an arm about her. "No decisions need to be made yet, my love. We must first find out who this man is. Where he comes from. Then we will go from there. Now splash that water on your face. You will feel better for it." She pressed another kiss to Alys' cheek and left the room.

"I should have told her," Alys muttered once the room was hers again. "I should tell him. I *will* tell him," she determined. "If he cannot remember who he is by May Day, I will tell him his name and suffer the consequences."

That gave her today to enjoy his company—if he didn't recall he was Kit Emory before then. Then she would let him go to live his life with Richessa, and she would make a new one for herself—one without Kit in it.

Calmly, she washed her face and took another glimpse at herself in the mirror. She seemed much as she had before.

Alys steeled herself and returned to Kit's bedchamber.

HE PACED THE chamber nervously, wondering what took Alys so long in retrieving a mirror.

It struck him that she had none of her own.

To think that a woman of her beauty had no idea how she moved him. He knew women—many of them. The last several nights he had dreamed of women. Had flashes of memories of his limbs entangled with other female ones. Even though he couldn't remember his own name, his gut told him that he had been with a score of women over the years.

Yet none could hold a candle to Alys de Montfort.

No matter whom he had encountered in his past, whatever his relationship had been with them, he wanted only one woman now.

Alys.

He heard her steps in the corridor and looked up as she entered his room. Instantly, he knew something was wrong. She was paler than when she had left, her eyes puffy.

She had been crying.

Without thought, he crossed quickly to her and cupped her face in his hands. He almost bent to comfort her with a kiss, but her eyes widened and she pulled away. Her arms crossed protectively in front of her, as if to ward him off. He saw the hand mirror clasped between her fingers.

He wanted to ask what had upset her, but he didn't know how to deal with whatever answer she gave him. Instead, he held an open palm out. She understood and placed the mirror in it. He stepped away and turned his back to her. Somehow he didn't want her to watch as he viewed himself.

His hand rose slowly, bringing the mirror to eye level. He brought it closer and moved it around, curious as to what he saw. Thick, dark brown hair. A high forehead, the knot over his brow now a bump. Brilliant green eyes. A strong jaw. A mouth that would enjoy kissing.

But no recognition came, no response from his body or brain. He studied the image dispassionately, as if it were a stranger before him.

Lowering his arm, he faced Alys. He could not read the odd expression upon her face. Wordlessly, he shook his head and stepped to her, returning the mirror.

"It stirred nothing?" she asked. "No memories?"

"None." His voice was flat. He hid the disappointment and hurt that began to well inside him. "I had hoped seeing myself might spark some recollection. It didn't."

She looked at him a long time, as if she tried to come to some decision. Then she brightened.

"I think you are ready to get some fresh air," she declared. "You must be tired of being cooped up in your sickroom."

"I am more than ready to fly my coop, my lady, if you will but join me. Might I see something of your family's estate?" He saw the flash of consternation cross her face. "I don't mean to ride yet, but I would enjoy a long walk. I need to regain my strength as much as my memory."

Alys visibly relaxed. "If you would like to see around the keep, Tilda would be happy to show you. If you want to see the castle grounds, I will see if one of our soldiers might escort you. You might want to watch our men training in the yard."

Disappointment sank in when he realized she would not accompany him. "And where will you be, my lady?"

A blush stained her cheeks. "I have neglected visiting our tenants this past week. I must make my rounds and see to some of our sick and ailing."

"Then I will come with you."

"Nay. I have far to walk."

He snorted. "You think me not capable of keeping up with you? I'm not an invalid, my lady. My bruised body is recovering. Movement will be good for me. As for my broken ribs, I promise not to run giddily about since you are releasing me from my sickbed. As long as I don't go lifting heavy objects, they will be fine. My legs have carried me many places over the years. I trust they can walk about the countryside with no problem."

"But you might become bored."

"Bored, you say? Bored is lying abed as I have for a week. The only interesting thing that has taken place is when you have come to tend to me or keep me company. I long to get out in the sunshine."

Still, she looked unsure. "It will only be walking to various workers' cottages."

"As you said, the fresh air will do me good. If I tire, I will return to the keep."

Alys nodded. "Then come with me to the herb room."

"Lady, I would travel to the kitchens if it meant leaving this chamber."

She burst out laughing. The sound brought a smile to his face then he, too, began laughing. And hurting. He wrapped an arm about his right side, holding it gently against his broken ribs.

Seeing what he did only made Alys laugh harder. Tears began to leak from her eyes.

"I am sorry, my lord. I don't mean to laugh at you. You are such a large man. I am sure you are fierce on the battlefield," she wheezed. "But to see laughter reduce you to . . ." She couldn't go on because she had erupted in peals of her own laughter again.

"I'm happy to see that I can entertain you," he said. "Now you laugh at my pain as well as my chess play."

His words caused her to double over in laughter again. "You . . . you aren't a bad player," she sputtered, "just . . . just one . . ." She sucked in a quick breath. "Sorry."

"Aye, my play has been sorry. Thank you for pointing that out, my lady," he said, teasing her.

Her giggles dissolved. She licked her lips nervously. The gesture tugged hard on him. He swallowed, his hands falling to his sides.

Now recovered, she nodded. "Follow me, my lord."

He did so, along a long corridor lit with a few sconces and down a sweeping staircase and into the great hall. The large room held trestle tables pushed against three of its sides and smelled of some sweet scent that coated the rushes they walked upon. A servant passed and dipped a curtsey to him. He gave her a nod. The woman eyed him with speculation and gave him a wink as she moved away, her hips swaying suggestively.

But it meant nothing. In the past, he knew he would have sought the woman out and spent a night with her. He imagined he had spent many nights in the company of such women, women who probably remained nameless to him. Ones he had used to pleasure himself with.

Now, he was interested in only one woman. Oddly enough, he wanted to pleasure her more than he would receive in return. He knew, in that moment, that something within him had changed. Fundamentally, he thought he had been a selfish man, one who thought only of himself and what others could do for him.

Yet a single woman with a magical smile and porcelain skin and a long, chestnut braid was making him into a new man. He wanted to be a better man than he had been.

For her.

He watched Alys round a corner and cut through the kitchens, already busy with women preparing the noon meal. The food Alys and Lady Merryn had brought to him had been tasty, much better than the fare he was accustomed to, at least that was what he thought. Though if he had fought on the battlefields of France, anything hot would have tempted his taste buds.

She entered a room and he followed closely behind her. Shelves lined the walls, with jars and many sizes of vessels sitting upon them. A large, rectangular table stood in the middle.

Alys placed two large baskets upon the table. She began filling one as she said, "This is the workspace Mother and I use. We bring our herbs in here to preserve them. We also blend all of our medicines here, tonics and the like."

"You have an impressive stockpile of items, my lady. I suppose this is where all my ginger has come from."

"Aye. Mother still believes it will aid in your memory being recovered."

She finished placing items in the basket and took it in one hand and gathered the empty one in the other. "Let me stop at the kitchens and have Cook fill this one."

"You take food to others?"

"Certain items. Especially to those who might need the extra help."

After the Kinwick cook had loaded the basket with breads, cheeses, and fish, he took it from her, waving away Alys' protests.

"It's not that heavy, my lady. I can hold it close so it won't bother my sore ribs in the least. In fact, let me have your other basket. It will help me build my strength back up."

"Nay, I am used to carrying it. Come. Let us go."

She led him through the inner bailey and past the training yard where steel swords clanged against one another. Alys waved to two men standing above the others on a raised platform. The taller one jumped down and headed in their direction. His stride held purpose, while his features noted his noble birth. His size and the grace with which he moved spoke of his skill as a warrior.

"It's good to see you out and about," he said. "I am Geoffrey de Montfort, Earl of Kinwick."

He shook the offered hand. "I am indebted to you, my lord. Many thanks for retrieving me from the attack I suffered."

"I know Merryn and Alys have taken excellent care of you. They like nothing better than to have a patient to fuss over."

He laughed. "They have both been most gracious and competent. I am mending fast, thanks to the salves they have applied." He reached to rub the bump on the back of his skull. "Now if they could only help me find my memory."

De Montfort sighed. "I'm sure you will be right in no time, my lord. Until then, our hospitality is extended to you."

"I hope I will remember something of myself soon, Lord Geoffrey. I do not want to wear out my welcome."

"Don't trouble yourself. When you are ready, you may join my men in the training yard."

Excitement filled him. "That's most kind of you, my lord. I hope I can do so soon."

The nobleman looked to his daughter. "I see Alys grows impatient with our conversation. Go, my sweet. I know you have others to tend to." He looked back. "I hope you will join us for the evening meal tonight, my lord."

"It would be my pleasure. Thank you for the invitation."

De Montfort excused himself and returned to watching his men.

He felt a pang of longing to be where those men were, swinging maces and swords. The sounds and smells of the training yard called out to him. He believed it to be his second home.

"Does your father always observe his soldiers' training sessions?" he asked as they continued on their way.

"He and Gilbert, our captain of the guard, often watch the men from the raised platform, but most times they both wind up amongst them, offering themselves up as training partners or pointing out ways the soldiers can improve their swordplay."

"You said Gilbert is the one who helps you train with your sword?" he asked.

"Aye. Gilbert has been with us since I can remember. He has great patience and skill."

"I would love to watch you in action with your sword," he said. He imagined her braid swinging as her sword came crashing down. The fire in her eyes. Her heaving bosom after exertion. And more than ever, he wanted her in his bed.

"My lady, would you look at the smithy's burn?"

He watched Alys rush past the stables to the blacksmith's shed. As he passed the familiar smell of hay, he wondered what had happened to the horse he rode when he was attacked. Seeing that Alys would be busy, he stepped inside the stable and saw a lad toting a pail of oats.

"Excuse me!" he called.

The boy hurried over to him. "Yes, my lord?"

"I was brought to Kinwick when—"

"Aye, my lord. We all know. 'Twas bad 'uns who set upon you. Lady Alys saved you." His eyes grew round. "She saves lots o' people. And animals. Our Lady Alys has a most tender heart."

"I have found that to be true," he agreed. "I wanted to ask if my horse might have been found and brought back here."

He looked puzzled. "Nay. No horse returned with you. Them thieves probably rode off on it. Or sold it at market, they did."

"I hadn't thought of that. Thank you."

He left the stable. He couldn't remember his horse's name or any attachment to one. Then a swift picture clouded his head. His war horse. He could feel the beast as he sat atop it. Feel his thighs pressed into its muscled sides. Look down and see the crinet protecting the destrier's neck. Feel the hard flanchard protecting the animal's flanks. His destrier was a dappled gray. He couldn't recall its name, but a tremendous sense of sadness overwhelmed him at once.

The horse had died in battle. He heard the swift swoosh of an arrow that flew through the air. The sound of it penetrating the destrier's flesh. The faltering step. The horse beginning to fall. His leap away so as not to be pinned under hundreds of pounds of horseflesh and the bard that the horse wore.

Cold sweat prickled along his spine, breaking out along his hairline, as well. The memory had been repressed, but now he would never forget it. He had loved the horse, which had been with him many years.

Slowly, he made his way toward the smithy's shed. He saw Alys bandaging the man's arm as the wife looked on in concern. Alys pulled a small jar from her basket and instructed them both on how often to apply it.

"I'll need to look at it in a week's time to make sure it hasn't festered."

"Thank you, my lady," the couple said together.

"Take care." She gave a wave of her hand and rejoined Kit.

"You didn't make it far before your first patient appeared," he noted.

"Fortunately, I carry all kinds of herbs and medicines with me. I never know what I might come across."

They managed to make it through the gates of Kinwick without another interruption. The open road lay before them, with green farmland to each side. He saw workers pruning and weeding as small children ran about, scaring the birds away.

"It's April," he murmured.

"Aye. And you know this how?"

"By what the workers are doing." He glanced up to the sky. "By the feel of the weather. It's warm but not overly so."

"You must be familiar with what happens on an estate, my lord. Not every nobleman would recognize what tasks workers did in the fields by the time of year."

"Most were pruning. A few weeding. The weeding will continue into May. Then come June, shearing and harvesting begin."

Alys gave him a smile. "You might not remember your name, but you do know about farming an estate. That's definite progress."

He hoped the progress would continue more rapidly than it had. But he had remembered his destrier. And now he knew about farming. Mayhap he had helped run his family's estate.

They walked for some minutes before Alys turned onto a small path.

"Our first stop will be to see Davy."

Before he could ask who Davy was, he saw a small cottage to his left. And a man running about in front of it—without a stitch on.

Alys sighed. "I suppose you will be seeing more of Davy than I expected."

CHAPTER 9

Alys braced herself, wondering if she would be meeting Good Davy or Bad Davy.

"Old Davy worked for many years at Kinwick," she explained to Kit. "When he began to grow feeble, both in mind and body, Father gifted him and his wife with this cottage."

She watched as the older man ran wildly in the open space, waving his arms as he called out.

"His wife passed away well over a dozen years ago."

"And Old Davy continues to live," said Kit drily.

She grinned. "Aye. He seems to have regained some of his strength over the years, but he has gone blind."

As she revealed that, Alys watched Old Davy sail through the air.

"He must have tripped on something." She moved closer to help the cursing man.

"Wait." Kit held her elbow. The heat from his fingers seared into her skin. Alys did her best not to react to his touch. "He could be dangerous."

"To you. Never to me."

"But he is raving like a madman, my lady. He could hurt you."

"He could. But he won't. Stay back and watch."

Alys had calmed Davy many times before. She knew the best way to reach him was through song. Though her singing voice was atrocious and she could never stay on key, somehow when she hummed, the melody sounded as it should. Girding herself, she began to hum. Softly at first, then gradually increasing the volume as she approached Davy.

Instantly, he stilled and then looked about. His angry face, red and frustrated, went slack. Davy remained frozen to the spot as she approached him. She knew all was well once he joined in, though instead of humming, he began to sing the words. She let her own voice fade as Davy's rich tone filled the air. Alys let him finish the song, knowing completing it served as part of their ritual and would calm him.

When his voice died down, she spoke. "Hello, Davy. It's Lady Alys come to see you."

A smile lit up his face as he turned in her direction. "Did you bring me bread?"

"I did. And soup."

"You haven't come 'round lately." He frowned.

"I know. I had to care for someone who was very sick. But he is better now. I brought him to see you."

"A visitor?" He grew flustered, wringing his hands. Davy did not take well to most people, much less strangers.

"He is very shy," she warned. "So shy that I don't even know his name."

That caused the old man to drop his hands. "I'm shy."

"I know you are. I thought that's why you might get along with him." Alys gestured for Kit to join them. "You could reassure him that he will be well taken care of at Kinwick."

Kit reached them, stepping gingerly instead of his usual stride. He stopped several feet short of them and waited.

Old Davy turned his head in Kit's direction. "Be you there, friend?" he asked.

"I am. Might I shake your hand?"

Davy thought about it. "I suppose."

Kit advanced carefully. He paused in front of Davy. "I would like to put my hand on your shoulder. May I?"

"You may."

Alys watched Kit gently rest a hand on Davy's shoulder. With his free hand, he reached down and bumped Davy's.

The old man grasped it and turned to Alys. "I made a friend, Lady Alys. Not you. A new friend."

"I see. Why don't we go inside your cottage? I can cut some cheese from the round I brought."

"And the bread. Can we have some of the bread? You know how I love bread."

"I know, Davy. Come." She went to his other side and took his hand. She and Kit led him back inside his cottage.

"Are you cold, Davy?" Kit asked.

"A little."

"I can find you something to put on," Kit volunteered.

"All right," Davy said, far more agreeable than he usually was.

Alys prepared the food for him and set it on the small table. She watched as Kit helped the old man into his clothes.

"You look good," he told the old retainer.

Davy snorted. "I haven't looked good in a score of years, young man. But I don't worry 'bout that no more. Being blind does have some advantages."

Kit led him to the table and helped seat him. "'Tis probably better."

"Why?"

"Well, I might frighten you."

"You sound like a nobleman. I doubt you would frighten me, my lord."

"But I am a mass of healing bruises. Lady Alys calls them my colors of the rainbow."

"I remember rainbows," Davy pointed out.

"I am very much like one now," Kit told him. "You see, I had some men beat me. They robbed me and left me for dead. And then Lady Alys came along and rescued me," he confided.

Davy grinned as he searched the table for a slice of cheese and brought it up to his lips and began to nibble. "Lady Alys does bring home her fair share of strays."

Kit laughed. "I hadn't thought of myself as a stray."

"Be it yea or nay, she brought you back to Kinwick. She will fix you up good and then send you on your way." Davy frowned. "Are you shy around people because they beat you?"

"A little," Kit told him. "And because they hit my head. I don't remember who I am."

Davy slammed a fist on the table. "Well, you're my friend. That's who you are. And Lord Geoffrey'll let you stay at Kinwick. He's a good man." A grin crossed the old man's face. "You could stay at Kinwick and visit me. Why, you could marry Lady Alys. She has no husband, and you sound like a fine fellow. You could visit me together. And bring me bread."

Alys sensed the blush that fired her cheeks. She avoided Kit's eyes though she knew he stared at her.

"So what did you search for when we first arrived, Davy?" she asked.

He chewed a piece of bread thoughtfully, trying to remember. "My hen. I went to gather eggs, and she danced up my arm and came out of her coop."

Kit stood. "Then leave it to me to retrieve this errant hen." He strode from the cottage.

After the door shut behind him, Old Davy said, "He seems like a nice one, my lady. You could do worse."

Alys chuckled. "I suppose I could."

Kit returned a few minutes later, telling Davy that the hen had been returned to her coop. He also placed five eggs on the table. "I gathered these for you, Davy. You know, that's what friends do for one another."

The old man placed his gnarled hands over Kit's. "Thank you, my lord. I hope you will come to visit me again. You, too, Lady Alys. I look forward to the days you stop by."

"We'll both be back. Soon," Kit assured him. "Good day to you, Davy."

Davy's lips trembled. "So be it. Till we meet again." He reached out to find Kit's hand and squeezed it.

Alys stood and brushed a kiss upon Davy's forehead. "Take care."

They left the cottage, each with a basket in hand.

"An unusual fellow," Kit said. "I'm still not sure why he danced about with no clothes on."

She shrugged. "It's hard to understand what goes through his mind. Some days his thoughts are clear and his conversation fine, but other times I find him in a fog. I think the time is coming where he will need to move in with another family who can care for him."

"And who might volunteer for that task? It would be trying on most families."

"You would be surprised. The people of Kinwick have always looked out for one another."

"It seems a happy estate."

"Very much so."

"I wonder if my home is such a kind and productive place."

"I don't know, my lord," she answered honestly. Alys only knew his father served at one time as an adviser to King Edward. She had no idea what the name of the Emorys' family estate was or in which direction it might be located. She did know his father was Lord Brentley. Other than that, she had no clue as to Kit's background. Whether Lord Brentley remained in service at court or even if Kit's mother was alive remained a mystery to her.

That sparked a selfish moment of hope within her. Richessa had been a sickly girl during the short time Alys knew her at court. Painfully bony. She wondered if once Richessa reached maturity that she became hale—or if she remained frail. What if she had passed on? The thought gave Alys a sense of satisfaction before guilt flooded her. How would she confess to such a sin? Father Dannet wouldn't know how to begin to tell her what to do if she admitted that she hoped an acquaintance from years before might be dead so that she could marry the woman's widower.

Alys sank her nails into her palms, trying to jolt herself back to reality.

"Where to next?" Kit asked.

"To the Bransons." She began walking briskly, trying to make her mind go blank. "Their son's wife, Tessa, is with child. She is due in another fortnight, so I want to see how she fares."

He fell into step next to her, still carrying the basket laden with food. "My lady, I thought you only visit those who are sick."

She laughed. "Speak to a mother who carries a child and has grown as large as the Kinwick stables, and she will tell you that she ails. Many women experience troubles throughout this time as their babe grows within their womb. Others are merely uncomfortable and cannot sleep."

Kit gave her an odd look. "What does sleep have to do with a babe?"

"As the babe becomes larger, it's hard for a woman to find a comfortable position. Even lying on her side won't bring her relief—especially with the babe kicking so."

"A woman can *feel* that? Inside her?" he asked, a look of horror on his face.

Alys tamped down the laughter that threatened to bubble up. "For a grown man, my lord, you seem quite naive. At least when it comes to giving birth." She couldn't help but tease, "I hope at least you know how a babe comes to grow in a woman's womb."

She did laugh out loud at the mortified look which crossed his face. "Don't worry. This is Tessa's first time for childbirth. A first babe traditionally takes its time coming into the world. Even if her water broke while we visited, it would be many hours before her babe came." She grinned. "Enough time for you to escape back to Kinwick."

His voice turned gruff as he said, "I suppose I have simply never been around any women in that condition."

If he had, Alys thought, surely he would remember. If Richessa had, indeed, married him as expected and given birth to his children, wouldn't he remember that? Then again, he could have been away fighting if and when that occurred. Or made himself scarce around her if he was at home. Many women in the nobility went into confinement, often not seeing their husbands for several months. Now that she pondered it, she decided many of the titled gentry probably had no idea how large their wife's belly would expand.

Her father was an exception. Throughout each time her mother found herself with child, her father had catered to his wife. Rubbing her feet. Bringing her sweets. Brushing her long hair and rubbing oil into her temples to soothe her. She smiled, knowing how lucky her mother was to have a husband wait on her in such a manner. Alys supposed part of it was due to the fact he had missed the months when she and Ancel grew inside her womb. Alys pushed the thought aside as they continued to the Bransons.

"You set a quick pace, my lady."

She froze in her tracks. "Forgive me, my lord. I'd forgotten you have been injured."

He laughed and kept walking. She hurried to catch up with him.

"As I told you before, I'm no invalid. Does my body ache? Of course. Do these troublesome ribs scream inside me? Aye." He raised his eyes to the sky. "But to be outdoors again, moving about? It's worth any slight inconvenience."

They walked in companionable silence after that until they reached their destination. Alys knocked on the cottage door and frowned when she received no response.

"Would Tessa be working out in the fields?" Kit asked.

"Nay. She is too close to delivering the child. I have given her strict instructions to rest as much as she can."

"And she would naturally follow them," he said with a smile.

"Of course." Alys decided to push the door open and slipped into the cottage. The single room had no windows, so she left the door open for light.

As she stepped deeper into the room, she gasped.

Tessa lay on the floor, moaning, surrounded by the water that had broken. A gash on her forehead led Alys to believe that the girl had fainted and struck her head. She might have been unconscious a few minutes—or several hours.

"Her time has come," she told Kit. In fact, Tessa was well past that time. She lifted Tessa's skirts and determined she had been laboring a good while.

"You cannot be here. Return to Kinwick and find my mother. Oh, please hurry!" she urged.

"What's wrong?" He paused. "I see now. She has hit her head. Will she deliver soon?"

"Aye."

"Then I will stay."

"Nay. Men do not attend births."

"But you need help."

She did. It was hard to admit, but much needed to be accomplished in a short time, and she could actually use Kit Emory's assistance if he was willing to stay and aid her.

"Put water on to boil. Stir the fire first. Fill that pot over there." She reached to her boot, where she carried her baselard, and removed it from its sheath. "Drop this into the water."

Kit grabbed the pot and went outside in search of water as she tried to awaken the girl.

"Tessa. Tessa. Can you hear me?"

The girl's eyelids fluttered. Alys continued to talk to her as she took items from her basket.

"The babe!" Tessa groaned. "It comes."

"Aye. You must have fallen and hit your head."

"Oh, Christ Almighty." Tessa let out a long wail just as Kit returned with the water.

Alys had no time to watch for his reaction. She had no time to coddle him when Tessa needed her.

"Tell me what to do," he said. "I am a soldier. I know how to follow orders without question."

She had him find a clean blanket and settle it in a corner. Tessa already shivered after lying in the cold puddle of water for so many hours. Alys started to lift her, but the girl screamed loudly.

"Let me." Before she could warn Kit about his ribs, he bent and swept Tessa up. She heard his quick intake of breath, but he did not falter as he carried her across the room and put her atop the blanket.

"I have no time for modesty. If you must leave, do so, my lord," she instructed.

"I want to stay and help," he promised.

Alys pulled up Tessa's skirts and rubbed rose oil along her flanks. She took another ointment that helped speed delivery and spread it across the panting girl's belly. She wished Kit had time to find vinegar and sugar for Tessa to drink but as Alys looked down, she saw the head starting to crown.

Tessa let out another screeching wail.

Alys looked to Kit. "Loosen her hair. Pull the pins from it and unwind the braid. It will give her some mild relief."

He followed her instructions and even rubbed Tessa's scalp, calming her. Then another contraction came and Alys thought the world might end, so loud was Tessa's scream.

"You need to push," Alys told the girl as more of the crown became visible.

"I can't," wept Tessa. "It hurts too much."

"Your pain will continue until you expel the babe," Alys said calmly. "The more you push, the faster your babe will come out to see you. Then the pain will be no more."

"Truly?" Tessa's eyes grew large.

"Push, Tessa. Hard. Now," Alys said as she watched Tessa's progress. She caught Kit's eye. He had continued to rub the girl's temples, attempting to sooth her. "Remove the pot from the fire. Pour some of the boiled water into a deep dish. Not much. We have need of it soon. Locate where the salt and honey are, but don't bring them to me yet. Instead, I need a small blanket and my knife. It should be clean enough by now."

He moved across the room as Tessa did as she'd been told by Alys, pushing and panting. Minutes later, the babe squirted from its mother's body in a rush of water and blood.

Alys held the babe in her hands, marveling at God's handiwork.

She realized Kit had come to stand next to her.

"You have a son, Tessa. A fine, handsome son." She took the knife Kit handed her and cut the cord. Turning the babe over, she gave him a light smack on his bottom. Immediately, a strong cry went up, one that could have matched those his mother uttered prior to his birth.

"Take the babe," she told Kit. "Place him in the blanket and rest him in your lap. Dip a small piece of linen into the boiled water and clean him. I want not a bit of the sticky covering to remain upon him."

Kit's eyes widened but, true to his word, he did not question her. He wrapped the newborn in the blanket and took the babe back to where the fresh water stood.

After some minutes, Alys helped Tessa with the afterbirth. Once that was completed, she called, "Is the babe clean yet?"

"Almost."

"Once he is wiped clean, rub salt over him and rinse him again with tepid water."

"Yes, my lady."

Alys heard the smile in his reply. She stood and retrieved some of the water and brought it back to bathe Tessa. She helped the new mother to her straw pallet in the corner and bound clean linen rags about her, explaining to her what had happened to her body and how often to feed her son. She also cleaned the cut on Tessa's forehead and covered it with a healing ointment.

"I'll be right back, Tessa. Rest a moment."

She went to where Kit rinsed the fussy babe. He looked at her.

"I have never dealt with a fish this slippery. Even clean, this boy wishes to fly from my hands."

"Where is the honey?"

He cocked a head to his left. Alys went and dipped her finger into the pot. She brought her finger to the infant's mouth and rubbed it on his gums. He smacked at it and stopped his crying.

"Why did you do that?" Kit asked.

"It will make him more eager to suckle."

"Ah."

Alys looked around and found a chest with the swaddling cloths on top. She quickly wrapped the clean child tightly in them and took him back to his mother.

"Keep him swaddled. Loosen it every three hours and clean him. Babies feel safe when swaddled. It's as if they are back in your womb. Now, try to feed him. I will stay until he is successful in nursing."

The babe missed in his first two attempts, but he understood what to do by his third pass.

"Oh!" Tessa exclaimed. "His pull is strong."

"A good sign," Alys assured her. "Now I shall burn your umbilical cord."

She brought it to the fire and tossed it in. Kit had remained on this side of the room to give Tessa privacy while she fed her child for the first time.

"And why do you do that, my lady?" he asked.

"Fire purifies. It's a way to counteract the sinfulness of his conception."

He frowned. "Do you think it sinful?"

Alys shook her head. "Nay. I believe God means for women to give birth. To revel in bringing new life into His world." She smiled. "Just look at how happy Tessa is. She glows."

"She has you to thank. If you had not stopped by the cottage today . . ." His voice trailed off.

"Don't think of that. Focus on the good that came from our visit."

And not dwell on how badly I wish you would bury your seed within me.

Alys would give anything—anything—to be a mother to Kit's child.

Mayhap that was the way she could keep a piece of Kit Emory with her always.

CHAPTER 10

He insisted on carrying both baskets as he followed alongside Alys after they left Tessa. The new mother, tired but glowing, urged them to continue making their rounds on the estate. They departed with the babe nestled in his mother's arms, fast asleep. Alys promised to return in a few days to see how they had adjusted with the new babe in the family.

"What you should do is go home and rest," he said.

"Why?"

"Because . . . you just delivered a babe," he sputtered. "I did very little. You and Tessa did all of the hard work. You must be exhausted."

She shrugged. "Tired or not, I still have a few who need my remedies. If you are tired, my lord, I insist you be the one who returns to the keep."

"Nay. I won't return to my bed until late tonight when sleep is unavoidable. I want to be up and about for as long as I can. I'm no infant who needs to be coddled."

Though the thought of Alys curled up next to him as Tessa's child had been with his mother caused his mouth to grow dry.

They visited four other cottages, with Alys dispensing advice and medicines at each and food at two others. Finally, she determined they could head back to Kinwick.

As they strolled down the lane, he asked, "Is this how you spend much of your days?"

"Aye. If I am not seeing to our people's needs, then I'm collecting herbs and flowers that I can use to create my medicines. I also help

Mother with various household tasks and before the boys went to foster with Lord Hardwin, I tended to and played with them."

"What of your sister, Nan? Is she also interested in healing ways?"

Alys shook her head. "Nan shows no interest in womanly tasks. If I take her in the garden to hoe, she turns the tool into a weapon and fights off imaginary dragons. If I bring her to grind herbs, she quickly loses interest and slinks about the room until I am occupied. Then she slips out and wanders the estate. She wants to be a page for Lord Hardwin as her brothers are. No matter how many times Mother and Father tell her that young ladies can't become a page, Nan quietly insists that the earl will take her on in due time."

She leaned down and picked a few flowers on the side of the road. He paused and let her drop them into one of the now empty baskets.

"I have taught her both letters and numbers. She reads voraciously for one so young, and she follows our steward, Diggory, around. He has let her start making entries into the ledgers. Listing the number of bales of hay put up or some such stuff. Diggory says Nan has quite a head for numbers. Father says it's important to allow Nan to follow her passion. I try not to worry about her overmuch and hope she'll grow out of such peculiar habits."

"She has visited me a few times," he revealed. "Told me the most outrageous stories as if they were the Gospel truth."

"Nan does have a vivid imagination. If you tire of her presence, let her know. She will flit off as a butterfly and move on to her next unsuspecting victim."

They reached the open gates of Kinwick and continued through the baileys. When they arrived inside the keep, Alys motioned Tilda over and requested that hot water be brought to both of their rooms.

"I am sure you wish to wash after such a long day, my lord."

"It was a long day," he agreed, "but a good one. Will I see you for the evening meal?"

"Of course."

He parted from her and went to his bedchamber. Soon, two servants arrived with water. He doffed his clothes and washed up, putting on his only other gypon and pair of pants. Lady Merryn and Lady Alys had each made him something to wear. He wondered, once more, how he would ever repay the de Montforts for their generosity in taking him in and caring for him.

A knock on his door drew his attention. When he answered it, he found Tilda standing in the corridor.

"Lord Geoffrey said to come to the solar for your evening meal now, my lord," she informed him. "Guests have arrived for tomorrow's May Day celebration. He would have you meet them."

"Thank you, Tilda."

He closed the chamber door and went down the corridor to the solar. As he drew near, he could hear raucous laughter from within. The door stood open, and he hesitated in the doorway.

A couple he had never seen before drew his eye. A petite, older beauty with dark hair and a striking dimple smiled up at a tall man with burnished red hair. His arm was wrapped possessively around her waist.

"Come in!" Lord Geoffrey called. "I wish you to meet my cousin and closest friend. This is Lord Raynor Le Roux of Ashcroft and his lovely wife, Beatrice."

Beatrice Le Roux was even more beautiful up close. Her dark brown eyes, rimmed in amber, held both kindness and mirth in them. She curtseyed to him while her husband offered his hand.

"I will tell you my name, my lord, when it comes to me," he said.

Lord Raynor's grip was strong. "Geoffrey told me about your situation. I'm sorry for what you suffered through."

"But under Merryn and Alys' care, you will be better in no time," Lady Beatrice assured him.

"They have been both gracious and helpful in my recovery," he confirmed.

Alys entered the room with her mother and both women embraced their guests.

"I am so happy you could come for the May Day celebration," Lady Merryn told them. "I only wish the children could have come with you."

Alys looked to him. "Raynor and Beatrice have two boys near my brother Edward's age and a girl who is eight. They are all precious children."

"I miss them every day," Lady Beatrice said. "But they will return from fostering when summer begins. You must bring everyone to Ashcroft, Geoffrey, when your boys have their break." She looked at him. "Ashcroft is but a few hours' ride from Kinwick. We are often back and forth between our estates."

"And Michael and Elysande should be here by the noon meal on the morrow," Merryn shared. "Lady Mary will accompany them." She turned to him. "Elysande is Geoffrey's niece. She married the Earl of Sandbourne, who once served as one of Kinwick's knights."

"And Lady Mary is my sister," Geoffrey added. "We are a large family and use any excuse to gather and make merry."

A feeling of emptiness sat hard in his stomach. Whoever he was, he did not have this in his life. If he did, he would know the joy he missed out on. This familiarity and warmth seemed almost foreign to him.

"Come," Lady Merryn urged. "Let's be seated. Cook has made Raynor's favorite berry tarts."

"Then we should start with the end and work our way backward through the courses," Raynor proclaimed.

Alys poured out the wine as Nan brought cups to those present. Kit ate until he thought he could eat no more—until he took a single bite of the tart.

"This must be the most delicious tart I have tasted," he exclaimed.

"King Edward tried on more than one occasion to steal Cook from under our very noses, claiming her fruit tarts to be the best ever baked in England," Lord Geoffrey shared. "But remember, we have the May Day feast tomorrow. Save room for that in your belly."

He listened as the Le Rouxs spoke of life at Ashcroft and the de Montforts shared what had happened at Kinwick since Lord Geoffrey had returned from the peace talks in Belgium. It surprised him that

Alys remained quiet. Around him, she was usually talkative.

When a lull occurred in the conversation, he said, "Lady Alys delivered a child today."

The women began peppering her with questions. As she spoke, he realized how modest she was being.

"Lady Alys took charge like a captain of a ship would. I served as a member of her crew," he said. "Frankly, I had no idea birthing a child was so involved—or so painful."

Alys chuckled. "Since men are not allowed to witness the labor or birth, why would you? But I appreciated your help today, my lord. Tessa Branson did well, too, and her babe is a sweet one."

"I will go with you when you check on her," Lady Merryn volunteered. "You know I cannot resist holding a new little one."

Suddenly, he saw a flash of a woman holding a pale infant in her arms. The babe did not move. She offered it to him. He felt himself shake his head and turn away.

Who was the woman, he wondered. *And had the babe been his child?*

HE CAME DOWNSTAIRS on his own for the first time and saw people streaming into the great hall. He supposed they had been to mass. He had no recollections of attending mass anywhere and did not venture a guess if he was a religious man or not. So much of him still remained a mystery and hidden from him. He tamped down the impatience threatening to rise because it would do him no good. Lady Merryn assured him his memory would return. He put his faith in her words and experience.

When it did, would he leave Kinwick at once, eager to arrive at his own home? Or would he delay his departure—the better to spend more time with Alys?

Lady Beatrice waved him over. He joined her and Lord Raynor. He liked this couple quite a bit and hoped that somewhere he had a friend as close to him as Lord Raynor seemed to Lord Geoffrey.

Lady Beatrice greeted him. "Good morning, my lord. It's good to see you up and about."

He seated himself next to her as her husband took the seat on her other side. "Other than my ribs aching, I'm almost myself," he told her.

She laughed. "Your face says otherwise." Then her eyes went large. "Oh, forgive me, my lord. I did not mean to imply that . . . well, that your bruises . . ."

"No apology is necessary, my lady. I saw myself in a hand mirror and know most of the swelling has gone down, but the bruises have turned nasty shades of colors. I suppose it will be another few days before I look as myself."

"I'm sure you are a handsome man when you have not been beaten by wild thieves," she said demurely, taking a bite of bread.

Lord Raynor put his arm about her. "My wife means well, my lord. Usually, she puts a little more thought into what she says. Today she is distracted, I believe."

He looked at her. "What troubles you, Lady Beatrice?"

"Nothing but excitement fills my heart," she confided, a brilliant smile lighting up her face. "Raynor and I are off today for Wellbury."

"But you have only arrived at Kinwick," he said. "I thought your visit would be longer."

"We'll only be gone today and the night, then we will return and stay a few more days with Geoffrey and Merryn," Lord Raynor told him. "Wellbury is the estate next to Kinwick. It was Merryn's home growing up, and her brother, Hugh, resides there now with his wife."

"Our three children foster with them," Lady Beatrice added. "Since we are nearby, I had Merryn send a messenger to Hugh and Milla to see if we might stop in and celebrate May Day with the Mantels. They said we were most welcome." She sighed. "So I will get to embrace my boys and my girl and spend the day with them before we return to Kinwick for the rest of the week."

"It's nice that they all foster together," he said. "And that Lord Hugh was receptive to the idea."

Raynor burst out laughing. "I'm sure the three women cooked up this scheme together before we ever left Ashcroft. This way, Beatrice gets to see our children and still spend time with Merryn. If you discover you are married, my lord, when your memory returns, I am sure you will be familiar with the way of wives."

He wanted to point out that it was the duty of a wife to obey her husband and not scheme behind his back, but Lord Raynor seemed quite lighthearted about the situation. He guessed the nobleman was also happy to see his children. Again, an emptiness lay heavy within him. If he had children, he had no recollection of them, much less if they brought such joy to him.

Lord Geoffrey and Lady Merryn joined them, along with Alys and Nan.

"Have you made any new improvements to Ashcroft since we were last there?" asked Lady Merryn after she took a sip of her ale.

"I always seem to keep Donaldus busy," Lady Beatrice admitted. "He is as much an architect as a carpenter at Ashcroft. I cannot wait for you to see the latest changes I've made in our steward's room. I had Donaldus make shelves to my specification, and now the ledgers are more organized."

"And what of Lord Gilbert and his children?" asked Alys.

"My uncle is quite well. He still tries to buy Fury from Raynor each time we see him."

"No one will ever buy my horse," Lord Raynor said, a scowl crossing his face. "That animal is like a brother to me. I think I like him even more than I do Geoffrey."

Everyone laughed. The conversation continued until their small meal concluded. As they stood so the servants could remove the dishes and the trestle tables could be returned to the walls, Alys whispered to him, "Ask Lady Beatrice if she will play for you when she returns tomorrow. She is a bit shy about it, but she has a lovely voice."

He nodded and turned to the noblewoman. "My lady, I have heard that you sing better than a songbird and hoped you might do so upon your return to Kinwick. I would enjoy hearing a bit of music."

"Oh, you must, Beatrice," Lady Merryn encouraged. She looked at him. "Beatrice plays her lute better than any troubadour, and she has a beautiful voice."

Lady Beatrice blushed at the attention brought her way but nodded. "I will do so if you insist. We should arrive back at Kinwick in time for the noon meal tomorrow."

"I look forward to hearing you perform, my lady," he said.

Lord Geoffrey said, "Come, we must head out to the meadow. The dancing should begin soon, and we need to let these two get on their way to Wellbury."

As the group left the keep, they stepped into a cool day with no wind and no clouds.

"I love a cool May Day with a little sunshine," Alys said to him as they descended the stairs of the keep. "I don't like it to be too hot for the dancing." She paused. "Do you remember any May Day celebrations, my lord?"

"Nay," he admitted. "I know very little about this custom. No images or knowledge of it comes to mind."

"At least at Kinwick, our people have been up since before daybreak. The women and girls have roamed the countryside to gather blossoming flowers and bushes. My favorites are the violets because of their vibrant color."

"And do the men also take part in the celebration?"

"They have gone to the woods to find the maypole. It's usually the trunk of a large, young birch tree which is chosen. Then they strip it of its branches except for those at the very top."

"Why are those left behind?"

"Those leaves symbolize new life, as May begins spring. The men will drag the maypole into the center of our meadow. They should have set it up by now. We will be able to watch them decorate it with the field flowers and ribbons."

Nan went flying by them, running through the gates ahead.

"She seems eager," he noted.

"Two years ago, Nan clung to Mother's skirts while the festivities went on. Last year was the first time she really understood what was happening and participated. She has talked of it ever since."

They arrived to a flurry of activity in the meadow. Nan came back and grabbed her sister's hand.

"Come on, Alys. Help me decorate the pole," she demanded.

"Go ahead," he told her. "I'll watch from here."

Music started up, with a piper playing a merry tune as the women adorned the maypole with garlands of the various spring flowers they had gathered. Once the pole had been trimmed, they began passing out ribbons to the younger children, both boys and girls. The men helped attached one end of the ribbon to the pole, then a drummer joined in playing along with the piper. Their lively tune started up the dancing.

He watched as the children held the colored ribbons by their ends as they circled the maypole, the boys moving in one direction and the girls in the opposite one. All the people joined in singing. He didn't know the words to the tune, but he appreciated the enthusiasm with which they sang. Finally, the song came to a close as the ribbons encircled the pole, entwined with the bevy of flowers.

Then a new tune began, and the children reversed their directions, unwinding the ribbons they had wound about the maypole. The voices grew louder in song as the children danced and skipped to the beat of the drum. He saw Nan in the thick of things, her eyes sparkling with excitement.

Something tugged at his heart. He wished he could have a little girl such as Nan—smart, strong, and pretty. Already opinionated at six years of age. He wondered what Alys had been like at that age and figured her to be much the same, full of joy and curiosity. He located her in the crowd as the music changed again. The girls and boys handed their ribbons off, and a new group took their places.

This time it was men and women who circled the maypole, singing and dancing with utter abandonment. His eyes were drawn to Alys. She moved with an innate grace, almost as if she flowed like water coursing in a stream. The circle became smaller and smaller until the ribbons surrounded the maypole and the music switched again, causing the participants to reverse direction and unwind the ribbons they held.

Alys handed her ribbons to a young girl and joined him. "You must come dance, my lord," she encouraged.

"I don't think I have ever danced," he said, appalled at the thought of giving himself over so freely to the music.

"Then it's high time you learned," she declared. Alys took his hand in hers and pulled him along. As they weaved in and out of the crowd, she turned and looked over her shoulder, her cheeks full of roses. He swallowed hard, taken by her simple, fresh beauty.

They finally reached the maypole. His heart began to beat faster. Her hand in his seemed the most natural thing in the world. Reluctantly, he released it when she took a long bit of ribbon from a girl and handed it to him.

"Dance, my lord," she said. She accepted a ribbon herself as a new song began.

He began moving to the beat of the drum. As a soldier, he knew he was a physical man. He had lain awake at night and pictured himself, sword in hand, arcing through the air. The weapon had seemed an extension of him. This ribbon now felt the same. He let his feet move as he became swept up in the melody. His ribs twinged unpleasantly if he moved his arms too high, so he lowered them and only waved them in small circles.

His body took over, and he experienced the happiness that he saw on the faces of those surrounding him. He looked across at Alys, who seemed to float through the air as a feather might. Her braid bobbed along as her feet did some intricate steps that he wouldn't bother to attempt. But looking at her brought a yearning that he decided must be satisfied.

Today.

Whatever had happened in his past. Whatever his present might be. Whatever the future held for him. None of that mattered.

Only Alys did.

It might be wrong, but he planned to kiss her this day. Leisurely. Thoroughly.

Passionately.

CHAPTER 11

"I AM SO out of breath!" Alys exclaimed. She tossed her ribbon to a young girl and moved away from the dancing.

In truth, it was Kit Emory who had taken her breath away.

She had grown warm as she watched him attempt to dance. At first, he had proved awkward, then his knightly training kicked in. He began to move with a physical grace for one so large. Though his feet did not attempt any complicated footwork, his limbs still moved well in time to the music. For the first time since he'd been brought to Kinwick, Kit smiled from his heart and a place of joy. She realized he was living in the moment, not worried about who he was or where he belonged.

Oh, but he had already found a place—though he did yet not know it. *'Twas in her heart.*

Alys determined to pull him aside after the feasting and inform him of his true identity. She had no right to hold the secret from him any longer. He must return to Richessa and whatever family he had.

Even though it would break her heart.

She looked up as a shadow crossed over her, marring the bright sunshine of the day. Kit stood next to her, his large frame dwarfing hers. She pushed aside the gloom that threatened to bubble up. He needed to enjoy these last few hours and she needed to enjoy them—with him.

"You left the dancing." He frowned. "Are you ill?"

"Nay. Just a bit tired. I have danced through several songs. I thought to take a bit of ale and cool down some."

Kit offered his arm to her. "Then let me escort you to where these refreshments are."

Alys slipped her hand through the crook of his arm and almost sighed. His very nearness allowed her to inhale his clean, masculine scent. She drank it in as one who thirsted but could never be satisfied.

As they drew close to the ale and various fruits and breads that had been placed outside for the revelers to nibble on, she saw her parents and waved. Geoffrey and Merryn joined them as Cook poured drinks for them all.

"I haven't seen you dancing, my lord," Kit said.

"I have been beating the bounds," her father replied.

Alys saw the puzzled look flit across Kit's face and said, "It's a tradition on May Day for the owner of a property to walk its boundaries."

"The custom allows me to reaffirm my rights to Kinwick," her father shared. He took a generous sip from his cup. "I find it thirsty work."

"And Geoffrey marks the various places where the fences need to be repaired," added her mother. "So our walk served a more practical purpose."

"You walked the boundaries with him?" Kit asked.

"Aye. We have done it together many years. It's time alone, which we rarely seem to have."

Alys saw the look pass between her mother and father and wondered if anything else had occurred as they beat the bounds.

A cheer rose, and she looked back at the maypole. "I think Jack in the Green has put in his appearance." Before Kit could ask, Alys explained, "Since May Day celebrates the new growth of spring and the hope of a fertile harvest to come, Jack in the Green always makes his presence known at some point."

Her mother said, "Our steward, Diggory, always disguises himself as Jack, the woodland spirit who guards the green woods of England. He will dance a little with the others and then slip away, returning to the woods."

Her father downed the remainder of his ale. He pulled his wife's cup from her hand and set both cups down. Then he snatched Merryn's hand and led her toward the maypole. Alys smiled as she watched the Earl and Countess of Kinwick join in the merrymaking.

"You are lucky, indeed, my lady," Kit said softly.

She turned to him. "Why?"

"You were brought up in a magical place. You have parents that not only love you and your siblings, but they adore one another."

Alys watched her parents dance around the maypole with abandon and nodded. "I am fortunate." Her eyes met his. "Mayhap you, too, came from such a family."

"Nay." His flat tone caused her to wonder if he had remembered who he was. She could not recollect ever seeing his mother at court, while her vague impression of his father was not that of a loving man as her own father was.

She knew now was the time to tell him of his origins.

"Alys!"

She turned and saw her cousin, Elysande, coming her way, little Tucker in tow. Her husband, Michael, followed closely behind, as did Aunt Mary.

"Elysande!" She ran to greet the woman, embracing her cousin tightly. "I am so happy to see you."

"Alys," a voice closer to the ground demanded.

"Good day to you, sweet Tucker," she told the boy, sweeping him up into her arms and kissing his nose. "I have missed you."

"I missed you, too," he said.

Michael came up and wrapped her in a hug and kissed her cheek. "And how is my favorite de Montfort?"

"Oh, Mother is doing well," Alys retorted. She nodded in the direction of the maypole. "She and Father just finished beating the bounds and are celebrating."

Tucker began squirming, so she released him and greeted her aunt. "Aunt Mary, I am delighted you could come. Father will be so pleased to see you."

"And I him."

Alys looked around. "Didn't Sir Charles accompany you?"

"Charles saw Gilbert and stopped to visit with him. He will be along in a moment." Mary looked at her intently. "How have you been, my child? I think I see something different about you."

"I am well, thank you," she said. "Kinwick thrives, so I am happy." Alys looked over her shoulder and motioned for Kit to join them. "But we have a guest I would like you to meet."

As Kit made his way toward them, Alys turned. Before she could say a word, she saw recognition on Michael's face.

"Emory? What brings you to Kinwick?" Michael asked.

Emory?

The image of a smiling, older woman with mischief in her eyes flashed before him. Then another quickly joined her, a man with gray hair and a beard. Both appeared so real that he reached out to touch them—but they dissipated.

"I beg your pardon, my lord," he said, his stomach churning. "You know me?"

"I made your acquaintance at King Edward's court less than a month ago. I am Michael Devereux. I was with my brother-in-law, Kenric Fairfax, the Earl of Shadowfaire." Michael frowned. "Surely, you could not have forgotten us so soon after we met."

Panic escalated within him. "We were at court. A month ago," he repeated.

"Aye. Kenric and I waited for Lord Geoffrey and Lord Raynor to conclude their report to the king regarding the newly-signed truce. We spoke briefly." Michael stopped and studied him intently. "You shared you were Kit Emory, son to Lord Godwin Emory, the Baron of Brentley and adviser to the king."

The same image of the bearded, gray-haired man flashed quickly before his eyes and vanished.

His heart beat wildly in his chest. He had trouble breathing. He looked at Devereux—and experienced no recognition of him.

Nor did the name Kit Emory stir any memories, other than the brief glimpse of the man and woman flickering in his mind.

"Excuse me, my lord. My ladies." He turned and abruptly stormed away from the crowd and noise. He would leave it to Lady Alys to make his excuses. He was certain she would tell them of his accident and his memory loss. Let her have at it. He was tired. Tired of not knowing who he was—even if he now had his name—one that meant nothing to him.

Anger poured through him, and his strides grew in length. He needed to get away from everything. Everyone. The music. The happiness. The love. He wanted to give in and sulk like a small child.

He left the meadow and entered the woods. Each step that took him deeper into them seemed to add to the hot flame that burned in his chest. He started to run, but it caused his ribs to ache. Still, he pressed on, rage permeating through every pore. Finally, he dropped to his knees and howled in frustration.

Then hot tears came. He could not remember the last time he had cried—or if he ever had. He was so weary of not knowing anything about himself.

A hand gently touched his head. He inhaled and knew Alys de Montfort stood by him. Today she smelled of lavender soap.

"I wish you had not sought me out, my lady."

Her hand continued to stroke his head. His hair. He closed his eyes and gave in to the feelings the simple gesture created. Gradually, the anger washed away. His body, once coiled tightly, relaxed.

She cupped his face in both her hands. Not soft hands, but callused hands that worked. Hands that tended the garden and prepared her herbs. Hands that sewed and cooked and delivered babes. Hands that brought a sweet sensation to him.

He opened his eyes and looked up at her, slowing rising to his feet. Tears caused her brilliant sapphire eyes to glitter.

"Please. Give it more time," she begged.

"I have given it nothing but time," he said gruffly.

"At least you have a name now. The rest will come. I promise."

He placed his hands on her shoulders. "Who knows if—or when—my memory will return? But what this experience has taught me is that I could die tomorrow and never have kissed you."

Her eyes went wide. "What?"

His fingers clutched her shoulders. "Who knows? I may have a wife and children. I may be the first son who inherits a vast estate and esteemed title or a fifth son with nothing. But I do know that I can no longer ignore what my heart has cried out to me ever since I first saw you."

He crushed her to him and brought his mouth to hers. Frantic at first. He wanted to gobble her whole. He couldn't get enough of her as sensations rippled through him. She clung to him, her knees buckling, her fingers digging into his shoulders. His arms tightened about her.

In that moment, his eyes closed, familiarity poured through him, as if he had embraced her in a similar fashion before, long ago. A sweet memory of him holding her. Comforting her.

Then other emotions took over as need coursed through him. The faint memory dissolved as he gentled the kiss and began leisurely exploring her mouth. His tongue playfully danced around in her mouth, stroking hers. He pulled her closer as shudders ran through her. His heartbeat pounded in his ears. He feared she would hear it and ask what drummer accompanied them.

He broke the kiss, drawing fresh air deeply into his lungs as he moved his lips to her ear. Her jaw. Her cheek. Her fingers ran through his hair, causing a racing heat to rush through him, tightening, extending through his arms and legs till his body vibrated as hers did.

He returned to her mouth. Their kiss grew more heated than before. His core seemed to melt as easily as candle wax. She had the power to mold him in any way she liked.

His hand dropped to cup her breast. It began to swell and fit his palm as he rubbed a thumb across her nipple, which pebbled in need. She cried out, small whimpers that caused his manhood to swell. Her hands ran down his chest, her fingertips dancing across his hard muscles.

Then they dropped lower to his member. As it pressed against her belly, her hand touched it. Stroked it. He groaned and captured her hands in his. His mouth remained on hers a moment longer, drinking in her sweetness, before he pulled away. Immediately, he missed the heat of her lips, her body pressed against his.

He rested his forehead against hers. "We cannot," he choked out, though his fingers remained entwined with hers. "Not till I know more about who I am and what commitments I have."

He raised his lips and touched them against her cheek, savoring the last touch of her silky skin before he released her.

Alys stood rooted to the spot, her lips swollen with their love play. "Kit?" she said hoarsely.

Hearing his name on her lips jolted him. He still did not recognize it as his, but he liked the way she said it.

"We must talk."

"Alys? Where are you?"

"It's your sister," he said quietly. "You should rejoin her."

"But I have much to tell you."

"Let it wait."

She gazed at him with a naked longing that she was too inexperienced to hide.

He took her chin in his hand. "Go to Nan. I will follow later. We will talk after the feast tonight. I promise."

Alys nodded reluctantly. "We have much to discuss." She turned and hurried away. As she did, she called out, "Nan! I am coming!"

He watched her depart. Loneliness crawled inside him with her absence. He sat down on a felled log and sighed.

"So my name is Kit Emory," he told himself, willing any memory to return.

CHAPTER 12

Kit entered the great hall amidst a buzz of activity. He had spent most of the day in the forest, alone, not wanting to join in the bevy of events surrounding the celebration of May Day. Only when his grumbling stomach continued to gurgle did he force himself to his feet and return to the keep.

He spied young Tucker Devereux riding on his father's shoulders, squealing in delight as the nobleman raced around. Near the dais stood Lady Elysande, a look of joy on her face as she watched the pair.

It was like a punch to his gut, seeing the happiness that the noblewoman radiated. He wanted a share of that happiness. He wanted a woman to share his life with.

And he wanted Alys de Montfort to be that woman.

He made his way to Lady Elysande. "I must apologize for my rude behavior," he said.

"Totally unnecessary," Devereux said as he stepped to his wife's side. He lifted his son from his shoulders and placed him on the ground. Tucker ran off.

"Merryn explained the situation to us," the nobleman continued. "I would have approached you differently if I had but known."

"Could you tell me about our conversation?" Kit asked. "Though I now have learned my name, I know nothing else of myself. Any clue you could provide might help restore my memory."

Devereux grew thoughtful. "Our discussion was brief," he began. "Kenric and I—and you, I gathered—had just returned from the fighting on the continent." He paused in thought. "We spoke of the truce. The ports England had retained. And the health of the king and the Black Prince."

Kit drew a blank at the information the nobleman related to him.

"Oh. We spoke briefly about Alys."

"We spoke of . . . Lady Alys?"

Devereux nodded. "Aye. I remember now. Somehow Lord Geoffrey's name was mentioned. You asked if he might be related to Alys. I gathered you had met her at court once many years ago." He thought a moment. "You mentioned something about the queen's death."

"Well, you could not have known Alys for long," Lady Elysande pointed out. "She left court immediately after Queen Philippa passed. She was quite upset by her death."

So he had known Alys. Years ago.

And yet she had said nothing to him.

Lady Elysande must have read his thoughts. "People change in appearance as they age, my lord. I'm sure Alys did not recognize you. Especially if you only met briefly." She paused. "Let me think. Alys returned home about six years ago. I am sure of it, for that was when David broke his arm. Remember, Michael?"

Her husband nodded his head. "Aye. He was only three at the time. We came to Kinwick to try and cheer Alys up after the queen's death. David broke his arm here, and Alys took such good care of him."

"Alys has always loved children," Lady Elysande explained. "Why, she was only a young girl herself at the time, mayhap ten and two. I know her well, but I don't think I would have recognized her if six years passed between times I saw her."

Kit understood Lady Elysande's reasoning. He knew how faces matured. How bodies filled out. Still, it troubled him.

"Again, I offer my apologies to you." Kit gave a curt nod and left their company. The boisterous noise in the massive room bothered him. He decided to leave the great hall and retire to his bedchamber.

As he made his way to the arched doorway, Alys and her parents appeared and headed toward him. He halted, not knowing how he could avoid them.

"I hear that Michael helped identify who you are, Kit Emory. It was a stroke of luck that he made your brief acquaintance in London."

Kit deliberately avoided looking at Alys as he responded to her father. "Yes, my lord, though hearing my name has not jarred any memories. I think if I return to my home and am in familiar surroundings, I will have a better chance at recovering them."

He saw Lady Merryn's eyes cut to her daughter's. He didn't wish to know what passed between them and looked away.

"An excellent idea," Lord Geoffrey declared. "I will provide a guard to accompany you back to Brentwood."

Brentwood. It was the first time he had heard that name and assumed it to be his home.

"You know where Brentwood lies?" he asked.

"Aye. To the north and west of London," Lord Geoffrey confirmed. "But we can save this discussion for tomorrow. Come and see me after mass. I will make the arrangements for you to return home."

Kit decided to push the matter. "I would like to leave now, my lord," he said firmly.

Lord Geoffrey grew thoughtful. "I see." He motioned their steward over. "Diggory, please find Gilbert for me. I need to see him at once."

"Of course, my lord." The steward left in search of the Kinwick captain of the guard.

"I will arrange the journey," the nobleman promised him. "But you must come and eat first. Cook has spent the past three days preparing our feast."

Kit allowed the three of them to pass, keeping his eyes to the ground as he followed. When they reached the dais, he took the seat on the end. Alys sat next to him.

Course after course came from the kitchens. Though they shared a trencher, no conversation occurred between them. Only an awkward silence hung in the air.

After several courses, Tucker grew restless. Nan took her young cousin by the hand and played with him in front of the long table from which they supped. She took a few apples and started juggling them. Kit thought Nan quite good. Tucker tried to imitate her, throwing one apple in the air at a time, trying to catch it as it came crashing down to the ground. He laughed every time he missed catching the fruit and even harder when it landed upon his head.

Kit glanced around the great hall. Whatever he returned to at Brentwood, it would not be like this. He looked to Tucker's parents who watched the children play with satisfied smiles on their faces. Further down from him, Lord Geoffrey fed a morsel to Lady Merryn. Love for her husband shone on her face. All around the room, people ate and drank and spoke, happiness abounding.

"It's the last course!" Nan proclaimed, grabbing Tucker's hand and returning them to their seats. "The best. I promise. Cook made two sweets. I want some of each."

A servant approached them with a tray, and Kit took both sweets offered. He recognized the ryschewys, a fried fig pastry. But the second sweet caught his eye. The name of it was on the tip of his tongue. He knew before he bit into it that the cake was a favorite of his.

Suddenly, Alys said, "May we speak after you finish eating, my lord? Alone?"

Kit didn't want it to be only the two of them, with no others present. He did not trust himself to keep his hands off her. Reluctantly, he met her eyes.

A different Alys looked back at him. Not one full of curiosity and mischief. Not the woman who was interested in the world about her. This Alys was stoic, as if she steeled herself for something unpleasant.

"If it pleases you, my lady."

He looked back at the sweet before him. "What is this?" he asked.

"It's called a cryspe," she replied. "A funnel cake coated in sugar."

He bit into the cryspe. As it melted on his tongue, a flood of memories exploded within him, as if he had been struck by a bolt of lightning.

Kit could recall eating this treat, his mother laughing how she spoiled him with it too often. He could see the great hall at Brentwood—and other halls. Places he had fostered. Too many of them to count. He heard his father berating him for being careless.

"I am running out of places to send you, Christopher," he admonished. "You have no respect and run wild no matter where you go to foster. You are an embarrassment to me. Think of my position!"

"He will remain with me. For now," his mother interrupted. "I will train him."

That was how he knew about farming and estate matters. He remembered riding around Brentwood as his mother poured all of her knowledge into him.

Then a rush of noises invaded his mind. The battlefield. He'd been reckless. Led a charge that failed. He could see his horse falling beneath him. Ralf, his friend, stumbling to the ground. He scooped Ralf up in his arms, the blood pouring from a chest wound and bubbling up, oozing from Ralf's lips. Fighting went on all about them as his friend died in his arms.

And it had been his fault.

He was not a methodical man. He was one who acted before he thought. Admired for his reputation of bravery, dashing into dangerous situations, expecting soldiers to follow him without question. He had no regard for his life or others. He spoke his mind, consequences be damned.

These memories brought him great shame.

Suddenly, Kit was struck with a rainbow of emotions, as the floodgates to other recollections emerged. Anger. Sorrow. Despair. Pain.

He leapt to his feet and raced from the room. He had to escape the gaiety. The noise. The laughter.

HE KNEW EVERYTHING.

That was Alys' first thought as she rose to her feet. She glanced over and saw that her mother had observed Kit's departure.

"Go to him," she mouthed, an encouraging smile on her lips.

Alys hurried from the great hall and paused in the entryway to the keep, wondering where he could have gone. Then she spied the door leading outside stood ajar. Glancing around, Kit was nowhere in sight. She believed he had gone outside, so she followed. As she flew down the stone steps, she saw a solitary figure pacing in the bailey. Though only a few torches were lit, she knew from the size and profile that the man had to be Kit.

She went and stood in the path that he marched. He was so deep in thought, he bumped into her and grabbed her elbows to keep her from falling. The look of anguish on his face caused tears to spring to her eyes.

"I sought you out," he said, his voice low. "Though years had passed, I remembered you from court. My mother needed a healer. I could think of no one else I could trust."

Her breath caught in her throat. So he had been on his way to Kinwick—to see her—when accosted on the road.

"But you knew me," he accused, anger sparking in his eyes. "You already knew me. And you said nothing." His fingers tightened, digging painfully into her flesh. "I came to you with a purpose. My beloved mother, the strongest person I know, was ill. She is all I have, Alys. The only one who cares for me."

Kit released her, shoving her away from him. She'd heard the quiet desperation in his voice and longed to comfort him. But the waves of rage coming from him had her keep her distance.

"You could never understand, surrounded by so many family members who love and support you. You live in a happy place and lead a charmed life. Mine has been far from that. Mother is all I have. My father spends most of his time away at court and when he was at Brentwood? He despised me because I was reckless and impulsive, nothing like him. Mother took time to teach me. She was always a calming influence on me. Under her tutelage, I learned and matured."

Kit raked his hands through his hair in frustration. "You delayed me, Alys. You withheld my identity from me. That may have slowed the memories from returning more rapidly to me." His eyes darkened in fury. "Worst of all, Mother has had no relief. She has lain at Brentwood all this time, waiting for me to return. With you. The healer I promised would solve what ailed her. Her illness might have worsened—and she's had no word from me." He swallowed. "She might think I am dead."

Kit had sworn she lived a charmed life but Alys only knew her heart was now torn asunder by the mistakes she had made.

"I have no way to make it up to you," she said quietly. "No apology will suffice."

He stood glaring at her. Alys gathered her courage and pushed ahead.

"Truly, I did not know you at first," she said quietly. "Your face was so swollen and bloodied from the beating you had taken. As you began to heal, I sensed something familiar about you. But six years had passed, Kit, and I had only seen you once. You'd grown from a boy into manhood. I wasn't sure it was you. Doubt plagued me. I didn't want to share with you who I thought you might be and give you false hope."

Even in the dim light, she saw the flush of anger that filled his cheeks. "The truth, Alys. I'll have it. When did you realize it was me? Because I can tell you knew before Michael Devereux called me by name today."

"When I was in your arms," she confessed, her gaze steady. "It was when I became absolutely certain." Her words came out in a whisper. His fingers relaxed. Then his hands fell to his side.

"You had held me before, Kit. We only met once in our past. I was fostering in the queen's household. You had just arrived at Windsor Castle. You . . . came to retrieve me. The king had need of me."

He stared off in the distance and nodded. "His head ached. He demanded that you be brought to him. Said no one could soothe his hurt as Lady Alys could." Kit looked back down at her.

"Aye. You came to the queen's rooms and escorted me to the king. He was feeling better by the time we returned. But Queen Philippa had asked me to summon her husband to her bedside."

Alys bit her bottom lip to still the trembling. "She died soon after we returned to her rooms. I was so upset." She wrapped her arms about her, the cold evening seeping into her, the black night enveloping her. "You were... kind to me. Comforted me. You held me close." She raised her eyes to meet his. "I felt safe in your arms."

She looked at him, hoping his anger was softening. "And that was how I felt when you embraced me again." She gathered her courage and admitted, "I have longed for your kiss all these years, Kit. That day, we shared something special between us. I never forgot it. No man has ever interested me. Not before and not since that day."

Alys placed a hand upon his arm. "I was about to tell you who you were earlier today. In the forest. But Nan interrupted us." Hot tears now cascaded down her cheeks. "I have wanted you for so long, and then I had you for a short while. I planned to tell you today who I suspected you were when we spoke after the feast. I realized I'd been selfish. I couldn't keep you here at Kinwick any longer."

She dropped her hand and took a step away from him. "You have a wife, Kit. I knew her briefly at court. She told me that the two of you were betrothed." Alys brushed her tears away in frustration. "And I have kept you from Richessa. Knowingly. I am... so sorry. I have no way to make it up to you." She dropped her head in shame.

Silence filled the night. Then Alys felt warm fingers under her chin, forcing her to look up.

"Richessa is dead." Kit held her chin firmly when she tried to look away. "We did marry, but no children came from our union. In fact, she could not have any more babes after she lost the last one."

Alys' hand latched on to his wrist.

"When I returned from France, I went to London to see my father and then left straightaway to Brentwood. Richessa had died two days earlier from Saint Anthony's Fire." A sad look crossed his face. "I confess the news brought me relief. She had been a spoiled, immature woman and never changed as time passed. Mother disliked Richessa intensely, and she thinks of nothing but the good in everyone she meets."

Hope sprouted within her. Her fingers tightened around his wrist. His anger had now subsided.

"So I know who I am, Alys. And that I am free. I have neither wife nor betrothed awaiting me at Brentwood." His large hands cupped her face. "But I must return at once. Mother will be sick with worry."

"You said you sought me out because she was indisposed. What signs of illness did she display?"

"Mother is never unwell, but she seemed listless and was feverish. It concerned me enough to seek a remedy for whatever ailed her. She is the reason why I traveled to Kinwick. I remembered how skilled you were at healing those at court. My mother means the world to me, so I wished to find you and bring you back with me to Brentwood."

"Then we must leave in the morning," Alys said, her heart beating rapidly as his thumbs caressed her cheeks.

"We will, my love," he said, his voice low and tender.

Kit bent and touched his mouth to hers. Her hands wound round his neck and pulled him closer. He teased her lips apart with his tongue, sending sparks shooting inside her. Her tongue mated with his. Heat began to rise within her. His hands captured her waist, easily spanning it, as he brought her to him.

He kissed her until she trembled from head to toe. Alys clung to him, wanting to burrow as close as possible. His mouth left hers, trailing hot kisses along her jaw, down her neck. His tongue flicked across the top curve of her breasts. She shivered in delight. His lips came back and found hers again, kissing her until she lost all track of time. All that counted was now. This moment. This man.

This love.

For Alys knew, as others in her family had discovered, when you kissed the one you were meant to be with for eternity, you would know.

Kit Emory was The One.

CHAPTER 13

WITHOUT WARNING, KIT swept Alys off her feet. He strode across the bailey in the faint moonlight, his strong arms carrying her as if she weighed nothing.

"Where are we going?" she asked breathlessly, tightening her arms about his neck.

"You'll see." His voice, husky and mysterious, caused her to shiver in anticipation.

They passed no one along the way as flickering torches lit the path he took to the stables. He paused at the entrance where a lantern hung and lifted it from its perch.

"We are going riding? At night?" She thought it most peculiar to want to ride a horse in the dark after they had shared such passionate kisses.

Kit laughed, a rich sound that came deep from within his belly. He continued into the stables with her in his arms, marching down a long row of stalls. A few horses nickered at them as they passed by. Then they stopped in front of an empty stall.

He gave her a long look, desire burning brightly in his eyes. "I don't plan to mount a horse this night, sweetest Alys. I plan to mount you and ride you to the stars and back."

His words shocked—and thrilled—her.

Kit eased her to her feet and opened the door. He hung the lantern inside the stall and looked around. Bending, he lifted some of the hay, resting it to create a small pile. He repeated the process several times until a bed of hay awaited them. The sweet smell of it surrounded her.

Alys locked her knees, fearful she would collapse. Kit returned to her and placed his hands on her shoulders. Slowly, he slid them down her arms till their hands met and their fingers entwined.

"I want you, Alys de Montfort. More than I have ever wanted a woman. I want to bury myself within you. Spill my seed into your womb. I want you now. And always. I will brand you as mine tonight, but know that I plan to take you to wife."

His voice, raw with emotion, turned tender. "I know who I am. That I am free to love you and plan a future with you. I want to bed you each and every night. My only wish is to wake up with you by my side every morning." He paused. "And never, ever let you go."

"I will always want you, Kit Emory," she boldly proclaimed. "Whether in dreams or awake, you are my one desire."

Alys squeezed his hands with affection. "When I decided to tell you your name, I made another important decision." She lowered her eyes, not wanting to see his reaction. "I told myself that I wanted a part of you to stay with me always. So I had planned to seduce you tonight. Either the experience would be burned into my soul and allow me to keep hold of a part of you forevermore, or I would find myself with your child growing inside me and always have something of you."

Warm lips pressed against her temple. "You would have seduced me, my lady?"

Alys bit back a smile. "I would have tried, my lord. And I usually am successful in my endeavors." She lifted her eyes to meet his and saw them gleam with passion.

"Then I will allow you to take the lead in this venture."

She hesitated. "I really don't know—"

"You do, my love. Simply follow your heart."

Alys saw that he yielded control to her. It intrigued her. It emboldened her.

He empowered her.

She released his hands and brought her own to his chest, flattening her palms against it. She felt the hard muscle beneath her fingertips and danced her fingers up slowly, savoring his clean, masculine scent. Her fingers lightly stroked his neck, and she watched his eyes darken. She pushed them into his thick, dark hair. Massaged his head sensually. Toyed with his earlobes. Listened to his breathing grow shallow then more rapid.

"You are too tall by far," she told him. "Come to your knees."

He knelt in front of her. Alys cupped his face, tilting it toward her. Then she brought her mouth to his and pressed it gently in a soft, sweet kiss. Slowly, she ran her tongue along his lips, tracing their outline over and over. A low groan from him made her smile. She flicked her tongue along the seam of his lips, urging them to open. When they did, she plunged her tongue inside his mouth, finding his so they could do battle together.

Alys had no idea how long they kissed, but she could have continued to do so all night. They warred for control, each one taking advantage and turning kiss after heated kiss into something much more. Each kiss broke new ground between them. Fanned the flames of desire within them. Spoke of promises that would join them as one for all time.

She reveled in the scrape of his stubble against her skin, but she wanted much more. Her fingers kneaded his shoulders, slowly dropping to his back. She gathered the material of his cotehardie and bunched it in her hands, pulling it up and over his head. His gypon came along with it. She stepped back a moment to admire what was revealed. Sleek muscles covered in shadows of the last fading bruises greeted her. A fine matting of dark hair, smooth to her touch, covered his chest, fading into a line that disappeared within his pants. Alys stroked him over and over, the muscles twitching at her touch.

Kit took hold of her waist and yanked her close. His head was level with her breasts, which seemed to have swelled as something pounded with need within her. His tongue returned to the top of her breast, then his teeth nibbled through her clothing. Bolts of lightning zipped inside her. Alys knew she must discard her clothes. Now.

"I need your skin to touch mine," she told him, her voice raw with need.

He rose and removed her sideless surcoat. Lifted her kirtle over her head. Pushed her smock down to her waist, baring her upper body to him. Alys took his head within her hands and guided him to her breast. His beard scratched the delicate skin as he began to kiss the globe. Lick the nipple. Tease it with his teeth.

"Oh!" she gasped, a great pull inside her beginning to drum as loud as any drummer she had heard.

He lavished attention first on one breast, then the other, giving each equal time, caressing them until they seemed sore and heavy.

"More," she commanded, still sounding in charge, but barely, for what he did was slowly undoing her.

Kit lowered her smock over her hips and brought it to the ground. She stepped out of it, and he tossed it aside. Only her shoes and stockings remained. But he didn't remove them.

Instead, his hands latched on to her hips. His mouth came to rest next to her belly and kissed it thoroughly before dropping lower. Alys knew what he would do next. Her mother's conversations about what pleased a man and a woman echoed in her mind. But what Merryn had spoken of and what happened now seemed like two very different things.

As he began kissing her, her legs started trembling, then violently quaking.

"I fear I must sit," she cried out.

Kit's eyes gleamed up at her. He stood and led her to the pile of hay that he'd gathered. She sat on top it, but he pushed her prone. Slowly, he removed her shoe and rolled the stocking down, his lips burning a path from her knees to her ankles. After both legs and feet were bare, he placed his hands around her calves and brought them up in the air, placing her legs on top of his shoulders.

"Keep them there," he ordered, bending close and grasping her hips firmly in his hands.

Then those intimate kisses began again, hot and wet. Alys felt the great heat of his mouth as the drumming inside her grew in intensity and volume. One hand left her hip and as he moved to kiss her belly, she felt his fingers touching her. Parting her. Entering her. One finger eased in, stroking her in a delicious fashion. Another one joined it, and the two began moving in and out in a rhythm that began to match the drumming within her.

He pulled them from her, and Alys saw they were wet. Kit licked them slowly, sensuously.

"Your juices run sweet for me," he said.

Breathless, she could not respond. She watched him return to her curls and realized when a jolt hit her that his tongue was now where his fingers had played. It stroked her with a fire and intensity that brought a growing warmth. She began panting. Writhing. Whimpering. Calling out his name. Her fingers dug into the hay at her side. The pressure grew, both from his mouth and something building within her.

Then it burst wide open, flaring like a thousand suns dancing across the sky, a warmth glowing brighter than anything she had ever known. Alys screamed at the intense pleasure, but suddenly Kit's mouth was on hers, absorbing the sound. His fingers entered her again, gliding inside her, and once more the burst of heat encompassed her. She rode a wave that never seemed to end.

Slowly, she came back to reality. She watched Kit stand and tear off his pants. Her eyes widened at the size of his member standing at full attention, and she wondered how he ever thought something so large would fit inside her.

He lowered himself until he hovered over her. "You are as ready as you will ever be. 'Twill be painful, love, then it never hurts again. I promise."

With those words, he plunged inside her as his mouth devoured hers.

Alys fought to rise, bucking against him, the pain excruciating. Kit did not move. Gradually, she became used to how he filled her. The pain faded. He seemed to understand that and slowly rocked against her. She clung to him as he began to move in and out of her. Then some primal instinct took control of her, and she started to move with and against him. The rocking motion became a dance, just as their tongues had danced with one another. The dance became faster and faster until she thought they would spin out of control.

Then the heat and warmth returned, more vivid than before. Desire for him mounted within her. Alys held on for dear life as they moved, going higher. Faster. Further. And then sweet release came again, for them both this time. They each made a triumphant sound. Then their mouths met, feasting upon one another as if they had come out of a famine and could not get enough of one another.

A heaviness suddenly invaded her limbs. Her hands dropped from him. Kit collapsed atop her, his weight welcomed. Alys brought her arms around his torso, slick with sweat as he buried his face in her neck. She held on to him tightly, her rapid breath beginning to slow. Then he rolled to his side and took her with him. She nestled in the protection of his arms, their hearts against one another, beating in time.

"You are mine. Forever," he declared.

Her hand touched his cheek. "And you are mine. Forevermore."

He kissed her gently, his passion reined in, but the promise of love now sealed between them.

"I need to speak to your father," Kit said. "He must know I intend to wed you as soon as possible."

"A wedding can wait," Alys said. "We need to return with haste to Brentwood and see to your mother. Once she is in good health, I will be more than happy to speak vows with you." She grinned. "And command you in our bedchamber."

His brows arched. "You think to make me dance to your tune in private?" Kit kissed her and sighed. "I believe that might be the wisest course of action."

THEY MADE LOVE again, this time more leisurely. Kit knew it was a luxury for them to do so. If the May Day feasting had not been in progress, they wouldn't have found the privacy the empty stables had afforded them.

He found a bucket and filled it with water and helped clean Alys. Surprisingly, she didn't seem embarrassed as he washed her. He assumed because of her experience with the sick and birthing babies that she had seen people in all states of undress and that made her less self-conscious than another virgin might have been.

As he dressed, he marveled at the fact that he had fallen in love. Utterly, madly, deeply in love. Alys de Montfort not only satisfied him physically with her glowing beauty and curvaceous body, but she had a keen mind and a healing heart. She would make a wonderful partner to him and, someday, a fine lady of Brentwood.

Best of all, Kit knew she returned his love. To find a woman of Alys' strength and character and fetching beauty was rare. Richessa had brought fabulous wealth to the coffers of Brentwood with her dowry, but she had never tempted him with her frail, sickly body or her shallow nature. She parroted what he said without forming opinions of her own. She never would have questioned him, much less stood up to him, the way he envisioned Alys would. They might have a few rocky times ahead when they disagreed, but Kit had found his missing half. A woman to equal him. And one who had him already hungry again for her touch. He chuckled, thinking himself like the other men in Alys' family. Strong men, of body and mind, who allowed love to rule them—and were better men for it.

He helped her replace her clothing, smoothing the skirts into place. Her braid had come undone, though, and no matter how hard he tried, he couldn't fix it. Alys pushed his clumsy hands aside and quickly twisted and flipped it till it looked as fresh as it had this morning.

Kit helped her to her feet. As she started to exit the stall, he captured her from behind, drawing her against his body, his arms wrapped about her. He lowered his lips to her ear.

"I will enjoy unbraiding your beautiful chestnut hair ever night," he murmured. "And I will brush it till it shines. Who knows? You might even teach me how to rebraid it."

Alys turned and looked at him over her shoulder. "In case we decided to come together during daylight hours?" Her soft lips gave him a wry smile.

His teeth grazed her throat. She shivered in his arms.

"Mayhap we shall connect in love play day and night," he said. "But it's time that we returned to the feast."

"The feast may be over," she warned. "I know not how long we've been away."

They left the stables and strolled back to the keep as workers from Kinwick began spilling down the stairs.

"It must have ended," Alys said. "Do you still wish to speak with my father?"

"Aye. If we are to leave tomorrow, I would have him know what is in my heart."

Only a few stragglers remained in the great hall. The trestle tables had been returned to the wall, and the usual group of servants had begun to bed down.

Alys took his hand. "Come. Let's go to the solar."

The corridor upstairs was deserted. They made their way to the end. Kit rapped his knuckles against the door.

Moments later, Geoffrey de Montfort opened it. After a quick glance, he ushered them inside. Lady Merryn appeared in the bedchamber doorway and looked at her daughter and then to Kit. She came to stand by her husband, a smile tugging at the corner of her mouth as she slipped a hand into the crook of his arm.

"You have a different look about you, Emory."

"I do, my lord."

"Would you care to sit?" De Montfort gestured to the group of chairs near the fireplace.

He and Alys went and took their seats. Lady Merryn sat across from them while her husband stood behind her, his hand on her shoulder. Alys propped her elbow on the arm of the chair and took his hand.

"I would first tell you that my memory has returned," Kit said. "All of it. I knew my name before, thanks to Devereux, and now I've recollected my past and present."

Lady Merryn gave him a generous smile. "That's wonderful news, my lord. I was hopeful your memory would come back before you left us."

"I also know that I had planned to visit Kinwick all along," he continued.

"But why?" Lord Geoffrey asked, a puzzled look crossing his face as he studied his daughter's hand in Kit's.

Kit looked to Alys, who nodded encouragingly.

"My mother has been ill while I fought in France. I wanted to find the best healer for her that I could. I had been introduced to Lady Alys when I arrived at the royal court several years ago. Though she was young, her reputation was unsurpassed. If the king and queen had entrusted her with their well-being, I knew she would be the one to seek out and help find what ailed Mother."

"So you came to Kinwick for my daughter." Lord Geoffrey's eyebrows rose. "And?"

"Not only did I find Lady Alys to be here, along with my memory, but I also found love."

"With Alys," Lady Merryn added, wanting confirmation.

"Aye, my lady. I am an only son to Lord Godwin Brentley of Brentwood. One day the estate will be mine. I would be most pleased to make Lady Alys my wife. She will be mistress of Brentwood and the keeper of my heart."

Lord Geoffrey rubbed his chin in thought. "Do you feel you know my daughter well?" he asked.

"I do, my lord. She is happiest caring for others and puts them before herself. She has an iron will and is a bit on the stubborn side. She likes to hum because her singing voice is terrible. Her beauty is only exceeded by her intelligence. She loves mundane tasks and is a most wonderful listener. She claims to be efficient with a sword, though I have yet to see that."

Kit paused and looked at Alys before continuing. "Most important of all, I love her. I love the joy she brings to me and those around her. I love her free spirit and her kind heart. I even love her every time she beats me at chess," he admitted. "I am a better man than I was before because she is in my life."

Lord Geoffrey nodded solemnly. "I always told Merryn that when a man knew Alys as well as Ancel—or even better than her twin did—that man would be the one for her. But that is not enough."

The nobleman turned to Alys. "I have heard how this man feels about you. I would ask if you return his feelings."

Alys' fingers tightened around Kit's in reassurance as she said, "I have waited all my life for Kit, Father. You know I have a mind of my own and would never settle, especially when it comes to marriage. I have always desired to find the right man to share my love and my life with, much as you and Mother have." She looked tenderly at Kit. "Kit Emory is definitely the man for me. No other can compare."

Lord Geoffrey took a few steps to close the gap between them and offered Kit his hand, a satisfied smile on his face. "I needed to be sure 'twas a love match on both sides."

Kit rose and accepted Lord Geoffrey's hand as the nobleman pumped it enthusiastically. Lady Merryn came and kissed his cheek, tears cascading down her own. She embraced her daughter. Kit felt surrounded by a warmth unlike any he had ever known.

"Welcome to our family, my lord." De Montfort grinned. "Where the women are far smarter than the men and their world becomes yours."

CHAPTER 14

THEY ARRIVED AT Brentwood three days after they left Kinwick and a round of lengthy goodbyes. The Le Rouxs had returned from visiting their three children at Wellbury, and Lady Beatrice knew at once something had occurred. She had to draw Alys aside, which led to both Lady Merryn and Lady Elysande joining in, all three women pumping Alys for details of her new love. While Kit was anxious to be off, Lord Geoffrey had pulled him aside and told Kit it was best that the women get their gossip out of their systems, else it might make for a long journey.

Father William was one of the first people Kit saw as they passed through the Brentwood gates. The old priest swung his head around and gaped at the large guard that accompanied him from Kinwick. Lord Geoffrey had sent some of his best men to escort them north, wanting his daughter to arrive safely at her future home.

"Good day, Father," Kit called. He slowed the borrowed mount from Kinwick. "How is my mother?"

"Worried sick about you, my lord," the priest affirmed. "Though I told her you were most likely on one of your frequent jaunts and had forgotten to send word to her."

He winced at the man's words. He remembered how, in the past, he'd charged off without a thought to the consequences, worrying his mother many times.

"I'm back now for good. No more wandering about," he confirmed. "And I bring both a healer for Mother—and my future bride."

Father William cast his eyes upon Alys and nodded with approval.

"My lady. 'Tis good to have you at Brentwood. I congratulate you for taming Sir Kit's wild ways. I hope you will be as successful in helping Lady Berengaria."

Alys gave the priest a sweet smile. "I'll do my best, Father." Then she cast a reproachful look at Kit.

He reached over and took her hand in order to press a kiss to her fingers. "I was no angel in the past," Kit told her. "But I promise to do my best under your watchful eye, my lady."

"Don't think I won't hold you to that, my lord."

They rode straight to the keep, and he helped Alys from her horse. She untied her case from the saddle horn as he gave instructions to Sir Gilbert to have his grooms take care of their horses and settle the Kinwick guard.

"There's plenty of daylight left," Gilbert said. "We'll spend it in your yard if you don't mind, my lord. My men would enjoy challenging new partners amongst your soldiers before we leave for Kinwick in the morning."

"I am sure our men would welcome the challenge, Sir Gilbert. I will see you all when we sup tonight," Kit said.

The dismissed guard rode off, and he escorted Alys into the keep. Dawkin met them.

"I'm glad to see you, my lord. Lady Berengaria has been informed of your return and would like you to come to the solar at once." The steward eyed Alys with interest.

"Lady Alys de Montfort is a renowned healer, Dawkin. Have our best guest room readied for her."

"At once, my lord."

Kit took Alys' case in one hand and her hand in his other. "Let us go see Mother."

She took a deep breath. "I'm a little nervous."

"Why? My mother will fall in love with you more quickly than I did," he teased.

She blushed at his words. "Lady Berengaria will be my future mother-in-law. I want to make a good impression on her. Mayhap I should change into fresh clothing."

"Nay," he said, leading her up the staircase. "She is eager to see me—and I am eager for the two of you to meet."

They arrived at the solar, and he tapped lightly on the door before entering. The outer chamber stood empty.

"Kit?" his mother called.

"Coming, Mother." They crossed to the opened bedchamber door and entered.

His mother was in her bed, an abundance of pillows behind her. Her pale face emphasized her dark eyes. Kit handed Alys her case and rushed to the bed.

Taking her hands, he asked, "How are you, Mother?"

She gave him a wry smile. "I am better now that I know my son is alive and back home."

"I've much to tell you. But first," he motioned Alys over, "I would like you to meet Lady Alys de Montfort, the healer that I sought."

Alys came forward. She set her case down and took his mother's hands. "I'm most pleased to meet you, Lady Berengaria. And I want more than anything for you to be healthy for your people. Your son has shared with me what a strong woman you are, both in mind and body, and how your leadership has kept Brentwood thriving for many years."

His mother eyed Alys carefully. "So you are here to discover what ails me?"

"I will do the best I can. May I examine you and ask you a few questions?"

"Aye. I can tell you that our priest believes I have dysorexy, with the occasional day fever mixed in, and that is what's caused my recent fatigue. I haven't been hungry for several weeks, and I have always possessed a hearty appetite in the past."

"Dysorexy does reduce a person's appetite," Alys confirmed, "but other factors might contribute to your weakened condition." She ran her fingers lightly through his mother's scalp and hair. Touched her face. Looked inside her ears. Had her open her mouth and stick out her tongue. Felt along her neck.

Kit became restless and started pacing the room. Alys continued to ask questions. She even had his mother blow her nose into a cloth and cough and spit into a different cloth so she could study the phlegm. He had to admit that she was quite thorough.

Alys finally pulled a chair next to the bed and sat, so Kit rejoined the women.

"From what you've said, I believe it's more than one thing troubling you. The nagging catarrh has lingered in your nose and throat, causing drainage. This is something seasonal and starts in the spring for some and the fall for others. Have you experienced it before?"

"Aye, always in the spring, but not to this extent."

"Sometimes, it worsens as a person ages. My Aunt Milla suffers from this springtime ailment. Besides her runny nose, she sneezes overmuch and has a cough that continues for a few months. Because of this drainage, it has caused you to lose your appetite. You also seem weak to me. That could be from not eating well, or mayhap it's chlorosis. To keep your energy up, you should eat more chicken, oysters, clams, and lentils."

His mother smiled. "I favor all of those foods."

"And since your bowels have not moved as often as they should have, you may have costiveness. In that case, it means eating more fruit and some oats."

"I will tell Cook."

"I would like to go and grind some herbs for you now to take in boiled water. It will help your nose and raw throat and keep the drainage at bay. The sooner you partake of this mixture, the quicker your appetite will return." Alys stood and retrieved her case. "I'll return soon, my lord. I would like to prepare this treatment for Lady Berengaria at once. For now, I will leave you to visit with your mother."

After Alys left, Kit took the seat she had vacated and reached for his mother's hands. "It's so good to see you, Mother. I feel as if I have wandered in the desert for years."

"You are so different, Kit," she said. "What has changed?"

"Everything."

He related his experience on the open road and how the band of thieves attacked him and then left him for dead. How the de Montfort party came upon him and took him back to Kinwick to care for his injuries.

"I would have sent word to you, but I knew not who I was. I suffered a severe blow to my head, and my memory became a blank. I did not know my own name. Where I lived. Who I was."

Tears welled in her eyes. She gripped his hand. "How awful for you, Kit. I cannot begin to know what you suffered or how helpless you must have felt." She gave him a sheepish look. "And here I thought you had forgotten about me and merely traipsed through the country on one of your merry jaunts. I feel guilty now."

"You shouldn't," he said firmly. "This experience has caused me to mature. I cannot say I'll always make the right decisions in the future. I know I was rash and impatient in the past, but I do believe that I've changed for the better—and that I am a better man."

"Because of Lady Alys," she said, an understanding smile lighting her face.

"Aye."

"I could tell from the moment you entered my bedchamber that something had changed in you." She pursed her lips a moment as she searched his face. "My goodness, Kit—you have fallen in love with this woman!"

"Hopelessly and utterly in love," he admitted.

She studied him for a long moment. "I must say that I envy you. I never had that with your father, nor did I ever discover love with another. I had no time to take a lover. I was too busy running Brentwood and the estate consumed me."

She squeezed his hand. "I am happy for you, my son. Lady Alys is not only incredibly beautiful, but she seems to have a sweet spirit."

"You'll be happy to know that I now understand what is important in life. I've always fought against rules and putting roots down. I was happiest charging into battle, not caring if I fell or found victory. While I will always fight for king and country if called upon, I am now content to remain home, here at Brentwood, with the woman I love."

His mother laughed heartily. "Surely, Lady Alys has worked a miracle. Christopher Emory wishes to become a man who remains at home?"

He joined in her laughter. "Indeed. I plan to marry the lady and make a life at Brentwood. I know I still have much to learn from you regarding farming the land and keeping the records. Alys has already taught me how to speak with tenants and truly show them that you care for them and their families."

A hopeful look danced in his mother's eyes. "And children?" she asked.

"I want to fill Brentwood with an army of children," Kit declared. "The more, the merrier."

Alys entered the room at that moment and wrinkled her brow, her look questioning their peals of laughter echoing throughout the room.

His mother held out a hand. Alys came and took it.

"My son tells me he loves you, Lady Alys. And because he does, I do, as well." She pulled Alys close and kissed her cheek. With a mischievous look in her eye, Berengaria asked, "So when is the wedding?"

A SENNIGHT PASSED, and Kit was delighted that his mother grew visibly stronger. She partook of the herbs Alys gave her in tinctures and hot water and ate everything put before her. She left her sickbed after only two days and returned to most of her duties around the keep. Each passing day seemed to bring a happier look to her appearance. She already treated Alys as the daughter she never had and the two seemed thicker than thieves.

He showed Alys around Brentwood's lands, having them ride the perimeter of the estate so that she could see its scope. He decided to wait for her to meet their workers until they had wed. He longed for the time when he could introduce her to the world as his wife. She agreed when he suggested the marriage take place soon. Because of his mother's rapid recovery, they would leave in the morning for Kinwick. The women packed upstairs while Kit readied a missive to be sent to his father in London, informing him that he would marry Alys de Montfort in a month's time. Kit only agreed to wait that long because his future bride wanted to send word to all of her extended family so that they could plan to attend. He looked forward to meeting more of her relatives and becoming a part of those she held dear.

Kit shared with her that he doubted his father would take time away from court to attend their nuptial mass, but he aimed to be a dutiful son, which was why he now composed a missive to send to London.

Dawkin knocked at the open door. He looked up and motioned the steward into the room.

"Your father approaches, my lord. I thought you would wish to know."

As usual, Godwin Emory gave no warning of his return. He so rarely came home to Brentwood that Kit had a hard time picturing him within the walls of the keep. He couldn't remember the last time his father had been at the estate.

"Give me a few minutes in which to greet my father and speak with him privately, then inform my mother and Lady Alys of his arrival," he instructed.

Kit pushed aside the parchment and ink. He wanted to apprise his father of his upcoming marriage before he introduced him to Alys. At least by his unexpected visit, his father would meet Alys in the flesh. Godwin would also know Lord Geoffrey from the nobleman's recent trip to court to discuss the truce with the king and his advisers. Between that and meeting Alys, Kit hoped his father would know what a wise choice he had made in his bride-to-be.

Kit left the room and hurried outside in order to meet his father as he rode in. As he reached the inner bailey, Kit heard the thundering of hooves and knew arrival was imminent. A large group of twenty horsemen or more rounded the corner, and he picked out his father at once since the man headed the party. Kit hid the shock he felt as the horses stopped in front of him.

His father, riding on his usual dappled gray mount, was visibly ill. He rushed to help him from the saddle. As Kit stood next to him, his father seemed to have shriveled in height. He was gaunt. His hair had thinned. He seemed unsteady on his feet. He looked nothing like the man Kit had seen in London merely a few weeks ago.

Immediately, he thought that Alys could determine what was wrong and help him. If she could, that would endear her to her future father-in-law.

"We weren't expecting you, Father," he said. "It's good to see you again so soon after our last encounter."

The nobleman began to wheeze and couldn't catch his breath. Without warning, deep, harsh coughs began to rack Godfrey's thin frame. Kit pounded his father's back as Godfrey brought a discolored rag to his face and spit into it. He quickly folded it and slipped it into a pocket. A sliver of fear cut into Kit. He'd never been close with his father, but he had never wished the man ill. With the speed that his appearance had changed and the sound of his lungs, Kit feared Alys would not be able to provide a lasting cure.

His father finally ceased coughing. He swallowed and said, "I have a surprise for you, Christopher."

Warning bells sounded within Kit's head. Usually, his father ignored him. He had never once, in all these years, given his son a gift, much less presented Kit with some surprise.

"What do you mean?" he asked cautiously.

The Baron of Brentley turned, his hand sweeping in a grand gesture.

Kit's eyes followed and landed upon a beautiful woman in the saddle atop a coal black horse. Large, brown eyes dominated her oval face. Her hair was as dark as that of the horse she rode. Full lips called out to be kissed. She was one of the most stunning women Kit had ever seen.

"Meet your future wife." His father motioned, and a soldier helped the woman from the saddle.

She walked slowly to them, her face a blank. If anything, an air of great sadness hung about her. She came and stood before him.

Stunned, Kit could only look at her. In the past, her type of beauty would have appealed to him. He would have bedded her more than once before moving on, but now his heart belonged to another. He must put an end to this at once.

"Lady Thea was recently widowed," his father revealed. "Her husband died while fighting in France."

The widow met Kit's eyes, a distant look on her face. She did not utter a word.

He would not embarrass this stranger in front of such a large group. He would see her safely inside and draw his father aside before he explained to him that he already had chosen a new wife. Kit would make sure Lady Thea returned to London with her dignity intact.

"Dawkin!" his father commanded. "See Lady Thea to our best guest chamber."

The steward looked stricken. Kit knew Dawkin had given Alys their best bedchamber when she arrived.

"Take Lady Thea to the blue room to freshen up," he told Dawkin, who looked visibly relieved at the command.

The steward led the noblewoman away. Kit turned to his father. "We must speak privately, Father. 'Tis urgent."

"Then come to the solar."

"Nay." He knew Alys would be there with his mother, helping her to pack for their trip to Kinwick. Kit wanted a chance to explain the situation to his father alone without the women being dragged into the matter.

"Let us go to Dawkin's records room instead," Kit suggested.

He watched his father take a few shaky steps. Kit took his father's arm firmly, guiding Godfrey up the keep's steps and into the small room just off the great hall. The older man collapsed into a chair, weariness hanging over him. Kit probably should see that food and drink were brought, but he didn't want to delay the news he needed to share.

"I can't marry Lady Thea, Father."

The baron gave him a withering look. Kit had been the recipient of that look many times over the years. But this time was different. He was here as a grown man, ready to fight for the woman he loved.

"You will marry her. I've already arranged things. The contracts have been signed."

"I signed no contracts!" Kit challenged, not hiding his anger.

His father eyes narrowed. "'Twas done by proxy."

Kit started to protest, but his father raised his arm, palm facing out, as if to block any words that might be uttered.

"Lady Thea is the daughter of a close associate of mine at court, a member of the king's council. She is related through her marriage to the Duke of Lancaster." His hand fell, and he sighed heavily. "The king and the Black Prince will soon be dead. That means Richard will be a boy king. And Lancaster, his uncle, will manage the throne until Richard comes of age."

"But—"

"No buts, Christopher. I won't tolerate another protest rising from your lips. Your marriage will help cement my position in the new court that comes to power. Your own, as well. It will be a most favorable alliance between our families."

Incredulous, Kit stared at him. His father could barely stand. He wouldn't live to see a new year, much less be a part of a new court and the power behind the throne. Still scheming, as he always had.

"I refuse," he said flatly. "I have found my own wife."

His father gave him a cold stare. "You will do *as I say*," he ground out, one word at a time. "You will honor the betrothal contract."

Godwin stared at his son. "Or I will disinherit you."

CHAPTER 15

ALYS CHATTED HAPPILY with Lady Berengaria as they decided what the noblewoman should bring to Kinwick. She had gotten to know Kit's mother well since her arrival at Brentwood and felt very comfortable in her future mother-in-law's presence. Though Alys knew she would miss her parents and all those at Kinwick once she and Kit wed, she already looked upon Brentwood as her home. She couldn't wait to start her new life here with her husband.

Just the thought of Kit warmed her cheeks. She longed for the nights they would spend together in their bed. Though it had been less than a fortnight since their love play in the Kinwick stables, Alys daydreamed about it constantly. She wanted—no, needed—Kit's touch. His hands on her. His mouth against hers. His member buried deep inside her.

"I remember your sister is Nan and your twin brother is Ancel. But tell me your younger brothers' names again. I want to make sure I know of everyone by the time we reach Kinwick."

Alys smiled at Lady Berengaria's eagerness. The noblewoman had revealed that once she came to Brentwood, she'd never left the area. Her husband refused to bring her to the royal court in London, saying she was more valuable to him running the estate. She had remained all these years in one place, and her excitement grew as the time came close for their departure.

"Hal is the elder of the two. He is a bright boy, full of mischief, but he has a good heart."

"He sounds much as my son."

She laughed. "I had not thought of that, but I do believe there are similarities between the two. Edward, named for our king, is the younger by two years. He is steadfast and loyal to his brother and follows him about as a puppy. They will be coming home for the summer from Winterbourne."

"And that is where your twin brother is a squire, correct?"

Alys smiled. "You have an excellent memory, my lady."

Berengaria sighed. "There are still so many names to remember. Your cousins and their husbands. And their children. Your Uncle Hugh and his wife, Milla. I hope I can keep everyone straight." She looked at Alys with apprehension. "I also hope they will like me."

"They most certainly will," she assured. "They like your son, and you are even more impressive than he is."

"Alys, you tease me."

She bit back a smile. "Mayhap a little, my lady. But they will welcome you with open arms. I sent word to them that we are coming. You will have a month at Kinwick to settle in and get to know everyone before the wedding. I daresay you and Mother will get along best of all."

"Kit tells me your mother is most beautiful and quite independent. And that your father worships at her feet."

A wistful sigh escaped Alys' lips. "Aye. Mother is the strongest, most capable woman I know. That's why I think you will take to each other, for you are cut from the same cloth. Father is a most respected man. I admire that he treats Mother as his equal. Together, they have built a successful life. They share everything between them and are very much in love."

Lady Berengaria paused and set aside the surcoat she had folded. She came and placed her hands on Alys' shoulders.

"I see your marriage to my Kit will be modeled after your parents' relationship. That makes me very happy." The noblewoman kissed her cheek.

She was moved by the gesture and embraced Berengaria. Though no one could ever replace her mother, Alys believed fortune now brought her a second mother in whom she could confide and be a true friend with.

A knock sounded on the door. Alys stepped around the open trunk they were going to use and left the bedchamber to answer it.

When she opened the door to the solar's main room, she almost gasped. A woman of ethereal beauty stood in the corridor, dressed in the softest shade of blue. Alys stepped back to admit her and she seemed to glide through the entrance.

Who was this noblewoman who swept in with a regal grace that rivaled that of Queen Philippa?

The woman moved to Lady Berengaria, who emerged from the bedchamber. "Greetings, my lady. I wanted to introduce myself to you since I have only arrived at Brentwood with your lord husband from the royal court. I wanted to make the pleasure of your acquaintance. I am Lady Thea, here to marry your son."

Alys sucked in a quick breath. This woman's words acted like a severe blow to Alys' belly. Nausea filled her at the thought of Kit with this beauty.

Lady Thea continued. "Lord Godwin shared with me how Sir Christopher lost his own wife a short time ago. I suffered my own spouse's loss. My husband was killed fighting in the French war." She paused. "My family and your husband believe our union will benefit all involved."

Lady Berengaria glanced to Alys, her eyes wide, her face stricken. Alys shook her head and mouthed, "Nay." She wanted to speak to Kit first. She didn't care to reveal their plans to this cool, assured beauty from court.

Then Lady Thea turned and looked at her. "And who might you be?"

Alys cleared her throat. "I have some skill as a healer, passed on to me from my mother. I came to help Lady Berengaria since she was doing poorly."

The newcomer turned back to Kit's mother. "You have been ill, my lady? I would never have guessed, for you look the picture of health to me."

Berengaria said, "I recently suffered from several ailments. My son retrieved Lady Alys de Montfort to see to my needs. Under her care, I have swiftly improved and am back on my feet."

Lady Thea's gaze returned to her. "Lady Alys?" She frowned, her brow wrinkling in thought. "Your name sounds familiar to me." After a moment, she brightened. "Oh, I have heard of you in London. You were at court some years ago, were you not?"

"Aye. I was in service to Queen Philippa for several years."

The noblewoman nodded in understanding. "People still speak of you and your healing ways, my lady. No wonder my betrothed sought you out."

The recent widow reached and took Alys' hand, a genuine smile lighting her features. A knife twisted inside Alys, though she kept her face placid at their contact.

"I must thank you for helping Sir Christopher's lady mother recover." Lady Thea's sweet look of gratitude almost caused Alys to run from the room screaming. The day had turned into a nightmare.

The solar door opened. A man Alys barely recognized as Godwin Emory entered. Not only had he aged horribly since she last saw him at Windsor Castle, but it was obvious he was quite ill. His ashen color and gaunt frame were far different from the memories of the robust man that she held.

Kit followed closely on his father's heels, a dark scowl on his face. His eyes found her and she saw anguish in them. The small hope Alys had held in her heart dissolved. She cast her eyes away.

"Greetings, Wife," the baron said, his voice thin. "I see you have met Lady Thea. She will be joining the Emory family soon." His wintry smile did not reach his eyes. "This will be a strong political alliance for us. Christopher's marriage to Lady Thea ensures the Emory influence will remain strong at court." He looked to his son. "And the Duke of Lancaster has promised to find a place for Christopher."

Alys found her gaze drawn back to a stone-faced Kit. Her beloved's eyes blazed in anger as he studied Godwin Emory at length.

Suddenly, Lord Godwin barked at her. "Who might you be? You look familiar to me, my lady."

She gave him a small curtsey. "We met at court years ago, my lord. I am Alys de Montfort of Kinwick, daughter of Lord Geoffrey and Lady Merryn."

"Lady Alys is a healer of some note," interjected Berengaria. "Kit brought her to Brentwood since I had been ailing in recent weeks."

"Well, you look the same to me as always, Wife," muttered Lord Godwin as he slid into a chair.

Alys made her decision in that moment. "She is, my lord, which is why I plan to return home tomorrow morning. Would you be so good as to arrange a guard to escort me? The one which accompanied me to Brentwood is no longer here. I find that I am eager to return to my parents and Kinwick."

"If that is the case, would you care to spend some time with me before you go, Lady Alys?" asked Thea. "I would like to learn a bit from you about herbs. I fancy myself planting a small herb garden here at Brentwood."

Alys swallowed. "Of course. I can help you unpack your things. In fact, I know I was given the largest guest bedchamber during my stay. It should now be yours. We can have a servant remove my things and I will help you settle in there."

She linked a hand through the crook of Thea's arm and looked to Berengaria. "If you will excuse us, my lady. I am sure you and your husband and son have much to discuss regarding his upcoming nuptials."

She led Thea from the solar. With every step away from Kit, her heart shattered into another piece. By the time they reached the corridor, Alys felt broken inside.

ALYS SPENT THE afternoon in Thea's company. It hurt her to do so, but she didn't trust being around Lady Berengaria, who would try to talk her out of leaving.

And she certainly did not trust being in Kit's presence. She wanted to avoid him at all cost. Already, the news of his unexpected betrothal had torn her asunder. Alys refused to add to her sorrow by speaking with him when nothing could be gained from their encounter. A betrothal was as good as being wed. Kit was a forbidden fruit which could never be sampled again.

Surprisingly, Alys found that she liked Lady Thea as the day went on. The noblewoman was friendly once they were alone and confided to Alys that she had presented herself to Lady Berengaria full of confidence when she actually trembled inside.

"Lord Godwin is a man of considerable influence at the royal court. My family—and my husband's family—both pushed for a marriage to his son when he offered the possibility to them. You have been at court, my lady. You know all about political alliances and how quickly they can be formed—or dissolved."

"Please, call me Alys," she asked. She felt no hatred for this woman. In fact, she believed Thea would make a good wife to Kit. She had a sweet nature and keen intelligence.

"Thank you, Alys," Thea said, embracing her. "I'm only sorry that you leave in the morning. Mayhap you can return soon for a visit. I have no sisters, and I feel a kinship with you."

"Mayhap," Alys said. She didn't want to make—much less keep—a vague promise to this woman. She would never, ever return to Brentwood, no matter how many years passed. She could not imagine stepping inside the solar and seeing Kit in the presence of his beautiful wife, children playing at their feet, a babe nursing at Thea's breast.

After she made sure Thea had settled in, Alys returned to the bedchamber where Thea had first been placed. She remained in her room the rest of the day and didn't bother to attend the evening meal. How could she sit there, trying to swallow the tasteless food, possibly sitting next to Kit for the last time?

Instead, she lay on her bed, dry eyed. She would weep tears of sorrow later when she returned home. At Kinwick, she would have the support of her family and could lean on their collective strength to see her through this ordeal. For now, she aimed to keep a tight rein on her emotions.

When a knock sounded at her door, she ignored it. She had no intention of speaking to anyone, least of all Kit, before she left Brentwood.

But the knocking persisted. It turned into pounding. Alys climbed from the bed and crossed quickly to the door. She opened it less than the width of her hand. As she expected, Kit stood on the other side, his eyes sparking with anger.

And desire.

"I cannot speak with you, my lord," she said, keeping her voice low. "Please leave—and do not return."

She began to push the door shut, but his hand slipped in and forced it open. Alys jumped back. Kit started toward her, his arms held out to embrace her. She ducked under one and fled the chamber, not wanting to be alone with him inside it. Not wanting to make love with him one last time. At least in the corridor, she felt safe from any assault.

He stepped out and looked in both directions before he headed toward her. Alys' heart began racing as she saw the hallway was deserted. She took off down it.

But Kit was beside her in an instant, his longer strides closing the distance between them in seconds. His hands captured her waist and pushed her against the stone wall even as his body blocked her escape.

"Alys. You must not go." His hands held firm, keeping her in place.

She raised her eyes to meet his. "I must," she insisted. "You have a betrothed, which means contracts were signed."

"Not by me," he insisted. "I am committed to you, my love. My heart. My mind. My soul. My body. All cry out. *For you.*"

She knew what he planned to do as he lowered his head and whipped her face away. His lips grazed her cheek and then his teeth nibbled on her earlobe, causing a sharp intake of breath. His tongue toyed with her ear, forcing her to catch her breath as she began to whimper. Her head fell back, exposing her throat to him, and Kit took full advantage of that.

Alys tried to keep her hands off him, but she gave in to temptation. Pushed her fingers into his thick, dark hair. Brought her lips to his. Kissed him with everything she had. In her mind, she rationalized that this would be their last kiss, the best, the sweetest of all. It went on and on and on until time stood still.

Finally, she broke it. "Enough," she pleaded.

"This can't be goodbye between us," Kit told her. "I beg you. Do not leave me. I care not that Father will disinherit me. I only know that I must be with you. I cannot live without you, Alys. I cannot. Don't ask that of me."

Anger coursed through her at the threat father had made against son, but she must convince Kit to do the right thing.

"Don't let Brentwood and its people suffer because of your selfish desires, Kit. You must remain here and become the baron when your father passes. You know that will happen soon."

She studied him. "And because you owe it to Brentwood, you know I could never stay. I cannot become your wife. I refuse to serve as your mistress. Nay, Kit. You have a legal obligation to marry Lady Thea. I spent a good deal of time with her today. She is kind and intelligent and lovely to look at. She will give you fine sons and daughters. You must honor her and the betrothal contract. I can never be a part of your life."

"But how will I live without you?" he asked, his voice breaking.

She understood his words, for she'd thought of nothing else during the last several hours.

"We will go on because we must," she said simply. "I refuse to be the cause of you losing all that is dear to you. I am not meant to ever love another man. Only you. I will love you till my dying day, Kit Emory."

Alys took his face in her hands and drank in one long, last look. "'Tis goodbye we must say now, my precious. I want you to live a good life with Thea. Forget me and our time together. Live in your present with your wife and the future to come. Promise me you will." When she saw the doubt in his eyes, she said it again. *"Promise me."*

Alys saw Kit was close to the breaking point, but he uttered the words. "I promise."

She pressed her lips to his one last time and then pulled away from him. Their tender farewell had ended. She must keep her resolve.

Without a backward glance, Alys hurried to her chamber and slipped inside. She closed the door and leaned on it for support. Her forehead dropped against the thick oak.

And then the tears came.

CHAPTER 16

Kit's spirits had never sunk lower in his life. His head told him that Alys was right. He couldn't let the people of Brentwood down and walk away—especially with his father so near death. Godwin Emory had no surviving brothers, nor did Kit have any male cousins that Brentwood could go to. If his father disinherited him for abandoning Lady Thea and the betrothal contracts, the estate would revert back to the crown. His mother would become homeless, her life's work all for naught. A new nobleman would lay claim to the title Baron of Brentley, and Kit could not guarantee that would be a good thing for their people.

If Alys had taught him one thing, it was sacrifice. She always did for others. Even now, she thought of the tenants and servants of Brentwood and his mother before herself. She wanted their futures guaranteed. She'd also encouraged him to marry Lady Thea and praised the noblewoman's good qualities.

But his heart remained broken despite Alys' advice to forget her. How could he push aside his memories of her? How could he go on when the love of his life was about to ride out the gates of Brentwood forever?

And how could he let her down? She had put great faith in him to do the right thing. To honor his family name and his people. Kit knew this was even harder on Alys than for him. He would look after Brentwood and its workers and keep his mother safe. He would make this marriage to Lady Thea work and father children, leaving them as his legacy. Kit would live up to the man Alys de Montfort expected him to be.

His heart told him Alys would have none of this. She would never marry nor have a companion to lessen her load and share her burdens and triumphs. Alys would carry him in her heart and forever be true to the love they shared.

That caused Kit grief beyond the pain he experienced for himself. Alys sacrificed her own happiness . . . so that he could be happy and fulfilled.

Without meaning to, he left his bedchamber. He had skipped mass and breaking his fast, not trusting himself to see Alys. He didn't want to be present when she and the guard from Brentwood rode from the bailey. And yet Kit's feet carried him down the stairs. He told himself he would merely step outside the keep and only catch a last glimpse of her. One final look that would have to last him a lifetime.

His mother rushed to his side. "Will you not stop her?" she hissed.

"Nay, Mother."

"But you love her, Kit. And she loves you."

"We spoke last night," he said quietly. "Though unhappiness fills me, this is what Alys deemed best. We love each other enough to . . . let go."

His mother stared at him, a hard look he had never seen in her eyes. "You would both let love go, something so rare and fine. Something that others seek and wait a lifetime for and never find."

Kit shook his head sadly. "I must respect her wishes, Mother. This is what Alys wants."

"You will never convince me of that." Her eyes narrowed. "You are no son of mine. *My* son would stand up to his father. He would show me that he is the better man he claimed to be because of the love of that woman. He would act boldly."

Kit laughed harshly. "The old Kit Emory *would* rush after her, I believe, and damn whatever consequences befell us. But Alys led me to understand that more is in play than the two of us if Father disinherits me. You. Lady Thea. This estate. The people of Brentwood. All would be sacrificed with nothing gained." His hands fisted by his side. "It's because of what Alys taught me that I know I cannot put myself first. That I am a good man and must think of others before myself—even if both our hearts will be forever bruised."

He saw understanding dawn on his mother's face as she contemplated his words. She took his hand and pressed it against her cheek as her tears spilled onto it.

"Oh, my son. You are truly a good man to give up the woman you love and your very happiness. I am sorry I judged you so harshly. Forgive me."

"There is nothing to forgive, Mother," he said softly. "But I want a last glimpse of her."

"Of course."

Kit left his mother and exited the keep. He glanced down into the courtyard and saw Alys tying her case to the saddle horn. A knight assisted her as she mounted her horse. He counted a guard of ten men that would accompany her back to Kinwick. He choked as the sun came out, shining down on her rich chestnut hair. He remembered his fingers gliding through the silken locks, his hands caressing her curves, their bodies joining as one.

Alys looked in his direction. Their eyes locked upon one another for a long moment. Neither raised a hand in farewell. She finally turned her horse. The sound of beating hooves filled the air as the escort party rode off.

Kit was beside himself. He fled back into the keep and ran up the dozens of steps until he reached the turret. He had brought Alys up here one afternoon. They had traded heated kisses. He told her this would become their private retreat, where they could escape the world for a few hours. Now he flung open the window so he could watch her ride away. The turret was the highest point in the keep, so Kit could watch her for the longest time. He caught sight of her russet cotehardie and chestnut hair and kept his eyes fixed on her until she was far into the distance. Alys reached the top of the hill and passed over it, dropping from his sight.

He ached more than when his body had been battered by the

thieves on the road. At least the bruises he had received that day had finally receded. Now, the scars left on his heart by Alys de Montfort would never heal. He closed the window, misery cloaking him.

"My lord?"

Kit turned abruptly and found Lady Thea standing in the doorway. They had never spoken to one another, yet here was the woman he was supposed to take to wife. To his bed. The thought of love play between them sickened him.

"What?" He regretted his harsh tone as she winced.

"May we speak freely to one another?" she asked.

"Aye. 'Twould be good to start doing so now," he admitted.

She closed the door and came to stand before him. Thea was lovely beyond compare. And yet even aware of her great beauty, it did nothing to move him, for he longed for Alys de Montfort more than ever while standing in this woman's presence.

"I overheard you last night."

Kit frowned. "What?"

The young widow gave him a sad smile. "Your conversation with Lady Alys. I heard it. You were in the hallway, near my room." She flushed pink with embarrassment. "I . . . I opened my door to see what was wrong. I couldn't help but listen to your conversation."

Guilt rushed through Kit. "My lady, I would never wish to harm you."

"You love her."

He sighed. He couldn't deny it. "I do."

"And you both acted nobly in this matter. You let her return to her home just now. You are willing to keep your commitment to me. A commitment you neither pursued nor made."

"Aye," he said, the ache within him heavy.

She squared her shoulders and looked him in the eye. "I believe in love," she declared. "Love triumphs over all. Love is what matters most. I did not share it with my husband. We were promised to each other years earlier. I only saw him once, when our betrothal contracts were signed. The next time was when we wed."

Lady Thea paused. "But I have known love. Great love—with another man. I have loved my Tybalt since we were children. We fostered in the same noble household together. I was separated from him when I wed. That made us both unhappy."

She reached out and placed a hand on his arm. "Should we both be unhappy the rest of our lives in order to please our inattentive fathers? Mine is close to death, which is why he did not accompany Lord Godwin and me to Brentwood. Your father is also suffering from poor health. Neither will live long enough to see any issue from our marriage."

Her words caused his mind to reel.

"My lady, are you telling me that we both need to take a stand—for love?"

She broke out in a sunny smile. "I am, my lord. I think we should go to London. I know enough of the right people to ensure that the king will grant us an audience."

Lady Thea's eyes locked with Kit's. "So what say you, my lord? Are you willing to risk all and hope that we can both find a chance at lasting happiness—only with other spouses?"

Hope burst inside him. Kit boldly picked the widow up by her waist and twirled her about. Laughter spilled from her lips. He joined in, his spirits soaring. Finally, he brought her back to earth.

"It may not work," he cautioned. "We must prepare ourselves for the king to reject our pleas."

"But we would regret forever not trying to change our fates," she insisted.

He smiled at her. "I agree. We will abide by what the king says. I only pray to Christ Almighty that this will lead us to our beloveds. And if not?"

Thea placed her hand atop his. "Then we will have made our best effort and must go forward with our own nuptials." Her eyes glimmered with unshed tears. "Thank you, my lord," she whispered. "Thank you for agreeing to try."

KIT TOOK LADY Thea to his mother. He found her pouring over ledgers, scattered parchments around her.

"Are you preparing for the hay harvest? Or shearing?" he asked as he ushered Lady Thea into the small room and closed the door. He seated his betrothed and looked to his mother.

She studied them, intrigue plainly written across her face.

"The two of you are up to something," she said. "I think I will like what you have to tell me."

"Lady Thea knows I am in love with Alys," Kit said bluntly. "She herself is in love with another man. We have no wish to wed one another."

"Though we will do so if absolutely necessary," the widow added.

His mother's brows rose. "How can I help you?"

"We wish to take our case to the king and see if he will allow the betrothal contract between us to be annulled."

"And you don't wish your father to know of this."

"Precisely."

Lady Berengaria steepled her fingers, her elbows propped upon the table. "Godwin won't be a problem," she stated.

"Can you keep Father here at Brentwood for a few days?" asked Kit.

She sniffed. "He is not going anywhere. Frankly, I don't know how he rode here from London. He has taken to his bed. By the looks of him, he most likely will never leave it."

"If he asks for me, put him off," Kit said. "Tell him I'm busy overseeing the hay harvest and want it finished before the wedding so that I may concentrate on my new bride."

"You can tell him I am troublesome," Thea volunteered. "That I have sent to London for a dressmaker for my wedding attire. That I am waiting to sort through different materials and deciding what I should wear. Make me sound as difficult as possible."

Kit watched his mother smile approvingly at Lady Thea's words.

"I'll also inform him that I have sent to London for a healer to look at him. Father William has usually seen to our needs at Brentwood, but Godwin never cared for the man." She looked to her son. "How long do you think you will be?"

"It depends on how long it takes for the king to grant us an audience. Lady Thea said it could be mere days—or weeks." Kit wondered at that moment when he would next see Alys. If his seed grew in her belly. If the next time he touched her, she would be round with his babe.

"You should leave at once," Berengaria suggested. "Although I sent our best men with Alys to Kinwick, we still have several good soldiers that can accompany you." She looked to Lady Thea. "It's almost June. What of the king's summer progress? London usually empties itself as the nobility flocks to their summer homes and the king travels about. Will that give you enough time to see him?"

"Fortunately, the king had not planned to go on progress this summer," Thea shared. "Between his declining health and that of the Black Prince's, he had decided to remain in London this season."

"That will certainly help," Kit noted. "If many courtiers vacate the palace, it might make it easier for us to acquire an audience with the king. I do think we should leave immediately. If we do, it will put us in London by noon tomorrow."

"I will do my best to keep Godwin in the dark as to your whereabouts."

"Agreed." Kit went and kissed his mother's cheek. "Thank you," he said.

"I hope it works out. For you both."

He escorted Lady Thea to her bedchamber. "Pack lightly," he advised. "Leave your trunk here at Brentwood. Take only a few things."

"I have a friend at court who will lend me clothes to wear. I can also stay with her. She serves the Black Prince's wife and is a fellow widow."

"Good. I, too, have a friend that will keep me close by." He took her hand and pressed a kiss to her fingers. "I must thank you, my lady. You have been gracious in this matter."

"I hope for both our sakes that we will meet with success, my lord."

"I will come to escort you to the stables once I've arranged for us to leave."

Kit decided to pen a brief missive to Alys. He wanted her to know what they tried. He started it three times and tore up each attempt. No, he would keep his actions a secret from her. If they proved to be unsuccessful, he did not want to dash her hopes. In case the king proved amenable, he would make sure Lady Thea made it safely to her Tybalt.

Then he would ride with haste to Kinwick. To Alys.

And demand to marry her on the spot.

CHAPTER 17

Both Kit and Thea went to work the minute they arrived London. He could tell that the ranks of court had already thinned and assumed many of the courtiers had started to return to their estates across England because the corridors of the palace were not lined with sycophants in clumps, whispering and preening. A few remained, but Kit felt optimistic of their chances for gaining an audience with the king sooner rather than later.

They had left Brentwood yesterday morning and arrived in town just after the noon hour today. Thea went to find her friend in the royal household and said she would speak to a few of the men in her father's circle. Kit went directly to the Lord Chamberlain, a man his father had worked in close proximity to for many years.

He entered the rooms of Lord Richmond and spoke to a few men gathered there as they dined at a small table. Kit requested a meeting with Richmond and was surprised that he was shown in right away. The rotund nobleman was also at a table, devouring a roasted chicken and fresh loaf of bread as he looked over a stack of papers.

"Greetings, my lord," Kit said as he approached him. "It's Kit Emory, Godwin's son."

Richmond gave him a tight smile. Kit always thought the man looked pained when he had to show any kind of happiness.

"What brings you to court, young Kit?" The nobleman paused, a serious look crossing his face. "Has your father passed?"

"Nay, though I feel certain his time draws near."

Richmond waved a chicken leg in the air. "To be honest, my boy, I don't know which man will pass first—your father or the Black Prince. Both are in terrible shape. And the king is not doing much better." He shook his head. "This court will change—and soon."

"I am sorry to hear that. Prince Edward has been such a stalwart figure for England."

"Well, who is to say? 'Tis up to a merciful Christ to decide when their times come. So why are you at court? Have you lost interest in fighting and decided you would rather push papers about, as I do?" Again, the tight little smile that Richmond favored was displayed on his thin lips.

"I'm here to gain an audience with the king," Kit said. "It concerns a private matter, but I will share with you that it involves my betrothed, Lady Thea. She is distantly related to Lancaster, you know."

They had decided not to give any details to anyone. Kit believed if others knew why he and Thea wished to visit with King Edward that their request would be flatly denied. He told her to lend an air of mystery to their request and to use her connection through her first marriage to the Duke of Lancaster, hoping it might be enough to secure them an audience.

"I see." Richmond stared off, considering Kit's words, then he turned back to Kit. "The king could see you for a very short time. On the morrow, as he breaks his fast. Is that to your liking?"

"Indeed, my Lord Chamberlain. I am most grateful to you, as I know Lady Thea will be. Until then."

Kit left, elated that time with the king had already been scheduled. He found Thea waiting at their prearranged destination and shared his good news.

"Richmond has always been a bit fond of me. I think he would like to have been the rebel I am known to be."

She laughed. "Believe me, your reputation made its way to my ears, my lord. I was horrified that I would wed another man who raced off into battle without a thought." She hesitated. "But you are nothing like the man I heard you were," Thea admitted. "You have surprised me."

"I have surprised myself, Lady Thea," he told her. "The man I once was no longer exists. In his place is a new one, mayhap a little wiser. And certainly one who has matured significantly from my younger days."

Her eyes sparkled at him. "I gather this involves the steadying hand and good influence of Lady Alys upon you?"

He grinned. "You guess correctly. Alys has changed me in ways I never could have imagined."

"Then I hope we will be successful in our venture, my lord."

He paused and gave her a long look. "If I had not fallen in love with Alys, my lady, mayhap we could have loved one another."

"Be careful," she warned. "You may be saddled with me if the king does not choose to support us."

Kit took her hand. "Alys will always have my heart, Lady Thea, but if we wind up wed? I suppose there are worse things." He looked around. "'Tis a warm day full of sunshine. Would you care to take a walk with me along the Thames?"

"I would enjoy that, my lord."

He guided her to her feet, and they spent the remainder of the afternoon strolling the streets of London. Lady Thea made for good company. She had amusing stories of her childhood. Kit shared some of the scrapes he had been involved in at the various noble households in which he'd fostered. They returned to partake of the evening meal at court and parted ways.

"Meet me in this same place. Early. We want to be at the king's door in plenty of time."

"I shall, my lord. Thank you for a lovely day."

Kit parted from her, eager for their meeting with the king.

KIT BARELY SLEPT and finally rose, splashing cold water on his face. He changed into the clean gypon and cotehardie that he had brought from Brentwood and set out last night. Slipping into the dim corridor, he ran his fingers through his hair as he made his way to where he had arranged to meet Lady Thea.

It surprised him to find her already there, looking fresh and rested in a pale yellow, sideless surcoat and matching kirtle. Her dark, sleek hair was pulled away from her face and fell into a long braid that rested over one shoulder.

"I had trouble sleeping," she said. "Part excitement. Part nerves."

"I would never have been able to tell, my lady. You look quite fetching this morning."

"Thank you, my lord."

Thea slipped her hand through the crook of Kit's arm and he guided them through the maze of corridors until they reached the king's rooms. Two armored knights stood silently at the doors. He seated Thea and stood next to her, leaning his tall frame against the wall.

An hour passed with only silence as their companion. Suddenly, a flurry of servants appeared with trays. The guards on duty admitted them. Close on their heels followed the Lord Chamberlain.

"Let me see how he fares this morning," Richmond said when he spotted them. "I will return for you soon after if he wishes to speak with you."

Kit forced himself not to dog Richmond's heels. He waited as patiently as he could, nerves bubbling within him. Thea gave him a reassuring smile. He placed a hand on her shoulder and squeezed it in return.

Minutes later, the servants filed back out. Richmond appeared at the door as they left and motioned for Kit and Thea to rise.

"His majesty is eating, but he's willing to see you for a brief conversation," the Lord Chamberlain said.

"Thank you," Kit told him.

He escorted Thea into the anteroom and through its doors. Another empty room awaited, so they pressed on and walked through a different set of doors. The king sat atop the royal chamber pot, a mug of ale in one hand and a slice of bread in his other. Kit felt Thea stiffen beside him, then he sensed her relax and steel herself for the encounter ahead.

"Sire." Kit bowed low while Thea dropped into a deep curtsey.

"Rise," the monarch commanded. He frowned at them. "I know you are Brentley's whelp."

"Christopher Emory, your majesty. And this is Lady Thea."

Edward eyed the beautiful widow with appreciation. "You are most lovely, my lady. I know I have seen you at court on occasion."

"Aye, your majesty." She demurely dropped her eyes.

The king swallowed another sip of ale. "So what is this about, Emory? Your father? By the Christ, he looked dreadful when he left London a few days ago."

"He is doing poorly, sire. But this is a personal matter Lady Thea and I wish to discuss with you."

"Hmm. Personal, you say." The king stuffed the remainder of the bread into his mouth.

Beads of perspiration broke out along his hairline, but Kit plunged ahead. "Everyone knows that your marriage to the queen was an arranged one, your majesty."

"As are all marriages for royals," the king snapped. "And my noblemen, for the most part."

"But it's also well known that you and Queen Philippa became a love match."

Edward's face softened for a moment at the mention of his dead wife's name. "Ah, we did not start that way. But my queen was a feisty young girl. Sweet—but most opinionated. We became friends. Good friends, and then—only then—did love grow between us."

"Love matches abound in my beloved's family."

The king frowned. He looked from Kit to Thea. "Is this not your beloved?"

"Nay, sire. Lady Thea is my betrothed. My father signed the contracts without my knowledge. But my beloved *is* my soul mate. I speak of Lady Alys de Montfort and her family. True love is present in all of the marriages the de Montforts have made."

"You said Alys de Montfort?"

"I did, sire."

"My Alys, from my wife's court?" King Edward broke out into a wide smile. "Oh, that girl was such a help to me and my dear Philippa, many times over. And I am most fond of her parents." He gave Kit a roguish grin. "I would marry Lady Merryn if no Geoffrey de Montfort existed. Of course, half the men in my kingdom would do the same."

The king paused. "Does Lady Alys resemble her mother? I have not seen her in a good number of years."

Kit nodded. "I am told she is the picture of her mother at that age. And looking at Lady Merryn, 'tis easy to see how Alys will only grow more beautiful as the years pass."

Edward grunted and looked to Thea. "And I suppose you will tell me that you, too, have a beloved, my lady? A man who is not your betrothed here?" The king studied her, rubbing his chin. "You were married before, if I am not mistaken."

"I was, your majesty. My husband gave his life defending England in the French wars, but he was not my heart's desire. I have loved another from childhood." Thea took a step closer to him. "Yet I was a dutiful daughter and did as I was told. I married my first husband—and then my father arranged for a second marriage to Sir Kit, who also had lost his first wife."

She fell to her knees. "We both have a second chance at love, sire. Sir Kit with Lady Alys and I with my Tybalt. I implore you, sire, to consider our request to set aside the betrothal contracts and allow us, this time, to marry our choices."

Kit helped Thea rise and watched as Edward mulled over their proposition. His eyes became watery with tears. When Kit saw that, he knew there was hope.

The king looked from one to the other. "I will agree to void the contract," he said gruffly. "Only because it 'twould please my beloved Philippa."

"Even if our fathers object?" asked Kit.

"Especially if they object!" The king tossed back his head and roared with laughter. He wiped the tears that now streamed down his cheeks. "I ask but one favor of you, Sir Kit."

"Anything, my king," he said fervently.

Edward looked first to Thea. "Is your sweetheart free to marry, Lady Thea?"

She nodded. "He would marry me tomorrow if he could, your majesty."

"Then tell him you have my blessing to do so."

Thea burst into tears and rushed to the king. She dropped to her knees again and took his hand, pressing a kiss to his knuckles. "Thank you. Thank you, sire," she said.

Kit assisted her to her feet. "And what may I do for you, your majesty?"

"I would advise you to avoid your father and head straight for Kinwick." He smiled. "I have such fond memories of stopping there on summer progress. The tarts their cook created melted in my mouth. I tell you now to marry Lady Alys with due haste and father a dozen or more children. I only ask that you name your first daughter Philippa after my beloved wife. Lady Alys served her well, and Philippa was quite taken with the girl. My queen's romantic heart would take pleasure in such a happy ending for Alys de Montfort."

"It would be our pleasure to name our daughter for such a wise, noble woman. I give you my word, sire. Philippa Emory will know who her namesake is and also be told of the generosity of our king in allowing her parents to wed at Kinwick."

"Then go. Tear up the contracts. In fact, I order you to rip them apart and burn them."

"We will follow your majesty's instructions to the letter. Thank you," Kit said.

He bowed and escorted Thea from the royal bedchamber. Taking her hand, he ran down the halls with her, oblivious to the odd looks tossed their way. They reached an outer courtyard, and Kit impulsively kissed her.

"Our first—and last—kiss, my lady. One of jubilation and celebration." He smiled down at her. "I believe I have made in you a friend for life. My first female friend."

Thea glowed with happiness. "You have given me new life, Kit Emory. I will be forever in your debt."

"I say we should remain friends. I would enjoy meeting your Tybalt. Would you and your husband like to come spend Christmas at Brentwood with Alys and me?"

"I can think of no better plans, my lord." She sighed. "You will take care of disposing of the contracts?"

"Nothing will give me greater pleasure than burning them to a crisp. Until I wed Alys, of course. She will always be first in everything I do."

"Then I will leave you to your task. Tybalt awaits me."

"Go to him, Thea. May the Christ be with you and yours."

"We will see you for the Christmas season," she promised. Then with another flash of a smile, she left him.

Kit pulled the betrothal contracts from where they rested inside his gypon and went to find the largest fire possible, a grin on his face. He couldn't wait to ride with all haste to Kinwick.

And Alys.

CHAPTER 18

ALYS LONGED TO reach home. She wanted this miserable trip to be over. Each league she traveled took her further away from a life with Kit. She said little to the men in her escort party, and they had left her to her own thoughts when they stopped for a meal or made camp to sleep for the night.

She noticed these Brentwood soldiers differed from her father's at Kinwick. Geoffrey de Montfort set a high value on men who performed their duties to perfection. Her escorts seemed lax to her. Alys had watched two of them cut corners when they were assigned to a task. At least no problems had arisen on the road. Thank goodness, they would arrive at Kinwick before tomorrow's noon meal.

The group bedded down for the night. Alys drew a light blanket over her and turned toward the fire. She listened as two men were ordered to stand guard on the first shift. It concerned her that the pair seemed to her to be the laziest in the group of soldiers. She wanted to warn the captain in charge of the escort party, but she didn't feel it was her place.

Alys lay awake a long time. Gradually, the snores from the other sleeping soldiers lulled her to sleep.

Suddenly, she awakened, her senses on high alert. Her eyes darted around the camp. She saw shadows moving. Alys reached for the blade inside her boot and silently pulled it from its sheath as she rotated onto her back. At once, a heavy weight sank on top of her. A rough hand covered her mouth, while another one clutched her throat. She must act fast.

With his arms stretched out to restrain her, the man above her was vulnerable. Alys slammed her knife into his throat and twisted it. He grunted. Hot blood poured from her attacker's wound, spilling onto her chest and throat. The man collapsed, his weight crushing her. Her belly roiled as the tinny smell of blood invaded her nostrils. She couldn't breathe. She tried to push him off and failed.

A noise sounded. Alys turned her head to see what happened. The shadows now slipped through the camp. She saw the glint of steel reflected in the faint firelight as throats were slashed. Within seconds, the onslaught ended. A chuckle broke the silence.

Fury poured through her. It gave Alys the strength to push off the dead weight of her attacker. She rolled and came to her feet, grabbing the sword of the dead Brentwood soldier who had lain next to her. She dashed and ran it through one man. Then another. She lifted it again only to have someone from behind wrap thick arms around her, pinning her arms to her side. Alys struggled but couldn't shake the man off. He tightened his grasp. She found it hard to breathe.

Someone ripped the sword from her fingers. A voice said, "She done killed 'em, Carac. Three be dead." Alys heard astonishment in the man's voice.

"I'll kill her," the one who held her fast offered. "But I want a bit o' fun with her first."

"Wait," a voice to her left commanded. "Bring her here."

The man restraining her lifted her off the ground and walked in that direction. Alys kicked her feet out and connected with a man's chest, knocking him into the campfire. The attacker yelped and rolled out of the blaze. She kicked again, but a second man dodged her feet.

Her captor stopped in front of the man she assumed to be the leader of this band of thieves. He was of average height and had a slender frame. A long scar ran from the outer corner of his left eye across his cheek and to his mouth. He gave her a mirthless smile.

"I can't breathe," she got out as she was lowered her to her feet.

"This one's full of spite," the man said over her shoulder as the band of his arms continued to crush her.

"But she's obviously of the nobility," the leader said. "That means she's worth something." He motioned. "Look around, my lady."

Alys did. Carnage surrounded them. Every man from Brentwood lay dead. She quickly counted six thieves, including the man who still held her and the one before her. She would bide her time and then make her escape.

"I won't run," she wheezed.

The man in authority said, "Release her."

"But Carac—"

"Do it!" he demanded.

Alys dropped to the dirt. She fell onto her knees and pressed her hands to the ground for support. She drank in the air, grateful that she was alive. Her heart still raced, but she rose to confront the one called Carac. She locked her knees, hoping that would still her trembling legs. Alys glared at the leader as he leisurely studied her.

"Ah, you are very much a lady," he finally said. "From your fine clothing to your haughty attitude."

Aly raised her chin defiantly.

"You seem familiar," he said.

"I don't know you. I don't care to know you," she told him, her voice dripping with contempt.

"No. You wouldn't." His piercing gaze swept over her. "It will come to me. What is your name?"

She dug her nails into her palms and remained silent.

"Your name, my lady?"

Still, she did not respond.

Carac slapped her. Hard. Alys stumbled. The dark night lit up with shooting white stars. She rested her hands on her knees. Blinked. Swallowed. Took a deep breath.

Then she raised her head and threw back her shoulders—and glared at Carac.

He raised a hand to strike her again, but Alys didn't flinch.

Carac slowly lowered his hand. Admiration appeared in his eyes. "You're no coward. I'll give you that." He thought a moment. "We'll bring her to Fendrel."

Dread coursed through Alys when she heard that name. She recognized it as one of the titled men who had fallen on hard times. His lands hadn't been producing, and workers abandoned him for other properties. With too few men to work the land and not enough crops, Sir Fendrel hadn't been able to pay the king's tax and had lost his estate to the crown. Alys heard Fendrel had gathered a band of men who stole for him, a motley group who attacked travelers at will. Since they were so close to Kinwick, Alys wondered if this group of thieves had been the ones who had assaulted Kit.

Carac looked to the man behind her. "Bind her wrists and ankles. She may be a pretty little thing, but I think she would run at the first opportunity. When you finish, set her against that tree."

Rough hands grabbed her and yanked her back. Arms snaked around her waist. Alys slammed her heel into the man's knee. She used the same foot to stomp on the robber's foot. He released her, but two other men moved toward her menacingly. How she wished she had thought to pull her baselard from her attacker's throat. She had no other weapon on her.

It took three men to restrain her. They tied rope around her wrists, binding them so tight that she lost feeling in her hands almost immediately. One thief wrapped more rope around her ankles several times. She pushed her legs outward as he did so, hoping it wouldn't be tied as tightly as her wrists. The largest of the three tossed her over his shoulder. He steadied her with a hand flat on her buttocks. He reached the tree and gave her a hard pinch before he placed her on the ground, her back leaned against the tree's trunk.

Alys watched as the thieves methodically went through everything at the camp. They removed every item from the guards' saddlebags. They gathered all the weapons from the soldiers and piled them in a heap, then they stripped the armor, clothing, and boots from the dead Brentwood soldiers and organized it. She thought they would sell what they could at market and wondered how large a cut Sir Fendrel would receive from their plunder.

Two of the men dragged the naked bodies away from the camp while another pulled out the remaining bread and a small round of cheese. He tore a hunk of bread off and stuffed it into his mouth.

Carac wandered the camp, supervising what the men did. He asked, "Is this all of the food that you found?"

"Aye."

The leader glanced at her and said, "They were probably close to their destination."

Alys hoped her face gave nothing away.

Carac crossed over his men, who now stretched out on the pallets that surrounded the fire. He squatted next to her, an evil smile playing on his thin lips.

"I know of you. You are Alys de Montfort." He lifted her braid and began toying with it. "I saw your mother years ago, and you are definitely her daughter. Merryn de Montfort was one of the most beautiful women I'd ever seen. The resemblance between the two of you is striking." He dropped the braid. "But you are even more desirable."

Alys spat in his face.

He laughed softly. "You are spirited. Fearless. You have the heart of a man, Lady Alys." He wiped the spittle away with a finger and then took the same finger and caressed her cheek.

Alys stared off in the distance, ignoring him.

Carac stood. "No one is to lay a hand on her," he called out. "Fendrel will want to ransom her. Lady Alys will be worth a few sacks of gold."

She caught disappointment in the eyes of the man who had latched on to her. She dropped her eyes to her lap.

Carac knelt again in front of her. "Sir Fendrel may want you for himself. He's never been able to resist a beautiful woman. Especially one with fire in her hair."

He grabbed her chin and forced her head up. Alys met his black eyes and swallowed the bile that rose in her throat.

"But he's desperate for gold coin. Once he ransoms you, I'll persuade him to let me be the one that returns you to Lord Geoffrey." Carac gave her a hard, swift kiss. "After I've had my fill of you."

Alys swore in that moment that she would kill him.

ALYS GOT NO sleep. She spent the remainder of the night listening to the snores of the ruffians as she plotted her escape. She knew she needed her feet free in order to run. She was an excellent rider. If she could make it to a horse, she could ride even with her hands tied.

But would she have a chance? There were so many of them.

She leaned her head back against the tree trunk and closed her eyes. They were gritty from lack of sleep. She opened them because the smell of the blood that covered her seemed stronger when she couldn't see it. Alys looked down and saw the dried blood had turned her yellow surcoat into a muddy brown.

The men began stirring. One man disappeared. He returned a short time later driving a cart. The vehicle must have been left down the road before the attack occurred. The men made many trips in order to load the items to sell into the cart. Two of them left with the wares.

Her chances for escape improved with fewer thieves to stop her.

Carac brought her a small bit of bread and gave her a few sips from a wineskin.

"I need to attend to personal matters," she told him, keeping her voice neutral. Defiance had gotten her nowhere, but she refused to meekly beg.

"You also need to wash the blood from you and put on new clothing. Fendrel doesn't have a strong belly when it comes to seeing or smelling blood."

He retrieved her change of clothing that sat in the dirt. Carac had instructed his men to leave it behind when they took the rest of the soldiers' clothing and armor to the cart. She had planned to change into the fresh outfit this morning before they rode the final leagues to Kinwick.

Alys longed to strip the blood-soaked material off, but not with Carac watching her. Not after what he had said to her last night.

He bent and sliced through the ropes around her ankles and pulled her to her feet.

"Come," he ordered. "There's a stream nearby."

She took a wobbly step before her knee gave out. He caught her elbow. Alys stood there feeling as if her feet weren't attached to her legs. Carac thrust her clothes at her and scooped her up into his arms. She didn't fight him. Her feet were now free. They would soon be alone. It might be her best chance to flee.

But not before she killed him.

She looked around as he strode from the camp, wondering what she could use. Her dagger had been removed from the neck of the man she'd killed and tossed into the pile of gathered weapons. Mayhap she could use something in the forest. A fallen branch. A heavy rock. She would take pleasure ramming a thick stick into this man's eye or slamming a rock against his skull.

As he carried her deeper into the woods, her feet began to sting as if bees attacked. The stinging turned into needles that jammed into her feet. Alys bit her tongue till she tasted blood. She would not cry out. She refused to let him see any sign of weakness in her.

Yet she couldn't stop the tears that came along with the pain.

She heard running water. The stream must be close. Carac set her on her feet but kept strong fingers secured around her upper arm.

"Walk now. It will help bring feeling back into your limbs."

Alys clutched the fresh clothes to her and took steps as small as a babe learning to walk might. They approached the stream and he halted their progression. He took the clothing she clutched and dropped it to the ground. With a sawing motion, he cut through the rope around her wrists.

If she thought her feet were bad off, her hands burned ten times worse as the feeling returned to them. Alys rubbed her wrists and hands repeatedly. She tried bending her fingers as the blood rushed back into her hands.

"I'll slit your throat if you run," he warned. "Fendrel need never know we came upon you. The animals in the woods would make quick work of you."

As she stomped her feet and shook out her numb hands, Alys knew he meant it. Her mother and father would never know what had happened to her. Kit would never know why she had disappeared. She knew she couldn't risk escape right now.

"Let me."

Carac took her hands and began working her fingers and twisting her wrists. She loathed his touch but tolerated it in order to have the feeling return.

"Can you walk on your own?"

Alys nodded.

"Go to the stream. Rinse off as much of the blood from your face and neck as you can."

She shuffled to the brook and eased down to the ground. She cupped water and splashed it on her face and then rubbed her fingers up and down along her face and neck. She continued for several minutes. Then Carac yanked her braid back, exposing her neck. He looked her over and gave a satisfied grunt.

"Stand," he ordered.

Alys did as he said. He clenched her sideless surcoat and lifted it from her then did the same with her kirtle. Only her smock and thin chemise remained. She glanced down and saw that the blood had penetrated to this third layer. Alys sensed his black eyes roaming her body.

"Hand me the fresh clothing," she said. Those were the first words she'd spoken since they'd left the camp.

Carac gathered the items and returned. But he didn't give them to her. A curt nod told her he wanted her to remove her smock. She did so, lifting it and the chemise over her head at the same time. She tossed them aside and stood before him in only her hose and boots. He didn't have the decency to avert his eyes and boldly skimmed her body. Alys stood, humiliation turning her pale skin bright red. The only man who had seen her this way was Kit. She remembered his loving touch and wanted to scream.

"Remove the rest."

She bent and took off what little remained. Anger caused her to close the gap between them. She grabbed her clothing and walked a few steps away from him. Then she armed herself with the only weapon she had and dressed quickly. Once every piece was in place, she turned around, relieved to have her bare skin covered. Her shoes and hose still rested on the ground. She hurriedly put them on since they didn't have any traces of blood on them.

His eyes gleamed at her. "You are perfect in every way, Lady Alys."

Alys felt more in control of her emotions now that she wore clothing again. "May I?" She pointed to a clump of trees.

"Of course. Don't take long, or I may have to come look for you."

She went behind the trees and hiked up her skirts in order to relieve herself. Her body shook uncontrollably. Alys took deep breaths and willed herself to be still before she rejoined her captor.

Carac led her back to the camp, his fingers digging into her arm, bruising the tender flesh. One man brought new ropes for Carac to bind her.

"Must you?" she asked. "I have nowhere to go even if I did run."

"Your hands then." He wrapped the rope around them, not as tightly as it was before. That brought her some relief.

And hope.

He bent and lifted her skirts. Before she could protest, he ripped a strip from her chemise and brought the linen to her face. Alys realized he intended to blindfold her.

Carac pulled the material across her eyes. He leaned so close that she could feel his hot breath against her cheek. His stubble touched her face and she shuddered. He reached and tied the cloth behind her head, knotting it several times.

She could hear the sound of men mounting the horses that had belonged to the dead. Carac guided her several steps and then stopped.

He released her elbow. Alys sensed that he climbed atop a horse. Then his hands locked around her waist as he lifted her up to join him. Alys found herself in front of him. He jerked her against his thin chest and brought his arms around her waist.

"Enjoy our ride together, my lady," he murmured into her ear.

As they rode, Alys thought of new ways to kill him.

CHAPTER 19

Alys couldn't tell how long they rode. She guessed it might have been for a couple of hours, but having no sight left her disoriented. The blindfold sat firm against her eyes and prevented her from seeing anything. She sensed the horses slowing and figured their destination loomed in sight. It couldn't be soon enough. Having Carac's body pressed against hers for an extended time had left her filled with disgust. Twice, he'd nuzzled his roughened beard against her neck. Alys refused to move a muscle, and finally he had stopped. Carac now halted the horse they rode. She felt him dismount, then he took her from the horse.

She hoped he would remove the blindfold, but he didn't. The outlaw hadn't wanted her to view the path they rode—and he was smart enough not to let her see the outside of the building where she would be held hostage. It would prove far harder to find the structure if she didn't know what it looked like. Alys reminded herself not to underestimate Carac in any way.

"Care for the horses," he said before walking her for a few minutes. Their progress was slow since she couldn't see where she was going and hesitated with each step.

He halted, and Alys heard a door creak open. He roughly pushed her inside.

At once, she knew the place was small and dark. The bright sunshine they'd ridden in quickly faded. Foul smells assaulted her nose. This was a place where men urinated in corners and threw the meat of their supper bones to the ground—where they remained. She heard the groan as the door shut behind her.

"Stay," he ordered.

Carac's footsteps didn't echo as he moved away from her. Alys twisted her toes and found a dirt floor beneath her. Then she caught the sound of snoring.

"Wake up, my lord," Carac ordered. When the snoring continued, he shouted, "I said awaken!"

"What?" a deep voice slurred. "Oh, 'tis you. You've been gone long enough, Carac. I hope you brought back more than your last foray. Even the food supply is low."

"You'll be most pleased, Sir Fendrel. I have returned with something that will put many gold coins in your hand. Behold, your treasure."

Alys heard a low chuckle. "My, she's a beauty. Bring her to me."

Strong fingers latched on to her arm and moved her in the direction of the voice. Knuckles bumped against the back of her skull as Carac untied and then lowered the blindfold.

Alys blinked and then focused on the rotund man before her. Food stains littered the front of his cotehardie. His beard and hair were both gray and unkempt. She licked her lips nervously.

"Where did you find her, Carac? She's exquisite—and much better than the whores you usually fetch me."

His uncouth words made her blood boil. "I am no whore. I am Lady Alys de Montfort, daughter of Lord Geoffrey and Lady Merryn de Montfort. I demand you return me to my parents at once."

The nobleman's brows shot up. "Ah, a true lady." He leisurely studied her. "Well, my dear. I have met Lord Geoffrey twice before and once saw your incredibly beautiful mother. Every man present coveted her. You favor Lady Merryn quite a bit, with your eyes of deep blue and gorgeous, chestnut hair."

"Then you know that my father will hunt you and this band of cutthroats down and slaughter you before you could beg for mercy," she said. "Unless you return me at once—unharmed. He will be mad with rage, but I can convince him to leave you in peace."

Alys gestured to the blindfold Carac toyed with. "I do not know where I was brought. I have no idea where this place is or what it looks like. Return me now to Kinwick, and I promise—"

"Return you?" Fendrel asked. "Without ransoming you?" He shook his head. "You are worth your weight in gold, my lady. And I have need of coin like you cannot imagine." He gave her a wintry smile. "Nay. 'Twill be a large ransom Lord Geoffrey will pay to me for your return. Are you a virgin?"

Her cheeks flamed at such a personal question. "Why would you dare to ask such a thing?"

Fendrel cocked his head and studied her. "I suppose I could rape you and then marry you. Send a bedsheet with your virgin blood to your parents. Your father would have to provide me with a dowry in that case."

Alys feared he meant it. What would happen if he did what he said—and found her to be no virgin at all?

The nobleman considered it. "Nay, I don't wish for another wife. I had one before. She left me for God and the convent when I lost my lands. I'd rather satisfy my needs with the whores Carac finds for me. Wives are a bothersome lot. By the look of you, you would be more trouble than you're worth."

The nobleman looked to his henchman. "You've done well for me, Carac. The ransom Lady Alys brings will go a long way for many moons. Let me pen a missive to de Montfort. You can work out how best to deliver it to him at Kinwick."

Fendrel turned back to her. "As for you, my lady, you will remain as my guest until your father sends enough coin to earn your release."

Alys added Sir Fendrel's name to her kill list.

———

KINWICK CASTLE CAME into sight on the horizon. Kit took a deep breath, eager to reunite with Alys. He'd pushed his horse hard as he rode from London so he could arrive at the de Montfort estate as soon as possible. He wondered how much Alys had told her parents about his unexpected betrothal. He knew she'd left Brentwood with a broken heart. He only hoped she would let him help her mend it.

Kit was glad Thea would be cared for. He looked forward to meeting her husband. He could see the four of them at the Christmas season, joking about the events that had occurred these past few days. At least he and Thea would be happy in the marriages they made.

He traveled the broad road that led up to the gates of Kinwick. Without warning, a rider burst out of the woods to his left some distance ahead. Kit wondered why the man rode at such breakneck speed. He urged his own mount on and prayed nothing was wrong with Alys. The man came to the gates of Kinwick and pulled up hard on the reins, bringing his horse to a sudden halt. He leapt from the horse and then tossed his arm back and quickly forward. Something sailed through the air and over the wall. One of the soldiers stationed on the wall walk ducked as it whizzed past him.

Kit watched the man jump back on his horse and tear down the road, dust kicking up behind him. Just before he veered off into the woods again, Kit came close enough to see him. The rider had a hat pulled low over his eyes, while a scarf wrapped around his neck concealed the lower portion of his face. He broke into the trees just as Kit reached him. Part of him wanted to follow and find out who this mysterious stranger was. Something seemed familiar about his posture.

Kit abandoned the idea, though. Holding Alys in his arms was what was most important. He approached the gate and called out to the gatekeeper. The man issued a warm welcome and signaled for him to be admitted. Kit waved as he rode through and spied Gilbert, Kinwick's captain of the guard, bending to retrieve something in the dirt. Kit determined it must be what the rider had thrown over the wall.

"Greetings, Sir Gilbert," he called out as he stopped his horse and dismounted near Gilbert.

"Sir Kit. 'Tis good to see you at Kinwick again." The knight glanced back at his hand. Kit saw that he held a scroll tied to a large rock.

"What the devil?" the soldier said. "This is addressed to Lord Geoffrey. Did you see who threw this?"

"Aye," Kit replied. "I could not place the rider since much of his face was hidden from view, but I believe I have seen him somewhere before."

Gilbert looked at him in confusion. "Where is Lady Alys? And your mother? The earl and countess expected you yesterday."

"They are not here?" Warning bells sounded in Kit's head. He quickly made the connection with the oddly-delivered missive and Alys. "We must go to Lord Geoffrey at once."

The knight fell into step with him. Kit handed his horse off to the nearby blacksmith, who promised to see it cared for in the stables. He and Gilbert hurried to the great hall. Servants shifted trestle tables from the walls to the floor as they readied the room for the evening meal.

"Sir Kit!"

He turned and saw Nan running his way. She hugged his leg. "Mother says you and Alys are going to be married."

So Alys had not sent word to her family about Thea's arrival at Brentwood. The last the de Montforts knew, their daughter headed to Kinwick with him and his mother in order to prepare for their upcoming wedding.

Two young boys ran over to them, eager smiles on their faces.

"These are my brothers," Nan told him. "Hal and Edward. This is Sir Kit. He's going to wed Alys."

At that moment, he saw Lord Geoffrey and Lady Merryn enter the room. "I will spend some time with you later, Nan. And your brothers. But I must speak to your parents at once."

He and Gilbert made their way toward Alys' parents. Kit saw the questioning look on Lady Merryn's face as they approached.

"Where is Alys? We thought you would arrive—"

"We must speak privately, my lord. My lady."

Lord Geoffrey took his wife's hand and marched from the room.

Kit and Gilbert followed them to the records room off the great hall. De Montfort closed the door and faced him, worry written on his brow.

"Alys healed my mother," Kit began. "You know of our plans to return to Kinwick for our wedding. But just before we left Brentwood, my father arrived from London—with my newly betrothed in hand."

Lady Merryn whimpered softly. Her husband put an arm around her to steady her and then led her to a chair.

Kit continued. "Lady Thea is a widow. We immediately discovered that we both loved another. To make a long story short, we traveled to London and were given an audience with the king. He granted our betrothal contracts to become null and void. I came straightaway to Kinwick, hoping Alys would forgive me for the pain she had suffered."

"Then where is she?" Lord Geoffrey demanded gruffly.

"She left with an escort party from Brentwood. They were to return her to Kinwick. I fear something happened to them on the road." Kit gestured to Gilbert.

The knight handed Geoffrey the rock. "This was thrown over the wall right as Sir Kit arrived, my lord. It's addressed to you."

Lady Merryn gasped. She rose to her feet and came to stand beside her husband.

The nobleman unrolled the scroll and scanned it. His wife began to cry as she read over his shoulder. Lord Geoffrey handed it to Kit and he quickly scanned it.

"So Alys is a captive, and all the Brentwood guards are dead," Lord Geoffrey said dully.

Rage raced through Kit. It was hard enough to hear that ten of their men were dead at the hands of highwaymen. But to know Alys had been kidnapped? Wild thoughts churned in his mind. He couldn't let them eat him alive.

"How do we get her back?" he asked the earl. "I will do anything. Go anywhere. I can't lose her, my lord. She is my life."

De Montfort's face had turned brick red with fury. Lady Merryn's was as white as a ghost.

"They ask for gold, Geoffrey. Do we have enough? Will we get our daughter back?"

"Aye. We have it," he assured his wife. "The ransom note tells me to bring it alone tomorrow. I will do as they ask. Then I will hunt the thieving bastards down and run my sword through every one of them. If they have harmed even a hair on her precious head..." His voice trailed off.

"Nay," Kit said. "I will go with you."

"We can't take a chance with Alys' life!" Lady Merryn cried. "We must do as they say. Geoffrey must go alone, as they have instructed."

Kit stared into Lord Geoffrey's eyes and willed the nobleman to agree with him. "I can hide in the wagon bed, my lord. You will need a cart to haul the gold anyway, instead of riding on horseback. Cover it in hay so that anyone you pass won't know what you carry."

He saw the moment Lord Geoffrey made his decision.

"He's right, Merryn. I would need to conceal the gold on the open highway. And I can use Kit's arm and his sword when we punish the men who have dared to take our Alys." He held out his hand to Kit. "Have a seat. We have much to plan."

CHAPTER 20

Alys sat in the corner of the filthy cottage. She had spent all yesterday and today in the same spot. Carac gave her a small bowl to use as a chamber pot and some watery stew with moldy bread after they'd arrived. The same meal had been repeated last night. She forced herself to eat it because she needed to keep up her strength.

None of the other men that had attacked their camp had entered the small cottage. She wondered where they were. If they slept outside somewhere, mayhap in a nearby barn. It was important to know what awaited her once she made her escape.

Sir Fendrel tried to engage her in conversation yesterday, but Alys remained silent. She had nothing to say to the nobleman. He finally gave up and had ignored her ever since.

She wanted him to forget about her. It would give her a better chance to get away.

Alys stifled a yawn. She'd only slept a few hours last night. She couldn't get comfortable with her hands tied. Once again, she'd lost feeling in them.

Sir Fendrel now stretched out on a pallet on the far side of the room. She doubted he could even see her sitting in the shadows on the opposite side of the one-room cottage. Carac had lain in front of the doorway last night. Alys guessed since he'd been generous enough not to tie her feet together, he protected the one way that would provide her escape.

But Carac disappeared at dawn, instructing his lord to bar the door. The outlaw hadn't returned yet. Alys believed he'd gone off to deliver the ransom note to her parents. She wondered how far she was from Kinwick. How long it would take Carac to get there and back. Fendrel had given her more of the moldy bread so she could break her fast, then he seemed to ignore or even overlook her. When it became time for a noon meal, she watched him cut into a round of cheese and eat some bread without bothering to offer her anything.

He'd left the knife next to the cheese.

Soon, he drank himself into a stupor and collapsed on his blanket and bed of straw underneath it. Alys waited patiently, barely breathing, not wanting to draw any attention to herself.

The snoring soon began. She wondered if all men snored. It seemed every man from Brentwood had as they rode from there to Kinwick. Did Kit snore? Tears sprang to her eyes as his image burned in her memory. Alys pushed aside all thoughts of him. She couldn't think of him anymore. Kit Emory was no longer a part of her life.

But a small part of her hoped that their coupling would produce a child. Their child. One she would love beyond measure—but never let him know about—for it might bring a world of trouble between him and Lady Thea. More than anything, Alys was determined to let Kit build a life with his new wife.

She waited a few minutes longer to make certain Fendrel wouldn't awaken, but she couldn't chance Carac returning. It was time to flee.

Alys pushed herself to her feet and tiptoed to the table where the knife lay. It was small, and the blade looked dull, but hopefully she could use it to free her hands once she escaped. She couldn't afford to take the time now to do so. The blade could also be used to protect herself if Carac came for her. Alys slipped it into her boot. She promised herself she would return with her father and an army of knights in order to confront the wicked Sir Fendrel for holding her for ransom.

She crept toward the door. Fendrel snorted, and the snoring ceased. Alys froze. She held her breath. Then the snoring started up again. Tiptoeing to the door, she quietly lifted the bar. Her heart pounded so loudly she was afraid it would wake the sleeping nobleman. She eased the door open, thankful that the Virgin Mary had answered her prayers since it didn't creak this time. Alys looked out and saw no one in the open clearing in front of the cottage. She closed the door behind her.

Her eyes swept the area. Beside the cottage, a small structure stood to her left. It was open on one side. She saw it was a barn. She hurried to it, hoping to find horses. She could ride without a saddle if she had to. But no horses stood there. Only a goat that was probably used for milk. He bleated at her. She petted him so that he wouldn't continue to bleat and give her presence away if any of Carac's gang hovered nearby.

As she scratched the goat under his chin, she glanced around the barn for a tool that might be sharper than the knife she'd stolen. She was weary of the restraints on her wrists. Seeing nothing she could use, she decided to move on. Even if she could find something to cut through the thick rope, she didn't dare risk staying here to saw through it.

She needed to leave. Now.

Alys lifted her skirts with her bound hands and took off running before someone discovered her. Before Fendrel awoke and found she was missing. She skirted the barn and darted into the trees. First, she would search for a road. Once she found it, she would look at the sun and determine which direction Kinwick lay. Alys knew she needed to keep her wits about her. Running blindly through the forest could cause injury and increase her chances of being caught and returned to Fendrel. She told herself not to panic. She would keep a cool head, just as she did when she delivered a babe or cared for a patient who had met with an accident.

It would be important to conserve her energy. After she ran for a few minutes, she slowed to more of a trot. It still let her cover a lot of ground and wasn't nearly as tiring. Already, her legs ached. Her calves burned. Her breathing was labored. Alys kept up this pace for as long as she could, until her breath came in gasps.

She slowed. Beating wings seemed to surround her. A coven of black birds flew up, frightening her. Still, she urged herself on. She didn't want to think of the consequences if she failed.

Especially if Carac was the one who found her.

A snap behind her caused her to draw up. Glancing over her shoulder, she saw nothing. As she stepped forward, she tripped over a fallen log and went down hard, biting her tongue. She tasted blood in her mouth. Alys spit it out and pushed herself up. She must keep going.

Again, she picked up her speed and ran again as if someone chased her. She wanted to put as much distance between her and Carac as she could. Alys could only imagine the man's rage when he returned to the cottage and found her gone.

Exhausted, she finally slowed her steps and began walking. The sound of water caught her attention, so she headed in that direction. Within minutes, a small stream appeared. Gratefully, she bent and drank from it. The cool water was the most delicious she had ever tasted. She drank her fill and then bathed her face. It had a calming effect on her.

Alys knew she must keep moving, but she didn't know if her aching feet could attempt another step. She had no idea if she had left any trail behind. She knew some men could follow others by clues left behind. She had to assume Carac was one of those who possessed this skill. He had proved far too wily for her to think otherwise.

As she stood, Alys realized she was too weary to continue on. She had to rest—but not here in the open. She forced herself to continue walking until she found a hollowed out tree. It was large enough for her to climb inside and not be seen.

She was so tired. Alys dropped to her knees. Her eyes drooped. She curled into a ball. She would rest her eyes. Only for a minute.

CARAC RODE AS quickly as he could through the woods. He looked over his shoulder several times to make sure that no one followed him. He thought the rider he saw approaching the gates at Kinwick might have, but he was too deep into the woods now. Something nagged at him, as if he'd seen the man before. He pushed it aside. It didn't matter.

Because he was about to be rich beyond his wildest dreams.

Delivering the ransom note to de Montfort had been risky. Usually, he wouldn't take such a chance. That was what his minions were for. But this would be a start to a new life for him. He wouldn't be sharing the ransom with anyone—least of all that fool Fendrel.

He only stashed Alys de Montfort at the fat bastard's cottage to keep her out of sight. He made sure each member of his crew had been sent on errands that would take them a few days. Carac had worked for Fendrel many years—first as one of his foot soldiers and later as the man who kept the stupid nobleman alive when he had lost everything. Fendrel trusted him, which was why he would succeed with this plan. He would collect the enormous ransom from Geoffrey de Montfort and never split it.

Every last gold coin would be his.

Carac read the note Fendrel wrote and knew exactly how much to expect. Part of him wanted to keep all of the treasure and Lady Alys. He'd never met a woman with more spirit and determination. She intrigued him, both her fearlessness and her luscious curves. But he didn't want to take the time needed to bend her to his will. He could do it, of course, but the lady had a stubborn streak wider than the sea between England and France. 'Twould take far longer than he wanted to spend. Besides, he didn't wish to be tied down to any woman, even one as lovely as Alys de Montfort. Carac enjoyed his sleep too much. Even when he succeeded breaking her, with Lady Alys he would spend the rest of his life in bed with one eye open, hoping she wouldn't stab him to death. He wouldn't put it past her.

He thought at first to leave her with Fendrel. Meet with de Montfort and claim the ransom. Tell the earl where she could be found. His gut told him the knight would not be trusting enough to part with the gold unless his daughter was in sight. So Carac would return for the lady. Spend a last night under Fendrel's pathetic thatched roof, then leave with a promise to return with the ransom.

But he would disappear instead. And Fendrel would never suspect a thing.

Carac wondered where he might go. Nothing bound him to England. He hated the French with a passion. Scotland would be too cold for his bones. The Welsh were too damned crazy.

Italy might be the place. He'd heard tales of its wine, women, and warm weather. He would definitely have the money to travel there and stay if he liked it.

He rode another hour and reached the small hovel that had become home to Fendrel. The man had gambled away most of his money at court. Then his lands grew barren—as barren as his wife. More peasants left the great estates each year, coming to London and other growing cities throughout the kingdom. Fendrel's tenants had run from the estate like foxes being chased in the hunt. Soon, hardly any remained, and the lord fell on hard times.

Carac thought the man deserved everything he got. The nobleman had been careless with his money and too hard on his soldiers for no reason. Fendrel drank more than he should and cared about no one but himself. Carac almost wished he could watch while Fendrel waited for his return. And waited. And waited.

He arrived at the cottage and tied his horse in the barn. The friendly little goat bleated a greeting to him. On a lark, he untied the animal and shooed it away. It went scampering into the forest. Just another nail in Sir Fendrel's coffin. Carac smiled.

The place had a deserted air about it with none of his men present. Carac strode to the door and rapped hard. He insisted that the nobleman keep the door barred. Even if pretty, little Alys de Montfort made it to the door, her restrained hands would have trouble with the bar. Fendrel could reach her easily in case she tried to escape.

He waited. When no one came, he pounded his fist several times and kicked the door for good measure. It swung open. Fendrel's greasy hair clung to one side of his face. His reddened eyes told Carac he'd been drinking a good part of the day. The last thing he had warned the nobleman about was not to touch a drop until he returned.

Carac pushed past him. His eyes perused the cottage.

"God's teeth!" He turned on the nobleman, but he already knew the answer. "Where have you put Lady Alys?"

Fendrel looked around sleepily as if he hadn't a clue as to who Lady Alys was. He scratched his chin. "She was here."

"You fool!" Carac unsheathed his sword. With both hands around the hilt and anger in his heart, he struck a mighty blow. Fendrel's head flew through the air. The nobleman's body seemed to hesitate before it crumpled to the ground.

Carac overturned the table. Threw a rickety wooden chair against the wall. Screamed obscenities. Kicked Fendrel's lifeless body—then kicked his head across the room. None of it brought back Alys de Montfort.

How long had she been gone?

She wouldn't have left moments after he did. Fendrel would have still been awake and sober. Carac saw the wine stains spilt upon the nobleman's cotehardie. The very smart Alys would have waited for the man to be deep into his cups. Fendrel had a high tolerance for wine. It would have been hours before he was so drunk that he slept through Alys slipping by him and unbarring the door.

No horse had been available to her, so she would be on foot. Surely, a delicate flower of the nobility could not have gotten far.

But this was Alys de Montfort.

Carac knew her to be clever and feisty. The beauty probably had the strength of ten men when angry, and she would have been plenty mad at being taken and held hostage.

He went through the pockets of the dead man and found a few coins. He also knew of the hidden place behind the cottage. He'd seen Fendrel digging one day and had waited for the nobleman to finish. In the dead of night, Carac had dug in the same spot and unearthed a small casket that held Lady Fendrel's few remaining jewels and some gold and silver coins. He replaced the chest and covered it with dirt and knew he would remember the location when the time came to end his partnership with the sloppy nobleman.

Carac went to the barn and couldn't find a shovel or any other farm tool. He returned to the cottage and took the poker from the fireplace. Between that and his hands, he recovered the casket after laboring in the dirt some minutes. There were fewer jewels than when he'd last seen the contents, but he found more coins inside. He would use some of them to buy a cart to carry his ransom. Nay. He had a better idea. He would order de Montfort from the wagon he brought with the gold inside. Let the man walk back to his castle.

But Carac knew the earl would never give him a single coin if he didn't produce Lady Alys. He must find her before the arranged meeting tomorrow.

He returned inside the cottage and found an extra gypon of Fendrel's. He dumped the contents of the chest inside it and tied up the ends. He attached the bundle to his saddle. Carac returned to the cottage and took some of the hay that Fendrel slept on. He placed it halfway into the fire and set the pallet next to it. He dragged the dead body and left it beside the pallet. Before he reached the cottage door, the fire had spilled out.

Carac left the burning abode and mounted his horse.

"Which way would she have gone?" he mused.

CHAPTER 21

ALYS AWOKE DISORIENTED. She reached to brush a stray lock from her face and found her hands facing each other, rope binding her wrists together. Then she remembered where she was and what had happened.

She looked out from the hollow trunk she hid within. Darkness had fallen. The sounds of the night came. A hooting owl in the distance. Crickets chirping softly. A gentle breeze. She couldn't travel at night because she couldn't see. The best decision was to stay put. Her stomach rumbled fiercely. It had been a long time since she'd eaten the small crust of bread Fendrel gave her. It angered her that she'd slept for so long, but the last two nights she'd gotten little sleep. The first had been when Carac's cutthroats attacked the Brentwood soldiers as they camped, then last night she had lain awake for several hours at Fendrel's cottage. Alys forgave herself for sleeping as long as she had. Obviously, she'd needed it.

Wondering how long until dawn broke, she decided to work on freeing her hands. She removed the knife she'd taken from the cottage and braced it between her knees. Squeezing it tightly in order to steady the blade, she laid the rope that bound her wrists against its edge. Alys rubbed back and forth, over and over, in a sawing motion. She stopped several times to rest. Finally, the rope began to give way. It renewed her strength. She moved her arms in and out over the blade until she had freed herself.

Immediately, she pulled the thick rope from her wrists and began bending and twisting her hands. As she expected, the pain shot through her quickly. It danced up her arms and into the center of her palms as the blood began to flow once again. Alys buried her mouth against her bent knees to muffle her moans. She couldn't afford for anyone to hear her.

Gradually, the feeling returned. She could, once more, wiggle her fingers and bend her wrists. She rubbed her hands up and down her arms, trying to warm herself. It had grown cool overnight. The sweat from her exertions chilled her and she shivered.

Alys sensed that morning approached. She watched as light began to peek through the thick trees in the forest. She listened carefully, fearful that Carac would discover her. Yet she couldn't let fear keep her hidden. She had to continue. Crawling from her hiding place, she decided to return to the nearby stream. She found it and drank her fill.

Her legs were sore and tired as she attempted to run, barely making it a dozen steps before she stopped. She decided to take her time and not rush. Locating a road became her priority. Once she found it, she could discover where she was and pick up her pace. It surprised her how in tune she was with every noise around her. She moved with caution for an hour or longer. Finally, she did find a road.

Alys left the forest and saw the sun now climbed in the sky. Based on the direction that the Brentwood escort party had ridden, Kinwick was to the south and east. She shielded her eyes as she glanced up at the sun and decided to head east on this road. She hoped to pass some landmark she recognized—another castle, a village—anything that looked familiar and that would help her establish her whereabouts.

More than anything, she must be wary. Not just because Carac would be pursuing her, but because of what had happened to Kit in this very area. England had groups of men who roamed the countryside, robbing travelers. She was a woman on her own and needed to exercise extreme caution.

Because of that, Alys decided to keep to the edge of the road. If she saw anyone coming in the distance, she could scramble into the woods. She could either wait until the other person passed, or she could skirt the woods and come out on the other side without being seen.

Alys tried to run and then decided she was too weary. She would press on by walking at a brisk pace. Despite trying to keep her mind a blank, her thoughts turned to Kit. How desperately she loved him. If only they had left Brentwood a day earlier, they would be at Kinwick now, making preparations for their wedding.

Or would they?

Lord Godwin had arrived with Lady Thea and a betrothal contract in hand. Alys knew a betrothal was as legally binding as the marriage ceremony. If they had missed Lord Godwin, he most likely would have come to Kinwick to put a halt to their wedding. And if she and Kit had married by that time, it would have been annulled since legally Kit was tied to Lady Thea.

Alys couldn't stop the tears that began to fall. She had to face the truth. She had lost Kit—forever. She fisted her hands and swung her arms angrily as she walked. Though she may have lost the man she loved, she refused to lose this battle with Carac. She would outsmart the thief and find her way home.

She only hoped her father would let her come with him when he searched for the bandit. Alys planned to bring justice to both Carac and Sir Fendrel.

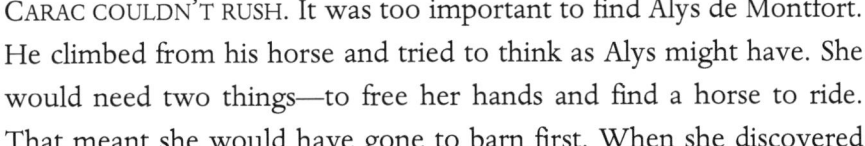

CARAC COULDN'T RUSH. It was too important to find Alys de Montfort. He climbed from his horse and tried to think as Alys might have. She would need two things—to free her hands and find a horse to ride. That meant she would have gone to barn first. When she discovered neither, she would have left.

He entered the structure again and walked around. This time he noticed small indentations that had to be her boots. He remembered watching her strip. Alys de Montfort had not worn feminine shoes but had on boots more like a man would wear. That meant she did plenty of walking. He went outside the barn and saw she had taken the path into the woods. Now he was getting somewhere.

Carac retrieved his horse and mounted it. He would go slowly and study the ground carefully, as well as the brush, anything the noblewoman might have touched in her haste to escape. He traced her path for hours, occasionally relying on instinct when he lost sight of the mark of her boot heel. Twice, he spotted a strand of chestnut hair floating on a low branch of a tree.

Darkness came. He could go no further. He tied up his horse and removed the saddle, using it to brace against as he dozed off and on throughout the night. When enough light peered through the trees, he resumed his search. Definite tracks led him to a stream. Carac paused and closed his eyes. He could almost smell her as he stood by the water. He could picture her bending and drinking.

She was close.

He knew it. The hair on the back of his neck stood up. He listened. Studied the ground. Then climbed on his horse again and headed for the road that he knew was ahead. He would no longer look for any sign of her. If she'd made it this far, he knew that she'd found the road. Ironically, it was on this very road where he'd arranged to meet Geoffrey de Montfort. The earl was already on his way to rendezvous at the assigned point.

And Carac had to find Alys before her father did.

He pushed his horse now and quickly covered a lot of ground. He arrived at the edge of the road and forced his horse to halt. A bent branch told him this is where she had crossed out of the forest and taken to the road. Carac hoped Alys had chosen to travel east. If so, he could find and detain her and still be close to where he would meet de Montfort.

He galloped down the road, passing no one. This was close to the stretch where his band of men had waylaid a single knight recently.

That was it.

Carac knew he had recognized the rider outside the gates of Kinwick. 'Twas that same knight they had attacked. He was sure of it. The man's horse had been injured and lost to them, which angered him. It was a magnificent beast and would have fetched an excellent price.

They'd beaten the knight to a bloody pulp and left him for dead, taking his armor and coin purse and clothing. Someone must have come across him and nursed him back to health.

Instinct told Carac that the de Montforts had been involved in that. Lady Merryn had a reputation far and wide as a healer. He'd heard one of her daughters also excelled in the healing arts and had even surpassed her mother's skill. He'd bet all the coins in his pocket that daughter was the beauty he now searched for.

Carac continued down the lane, his horse's hooves thundering along. When he thought he'd ridden close enough to have caught up with Alys, he reined in his horse. The de Montfort woman was shrewd. She would be looking for him. Alys would never walk down the center of the road. Instead, she would cling to its side. Mayhap even travel parallel to the road and stick to the woods. It was what he would have done if someone pursued him with a vengeance.

He did the same now, clinging to the edge of the road. He'd taken to his feet and led his horse behind him. Carac kept his eyes peeled ahead, darting from side to side. She might have stayed on the left side for a bit and then switched to the right to confuse anyone who pursued her. He wore hunter green and would blend in with the foliage. He remembered Alys had changed from the bloodied yellow gown to one of sky blue. That would stand out—and give him an advantage.

He walked another half-league and then spotted a flash of blue in the distance. His heart jumped into his throat. He froze and watched the blue move forward toward the horizon.

"Oh, I've found you now, Alys," Carac said to himself. "You clever girl."

He pulled his horse into the woods and mounted it. He could reach her faster by riding. He trotted along until he came within her hearing distance and then stopped and tied the horse to a bush. It would be easier to creep up on her if he was on foot.

Carac slipped quickly through the woods. He sighted the sky blue again and slinked closer. Her burnished red hair had come loose from its braid and now hung to her waist. Between the red on the blue, following her proved easy. Yet he didn't know how much time he had left. He needed to reach her before her father did, so he increased his speed.

As he drew near Alys, he saw she moved with caution. He stepped on a twig and cringed when it snapped. Carac jumped behind a tree and waited. He was close enough to hear her footsteps. She paused a long moment and then kept on.

Carac sprang from his hiding place and narrowed the gap between them in seconds. Alys must have sensed him behind her. She started to turn as he was upon her. Carac clamped a hand over her mouth and threw his arm around her waist. She bit his hand immediately, but he left it in place, pressing it tightly against her mouth and over her nose. Alys bucked in his arms trying to win her release. He held on even tighter, determined to rein her in. Her struggles lessened, and he knew she'd run out of breath when she gasped for air behind his hand.

He needed to take advantage of her weakened state. Carac threw her to the ground. He slammed a hand into the small of her back and then straddled her, facing her feet. Pinned to the ground, Alys flailed her limbs. He pulled up her skirts and found her already-torn chemise. He yanked hard on it, and the material ripped. He kept tearing until he had a huge chunk of it. While continuing to sit on her, he tore the material into several strips.

Alys realized what he was doing and she bucked even harder, slamming her fists into his sides. His weight held her down, though. Carac slipped a long strip under her ankles and then encircled the ends in opposite directions. He knotted it when he'd looped it around several times. He grabbed another strip from the chemise and crouched to face the other direction. It took him longer to gain control of her arms. He yanked them back and used one hand to hold her hands while he wrapped the linen around her wrists several times. He tied it off, using several knots to ensure the linen would hold her fast.

She hadn't screamed before now, but Carac knew that was coming. He captured her chin and lifted her head back. She whipped her head from side to side to prevent him from silencing her.

"Be still, Alys," he commanded.

She screamed. Carac rolled her on her back and clamped a hand over her mouth as he straddled her again. Her sapphire eyes flashed in anger as his hand stifled her shouts.

"I haven't hurt you up till now. I don't intend to. Unless you force me," he warned.

Alys quieted, but he kept his hand in place, forcing her head to remain against the ground.

Carac took his free hand and brushed his fingers lightly against her breast. Her eyes widened. Muffled protests erupted from her. He flattened his palm and rolled it slowly over her nipple. Then he tightened his hand, squeezing hard. His fingers pinched and twisted the nipple. Her eyes squeezed shut. He stopped as quickly as he started. The blue eyes opened and searched his.

"I can bring you pain, Alys. I can rob you of your dignity. Strip you of your virginity. I don't want to do that. I want to return the spirited girl I've come to know to her father. But you must cooperate. Do you understand?"

"Aye," she grunted beneath his hand.

"I will place a gag around your mouth. You will not utter a sound. If you do, I will punish you. Nod if you understand."

Alys did.

Carac removed his hand. His saw that beautiful rosebud mouth trembling. For a moment, he did want to take her, then and there. Plunge into her sweet, tender folds. Suck on those full breasts. But a few minutes of pleasure did not equal a lifetime of wealth. He would remain focused on his task.

He got off her and brought her to her feet. Carac gagged her with the remaining bit of her torn chemise. He made sure the knots were firm. He couldn't afford to have Alys call out a warning.

He spun her around so that she faced him. It saddened Carac when she dropped her head in defeat. He forced her chin up and told her, "I admire you, Alys de Montfort, for what it's worth. You are the strongest, most fearless woman I have ever met. The man you marry will be a lucky man, indeed."

The look she gave him might have struck another man dead, but Carac only laughed.

CHAPTER 22

Kit watched as a grim-faced Gilbert placed four sacks of gold in the wagon in the midst of many bales of hay. The knight climbed down from the bed and came to stand next to Kit.

Kit glanced over at Lord Geoffrey and Lady Merryn. Both stood resolute. After their planning, they all believed they would see Alys safely within Kinwick's walls by the time the sun set tonight. He moved to where the couple stood, wanting to reinforce that belief.

"I give you my solemn vow, my lady. We will be home soon with Alys."

Merryn gave him a hard look. "I don't just want Alys returned to me. I want the head of every bastard who laid a finger on my daughter."

"I feel the same way, my lady. Alys is a strong woman. Mayhap even stronger than you. She will be sure justice is done this day."

Kit went to the driver's seat and hoisted himself up. He unsheathed his sword and placed it in the cart's bed, directly behind where Lord Geoffrey would be sitting to guide the team of two horses. The nobleman did the same and handed up his sword. Kit set the weapon down next to his own. The ransom note had instructed the earl to come unarmed, but they had decided once Alys was safely in hand, her kidnappers would be in for the fight of their lives.

"Are you sure I cannot follow you, my lord? At least with a few of our men," Gilbert asked.

"Nay," said Geoffrey. "We can't be sure who is watching. There might be spies hidden outside the gates of Kinwick right now." He shook his head. "I'm sorry, Gilbert. I can't risk it. That's why Kit will hide in the cart now and not wait until we are closer to where we've been instructed to rendezvous with the kidnappers."

The earl placed his hands on his wife's shoulders. "Have faith, my love."

"I've always believed in you, Geoffrey. Be safe." She pressed a soft kiss to his lips.

Kit lowered himself into the cart, centering himself between the two swords. Gilbert covered him with a horse blanket. That way if anyone rode by, he would be hidden from view. It would be hot, but it was a small sacrifice to make for Alys. He would ride through the fires of Hell itself to save her.

The wagon tilted slightly as Geoffrey got into the driver's seat. Kit heard the click of a tongue and the two horses started through the bailey.

Geoffrey spoke up several minutes later. "We've passed through the gates. I'll tell you if I see anything suspicious. It should take us three-quarters of an hour to reach the spot the missive specified."

Kit forced himself to relax. He had no reason to be on edge until the time came. He closed his eyes and allowed his thoughts to turn to Alys. He could see her image so clearly, especially the mischief in her sapphire eyes. He could hear her throaty laugh. Remembered the feel of her silky locks when he ran his fingers through them. Touching her body with reverence. He smiled thinking how sensitive her ears had proven to be. How he could play with the lobes and bring shivers of delight to her.

More than anything, he recalled how she called out his name in passion as they came together as one.

Kit promised himself that Alys would do the same again when he pleasured her many times in the years to come. They would spend every night in love play, and he would never let her go. Once they had rescued Alys and destroyed the men who'd taken her, Kit didn't know if he could wait for her family to gather for their wedding. He wished he could marry her on the spot.

He heard workers in the fields greet their lord and Geoffrey call out in return. The wheels turned on the cart. Silence again.

"Nothing so far," the nobleman said. His voice was low, but that was why they had determined Kit should ride where he did. It would be close enough for them to communicate and, hopefully, prevent him from being seen by the kidnappers once they arrived at the exchange.

"Are you all right?" Geoffrey asked.

"I will be once Alys is safely in my arms," he replied.

"I would feel the same if Merryn had been taken from me. We will get her back." Kit heard the determination in Geoffrey's voice. He thought Alys was a combination of the best of both her parents.

Silence fell for what seemed like an eternity. Kit wiped his sweating hands against his cotehardie. Anxiety filled him. It never had all those times he'd ridden into battle because he hadn't cared if he lived or died. But now he wanted to live—for Alys.

His thoughts were interrupted as Geoffrey spoke.

"Up ahead. A lone man in the road. Standing. No horse. There could be others hiding in the woods though I see no one else."

Chills ran through Kit. He flashed to the line of men blocking the road when he'd been attacked. He was certain he and Geoffrey were close to the spot where that incident had occurred. More than anything, he saw the one with the long scar who'd held the club. Kit remembered how brutal the man's blows had been.

"Lord Geoffrey, look to see if he has a scar that runs from his eye to his mouth."

"You think the brigands involved in the assault on you have Alys?"

"We're in the same area. I believe it's a strong possibility."

The cart rumbled on, then the earl quietly said, "I can see his scar."

Less than a minute later, Kit felt the vehicle roll to a stop.

"Be you Lord Geoffrey de Montfort?" a voice called out.

"Aye. Where's my daughter?"

"Very close, my lord. Be patient. For now, I need you out of the wagon."

Kit felt the wagon rock as the earl's weight left it.

"Raise your arms. Keep them up," the man instructed.

"I have no sword or any weapon on me," Geoffrey said calmly. "I have done all that you asked. I am alone. Unarmed. And I have the ransom for you."

Kit knew the tricky part came next. Lord Geoffrey needed to show the kidnapper the sacks containing the ransom and, at the same time, make sure Kit was not exposed during the process.

"Show me the gold," the voice commanded.

"The bags are hidden amongst the hay."

"Prove it."

Kit heard footsteps moving toward the rear of the cart and held his breath. This was the time when Geoffrey would be most vulnerable. Yet they'd decided for the nobleman to keep up a running dialogue so Kit would know what happened.

"I'm reaching for one of the bags. Shall I untie it for you?"

"Nay, toss it to me."

Kit heard the jingle of coins as the thief caught the sack. He waited as the man must be untying it.

"Sink your teeth into every coin," Geoffrey said. "They are all real."

A rustling sounded. The robber must be sifting through the coins in the bag and sampling some.

"There should be more."

"Aye. Three more bags," Geoffrey said. "I'll show you."

Kit felt the wagon dip as Geoffrey climbed into the back of it.

"There. I've retrieved the others. Check them all. You'll find it's what you came for."

Kit kept perfectly still as the thorough kidnapper must have checked the contents of each bag. His heart beat frantically. *Where was Alys?* He wondered how far away she might be.

"You did well, my lord."

"I'll ask again. Where is my daughter?" Geoffrey demanded.

"First, place the sacks where they were," the thief instructed. "Hide them well."

Kit supposed Geoffrey did as he was told from the movement he felt. Then the cart bounced as the earl landed on the ground again.

"I want my daughter. Now."

"And you shall have her, my lord. Look down the road. Far down on the left. Do you see the sky blue of Lady Alys' cotehardie? Her fiery hair against it?"

Kit heard Geoffrey's intake of breath.

"She's waiting for you with my men up ahead. They are watching every move we make. I want you to stand away from the wagon. I'll be taking it. I thank you for so cleverly concealing the sacks of gold coins." The man chuckled. "As I pass, I will signal my men that I have the ransom so they can release her and ride away. You can run to her after that."

"If you've harmed—"

"Nay!" The voice laughed. "If anything, you should ask if I've been harmed. Lady Alys is full of courage and determination. She killed two of my men with a sword and another with her own dagger. Drove it right through the man's throat without hesitation. I won't forget Lady Alys de Montfort anytime soon."

Alys had told Kit she knew how to use a sword. A smile came to his face as pride filled him that she had the ability to take down three of her captors.

"Step back more, my lord. More. I want you to start walking in the direction you came from. Count loudly and steadily to one hundred. Don't rush. Once you reach the last number, you may turn and come back Alys' way. I'll keep an eye on you as I go, so don't think to cheat me."

The cart shifted abruptly. Kit knew the kidnapper had climbed into the driver's seat. The horses started up. He heard Lord Geoffrey counting, clearly at first and then his voice faded as they drove away.

Kit wondered how many men guarded Alys up ahead and when he should make his move.

The cart slowed slightly. He heard the voice next to him call out, "Your father will be here to claim you soon. 'Twas a pleasure to make your acquaintance, my lady. I will think of you often." He chuckled. "I hope you'll think of me."

Kit heard a muffled response. Alys must be gagged as well as bound. The wagon picked up speed. He realized the man hadn't shouted any instructions to free Alys. Instinct told him that no other criminals had come. This kidnapper who drove the cart away must have wanted the entire ransom for himself.

He eased the blanket from his head and saw the back of the man so close that he could touch him. Kit looked behind them and saw Lord Geoffrey racing down the lane, a speck in the distance. He also saw Alys still tied to a tree, looking back at her father. White-hot anger seared through Kit. He ripped the blanket off and slammed his hands into the man's back.

The thief fell forward and became tangled in the reins and the harnesses of the horses. The two animals cried out as the man fought to free himself. Kit grabbed his sword and leapt from the vehicle and yanked the stranger free and then tossed him to the ground.

The man scrambled to his feet and whirled to face him, fisted hands springing up in protection. Kit's heart pounded furiously the moment their eyes met. Instant recognition crackled between them.

'Twas the scarred criminal who'd led the band that attacked him on the road to Kinwick.

The thief wore no sword. Kit could have cut the man down with one blow but he chose to toss his sword back into the wagon. He sought revenge now. The bastard needed to suffer. Not only for the assault he'd directed on Kit—but for abducting Alys.

He slammed his fist into the thief's nose. The crunch that followed sounded as music to his ears as blood spurted like a fountain. The thief growled an obscenity and threw two quick punches to Kit's gut, though Kit turned so that the second barely grazed him. He brought his fist upward, connecting with the bastard's jaw, snapping his head back. The man stumbled backward but did not lose his balance.

Instead, he launched himself in the air, both feet crashing into Kit's chest, knocking him to the ground. Kit rolled to his side as the thief landed where he had just been. Both men sprang to their feet again and the scarred criminal moved more quickly this time, his fist ramming into Kit's eye.

With a loud roar, Kit threw strike after strike into the man's face, giving him no time to return a blow. The last one spun the man around and he fell to his knees. Scrambling away, he came to his feet and began to run. Kit tackled him, pummeling him repeatedly in his side till he heard ribs snap. The thief tried to crawl away, clawing the dirt in an effort to escape. Kit bunched the man's tunic in his fingers and dragged the bastard to his feet, spinning him around so he could see that ugly scar once more.

Throwing the most punishing blows of his life, Kit battered the criminal till the man's cries ceased. He collapsed on the ground and lay still. Only then did Kit find satisfaction. As he looked down, he couldn't determine if the scarred man was dead or merely unconscious. If he proved to be alive and came around, he wouldn't get far.

Kit turned and saw that Lord Geoffrey had reached Alys. Kit ran full speed to close the distance between them.

He arrived at her side as her father lowered the gag from her mouth.

"I'll kill the bastard!" Alys shouted for all the world to hear.

That was his woman.

Even bedraggled, she was the sweetest sight Kit had ever seen. He had to touch her.

Kit nudged the nobleman aside. His hands cradled Alys' face. Her eyes lit up. Kit saw all the love and longing that beat within him reflected in her eyes.

"I love you, Alys de Montfort," he declared. "It's always been you. You are my soul mate."

His mouth crashed down on hers. Kit drank in the sweetness of her taste as his tongue danced happily with hers. His fingers pushed into her glorious chestnut hair. He kissed her till neither of them could breathe—and then he kissed her some more.

Finally, he rested his forehead against hers. His hands caressed her shoulders.

Someone cleared his throat.

Kit sprang back, aware that they had an audience of one. "My apologies, my lord. I . . . I forgot you were here."

Geoffrey de Montfort laughed heartily. "No apologies are necessary, Kit Emory. To see how well loved my sweet Alys is, makes me a very happy father." The earl clapped Kit on the back, a welcoming smile on his face.

Another throat cleared, and both men turned back to Alys.

"It would be nice if I could run my fingers through Sir Kit's hair. Of course, that would mean someone would have to free me from these restraints," she said drily.

Kit kissed her hard and swift. "Whatever you say, my love. I plan to spend the rest of my life waiting on you hand and foot."

He pulled a knife from his boot and cut through the linen strips that held her wrists and ankles and the rope that anchored her to the tree. Alys swayed unsteadily on her feet, so Kit swept her up into his arms. She linked her fingers together behind his neck, satisfaction evident on her face.

"I'll see to the thieving bastard and bring the cart around," Lord Geoffrey said.

"Don't kill him, Father."

The nobleman stopped. "Your mother did ask for his head."

"Then let me be the one to give it to her," Alys said. "Better yet, we should return Carac to Kinwick. I would see him brought to justice in front of many. He and the other band of outlaws he leads. And Carac takes his orders from Sir Fendrel. He is the one who wrote the ransom note."

"Fendrel?" asked Geoffrey.

"I can lead us to him. I escaped from the cottage where they held me."

Kit gave her an appreciative squeeze. "It seems you know how to take care of yourself, my lady. But I hope you will allow me to help every now and then."

He watched Lord Geoffrey start in the direction of the one Alys called Carac. Kit was grateful for a moment alone with her.

"Do you mean it, Kit, that we can spend our lives together? What of Lady Thea and your betrothal?"

He caressed her cheek. "The widow is in love with another man. We are no longer betrothed, thanks to the king."

"The king? You went to the *king*?"

"Aye, Lady Thea and I did so together. Once we explained the situation to King Edward, he was most cooperative. I think 'twas because it involved the de Montforts. He has very fond memories of coming to Kinwick."

Alys smiled. "He did enjoy eating Cook's tarts."

Kit's finger twirled a lock of her hair round his finger. "He mentioned that. And that he would wed your mother if not for your father already being her husband."

She giggled. "Mother has that effect on many men."

He tugged on the curl, tilting her head back. "He allowed us to burn the betrothal contracts with one request."

Her eyes widened. "What?"

"That you and I name our first daughter after his late wife. It seems Queen Philippa thought a great deal of you, as did the king."

Tears sprang to her eyes. "I was devoted to the queen. 'Twould be an honor for our child to bear her name. Philippa Emory," Alys said softly, trying the name out.

Kit released her lock of hair and cupped her face in his hands. "Lady Thea will soon wed her Tybalt. In fact, I have asked the two of them to come spend the Christmas season with us at Brentwood. I think they will become close friends of ours." He smiled down at her. "That means we also need to marry. I want to wed immediately. If we could, I would have us do it here. Now. If we pass a priest on the way back to Kinwick, I will make sure it happens."

"Truly?" Her smile almost blinded him.

He gazed into her eyes. "Alys, you have taught me many things. I expect you will continue to teach me many more in the years to come.

Being here, with you in my arms, I know I have come home. I swear never to be parted from you, not for a single day. Our forever together starts now."

Kit lowered his mouth to hers. The kiss was deep and long and full of the promise of their love.

EPILOGUE

Brentwood—Christmas, 1375

KIT AWAKENED TO the sound of Alys softly snoring. She was nestled in his arms, bringing a warmth to him that went beyond the physical. His hands rested on her protruding belly. Their first child would be born in early spring of the new year. Alys had started snoring shortly after she discovered she was with child. He didn't tell her she did so, but he loved to lie in bed next to her and listen to the sound all the same.

A kick under his hand caused him to smile. He gently stroked her belly with his fingertips and lightly tapped back. Another kick came as if the babe within responded to him. Kit lifted a hand to her long, chestnut hair and combed his fingers through it. He would never tire of touching this woman. He found himself more in love with her each day.

Alys stirred and turned. He looked down as she opened her eyes.

"Good morning," she said sleepily, rubbing her cheek against his bare chest.

That was all it took to heat his loins. Kit cupped her face and gave her a lingering kiss. Alys stroked his chest, raking her nails down it, teasing his nipples. He deepened the kiss as she pushed against him, rolling him to his back. She climbed atop him, hiking her night shift up to her thighs.

At first, as the babe grew within her, Kit worried about their heated love play. Alys proved insatiable, wanting them to make love day and night the larger she became. She calmed his fears, telling him she knew enough about babes and that the love they shared would cause no harm to their growing child.

Kit took the edge of the gown and pulled it up over her head. He tossed it aside and gazed at the woman he loved. Her breasts had grown even fuller. Her skin glowed. And she had that hungry look in her eyes that he'd grown fond of.

"So you need your fill of me again," he teased.

Her lips curled into a smile. "I can never get my fill of you, my lord," she said seductively. "Feel. I am already dripping with desire for you."

His fingers touched her folds and found her already wet. He toyed with her a few minutes, stroking her, finding her nub and teasing it to a peak. Her breathing became rapid and shallow as his fingers pleasured her. Alys cried out, calling his name.

Just as he liked it.

Kit let her guide his stiff member inside her. She enjoyed being on top, especially as her belly expanded. She'd told him once it was like riding a horse.

"And you know riding is one of my favorite things to do."

Nowadays, when she told him she wished to ride, he knew what she meant and quickly escorted her to their bedchamber. He craved her touch and knew she felt the same.

Alys now moved slowly, teasing him as he had her. She leaned down to press her lips against his throat, her teeth nipping where his pulse beat strongly. Kit felt her clench tightly as she quickened her pace and then rode him with abandon. He flew higher and faster and further than ever before until he cried out her name, over and over.

She collapsed against him and then rolled to her side.

"We should dress. I need to make ready for our guests."

"They aren't supposed to arrive till the noon meal," he said. "And everything is already perfect."

"We can't stay in here all day."

"We can the entire morning." With that, Kit kissed her.

THEY MADE IT downstairs in time to greet their many guests. Kit knew Alys would miss not being at Kinwick for Christmas, and he told her that Geoffrey and Merryn must come to celebrate with them at Brentwood. Of course, they would bring Ancel, Hal, Edward, and Nan along. Though Kit longed for many sons, he secretly wished for this first babe to be a daughter. Nan had stolen a piece of his heart. He hoped he and Alys would have a girl much like young Nan.

But many others were due to arrive. Geoffrey's cousin, Raynor, often brought his wife and their three children to spend Christmas at Kinwick. Alys had told Kit that they couldn't possibly leave Raynor's family out of the celebration. Then she decided her cousins, Elysande and Avelyn, must also come and share in the Christmas joy. Kit had met their husbands, first at court when he'd returned from fighting in France and again when he and Alys wed. He had also been reacquainted with Michael at the May Day celebration. They had five—or was it six?—children between them. He couldn't remember.

Last of all, he had invited Thea and Tybalt to visit with them months ago. The newly-wedded couple had already come once in the fall to Brentwood since they lived only two hours away. Thea, too, was with child and would deliver in late spring. Kit was pleased at how well Alys and Thea got along. He, in turn, enjoyed Tybalt's company.

Soon, the great hall burst at the seams with all of their visitors. His mother and Alys made perfect hostesses, making sure everyone was shown to their chambers and providing toys for all the young cousins to play with. They made for a merry group as they dined at noon and then sent the children off to explore.

Alys came to where Kit was seated and stood behind him, wrapping her arms around his neck. "The ladies are retiring to the solar," she murmured against his ear.

"I'm sure you'll have plenty to gossip about," Kit told her.

"No more than you men," she said saucily.

"Watch that one," Michael teased. "It seems she's been taking lessons from my Elysande."

"Or my Avelyn," chimed in Kenric. He gave Kit a solemn look.

"You have to watch the women in this family. They need a firm hand." Then he threw back his head and roared with laughter.

Kit called for more mead. Alys had learned the recipe from her mother and had made it for the Christmas season. He already wondered how he could convince her to make it year round.

"You look like a man in love," Raynor said to Kit. "Doesn't he, Geoffrey?"

Alys' father smiled. "He does, indeed." Then Geoffrey grew serious. "You may think you love Alys now, Kit, but it's only a fraction of how much you'll love her when you hold the child you made together in your arms. And as each day passes, as months turn into years, and years melt into decades—you will love her more than you can ever know."

Kit understood what Geoffrey de Montfort meant. The women in this family were all special in their own way, and their men were lucky to have them.

Kit raised his glass and the others followed suit. "To our wives. May we live with them long and may love always be with us."

The End

About the Author

As a child, Alexa Aston gathered her neighborhood friends together and made up stories for them to act out, her first venture into creating memorable characters. Following her passion for history and love of learning, she became a teacher who began writing on the side to maintain her sanity in a sea of teenage hormones.

Alexa's historical romances use history as a backdrop to place her characters in extraordinary circumstances, where their intense desire for one another grows into the treasured gift of love.

She is the author of *The Knights of Honor*, a medieval romance series that takes place in 14th century England during the reign of Edward III and centers on the de Montfort family. Each romance focuses on the code of chivalry that bound knights of this era.

A native Texan, Alexa lives with her husband in a Dallas suburb, where she eats her fair share of dark chocolate and plots out stories while she walks every morning. She enjoys reading, watching movies and sports, and can't get enough of *Fixer Upper* or *Game of Thrones*. Alexa also writes romantic suspense, western historicals, and standalone medieval novels as Lauren Linwood.

Alexa loves to hear from her readers. You can connect with her through FB, Twitter, and her website: alexaaston.com.

Facebook:
facebook.com/authoralexaaston

Twitter:
twitter.com/AlexaAston

Newsletter sign-up:
madmimi.com/signups/422152/join

Amazon Page:
amazon.com/author/alexaaston

Made in the USA
Middletown, DE
29 August 2017